THE NIGHT WE FIRST MET

CLARE SWATMAN

Boldwood

First published in Great Britain in 2022 by Boldwood Books Ltd.

Copyright © Clare Swatman, 2022

Cover Design by Leah Jacobs-Gordon

Cover Photography: Shutterstock

A CIP catalogue record for this book is available from the British Library.

Paperback ISBN 978-1-80280-662-5

Large Print ISBN 978-1-80280-663-2

Hardback ISBN 978-1-80280-661-8

Ebook ISBN 978-1-80280-665-6

Kindle ISBN 978-1-80280-664-9

Audio CD ISBN 978-1-80280-656-4

MP3 CD ISBN 978-1-80280-657-1

Digital audio download ISBN 978-1-80280-659-5

Boldwood Books Ltd
23 Bowerdean Street
London SW6 3TN
www.boldwoodbooks.com

For Serena, with love

1

13 DECEMBER 1991, 10.30 P.M.

Ted

It's bitterly cold on the last day of my life, the snow dropping in scrappy flakes and smothering the city in a blanket of quiet white.

I watch it from the window, five floors up. It's peaceful up here. The heating has gone off and I shiver, but I don't dare put it on again. I'm taking enough liberties sleeping on Danny's sofa without costing him more cash too. But he won't have to worry about me taking up space for much longer.

Because after tonight, I'll be gone.

I puff out my cheeks, stamp my feet on the carpet and turn away from the window, away from the cars streaking past below and the Londoners going about their everyday business, and sling my battered rucksack over my shoulder. I've been thinking about this for far too long now, it's time to just get on with it.

I've always been logical, methodical. Which means that, even while thinking about the best way to end my life, I have made lists of people who might be affected, trying to work out whether I'd hurt anyone, and how I could get it over and done with while causing the least amount of drama. And it certainly feels as though I've finally come up with the best, most simple solution: to just slip away into the night, sink into the Thames and quietly disappear. The only people who will notice my absence are Danny, when his sofa is empty again, and my father, who probably won't find out for a few weeks anyway when he rings to check up on me from his flat in Spain.

So that's that.

Don't get me wrong, it's not a decision I've taken lightly. Since returning from the Gulf, I've really tried. For the last eight months, I've done everything I can to stop the nightmares, to block the terror, and feel normal again. But nothing's worked. So I'm not being flippant when I say this is for the best: one less person taking up space in the world. It's the easiest thing for everyone. Including me.

Minutes later, I'm at ground level, walking along the road, head down, blinking away the snow that's driving into my face. My coat isn't thick enough and my skin burns where the wind whips through the fabric, but it doesn't matter. Soon, I won't feel anything, so it's good to feel something for now. I spot the headlights of a bus approaching and quicken my pace to beat it to the bus stop. I'm not exactly on a tight schedule, but it somehow feels important to get on this bus and not have to sit and wait for the next one. Just in case I change my mind.

I make it on and clamber up to the top deck, drop my bag on the seat next to me and pull out the glass bottle that's been my friend these last few months. I tip my head back and take a deep swig, feeling the amber liquid burn my throat as it slides down, the warmth spreading to my arms, my legs, my fingertips. Booze has been the only thing to numb me enough to get me through each day, and now it's helping me to keep my mind off what I'm about to do. I polish off the rest of the bottle, and when the bus reaches my stop, I stand and stumble, almost falling before I manage to grab the yellow handle and pull myself upright. A woman a few rows down turns her head and watches me, then shrinks closer to the window away from this mad man who's clearly drunker than he should be.

The fresh air hits me like a hammer in the face and I stand still on the pavement for a few moments as the bus drives away. The lights strung alongside the Thames whip back and forth violently in the breeze, and I notice it's stopped snowing now, the piles of filthy slush along the edge of the pavement the only sign that it ever was.

On jelly-like legs, I cross the road. The traffic's light down here at this time of night, too late for pub closing time, too early for the early bird commuters. The yellow lights of black cabs blur as they crawl past, hoping for custom. I reach the other side and approach the barrier separating me from the mighty strip of water below. It's dark and choppy, the lights from the buildings lining the river reflected in shards and flashes, glinting like diamonds in candle-light. I can't think about how cold it will be, how much my body will resist as I walk slowly into the murky depths. Instead, I feel inside the pockets of my jacket and my hand hits the ragged edges of a small rock. I'd collected a few large stones and small rocks when I was still trying to decide between the oblivion of freezing water, or the escape of pills. I chose this way in the end so that Danny didn't have to walk in and discover my body. It didn't seem fair after everything he's done for me.

And so here I am. I peer down at the black water again, at the small semi-circle of sand and rubble that abuts the river wall from where I'd planned to walk out. Can I really just walk into the river and let the weight of the water take me down? I had thought it would be easy, but now I'm here, confronted by the river itself, doubts are starting to creep in. I glance to the left, and then to the right, up at Waterloo Bridge. Maybe that would be easier after all. A quick jump from the railings of the bridge, and that would be it. Over. No time to change my mind.

I push away from the wall, walk towards the bridge and trudge up the graffiti-covered concrete steps. The wind is stronger up here and bitterly cold. I pass the occasional person, dressed for a night out, but otherwise it's eerily quiet. I walk halfway along the bridge then stop, wrap my fingers tightly around the white metal railings and study the scene. The black river in front of me, the Royal Festival Hall to my left, empty and silent like a sentinel at this time of night, Charing Cross Station to my right. The barrier between me and the drop only reaches just below chest height – it would be so easy to just leap over and let go.

I glance left and right again, making sure no one is watching me. The coast seems clear, so I press my trainer into the bottom railing and swing my right leg over, dropping my foot until it reaches the curved narrow ledge of concrete below. My left leg follows and I grip the rail even more tightly, my fingers numb from the cold. I try to turn slowly round to face the water. I need to be clear what I'm doing, where I'm going, it seems important somehow to face up to it. And then I lean out, letting my body tip forward forty-five degrees, the wind whipping me gently back and forth, my arms straining to hold me up, keep me rooted to this life.

I breathe in deeply. I have to do this. It's all planned. I can't keep going on like this. *Come on, Ted, stop being so pathetic.* It's funny – perhaps not funny, but certainly significant – that it's my father's voice I hear now, egging me on. Not because I believe for one second that he'd want me to do this, but because it's always his voice I hear when I can't do something, when I'm struggling. Not to encourage me, but to shame me into it.

Pathetic.

He's right. I am pathetic.

I'm about to let go when there's a sudden movement to my left. I turn my head quickly. There's a fairy next to me, clambering over the railings. I shake my head. *Am I hallucinating?*

I blink, but she's still there, standing next to me now on the wrong side of the railings, teetering wildly over the chasm, her wings flapping ridiculously, her foot slipping perilously close to the edge of the tiny platform. A halo bops above her head, attached to a piece of wire, and her hair covers her face so she has to release one hand to push it away before replacing it quickly.

What the fuck is going on?

I stare at her and she keeps her eyes on me, her gaze steady.

'Hello,' she says. Not 'stop' or 'wait' or 'don't'. Not even a wobble to her voice. Just a firm 'hello' as though it's perfectly normal for her to be chatting to a man hanging off the edge of a bridge in the middle of the night.

I can only manage a nod.

'Could you—' She tips her head towards the pavement, her hands turning blue beneath her lacy gloves. 'Do you think you could come off there?'

Just like that. Completely calm.

And that's what makes me wonder whether, actually, I should come off here after all.

'Can – can you just stand up straight?' she says.

She reaches over to grab my arm and I snatch it away, then I swing wildly to the right, my whole body weight being supported by just one arm. I don't know what I want to do now, but I am absolutely certain that I don't want this young woman to witness me ending my life. I know what that can do to a person. And so, slowly, I swing round to face the railing and pull myself up to lean against it.

'Thank you,' she says. I'm so surprised by her serenity that I don't know what to say, so I just shrug. Fairy Girl is watching me, a deep crevice between her eyebrows, her face pale beneath the glitter that keeps catching in the streetlight. She looks frozen.

We stand in silence for a moment, both of us on the river side of the bridge. I don't know what to do next, and I search her face for signs that she might have a clue. I don't think there's a rule book for this sort of thing, so slowly, I lift my foot onto the railing and pull myself back over to the other side, then help her to do the same. Then we both slump onto the damp pavement, our backs against the icy metal. Snow seeps through my clothes and numbs my skin, and we sit in silence as a half-empty bus slips quietly by.

'Sorry,' I say, my voice catching in my throat so it comes out half-strangled. I stare down at my hands.

'I—' She stops, clears her throat, then says, 'Why?'

I shrug. It all seemed so clear to me before, but now I can't seem to find the words to explain.

'Look, I've had a pretty shit night too, as it happens, so I'd much rather not be sitting here freezing my arse off if you're not even going to talk to me,' she says, and I'm so shocked that she's telling me off rather than sympathising I want to laugh. Who *is* this girl?

She pulls herself up so that she's standing in front of me, her indignation seeming to ebb away as she looks at me, being replaced by – what is that? Pity? I stand too and step towards her, suddenly desperate for her not to leave.

'I—' I stop and look up at the sky. What am I trying to say? I take a deep breath and carry on. 'I'm sorry for scaring you. I'm just – I'm not very good at this.' I wave my hand between us. 'Talking.'

'I can see that.' She rubs her upper arms vigorously. 'So why were you trying to kill yourself?'

Again, I'm surprised by her bluntness, and yet also impressed.

She's not scared of anything. 'There's nothing to live for,' I say, truthfully.

'There's always something to live for if you look hard enough,' she says.

I shake my head. 'Not this time.'

'Oh, don't be so self-pitying. Nothing can be that bad that you need to throw yourself off a bridge.'

I don't know what to tell her. What is it that finally tipped me over the edge, brought me to this moment? Was it my father? Kuwait? The fact I can see no future?

'I killed someone.' The words surprise me, as I realise it's the truth. That *was* the final straw, the thing that I can never forgive myself for, that I can never see a way of forgetting. Images of that moment flash in front of me and I rub my eyes to get rid of them.

'What?' she says.

'In Kuwait,' I tell her, simply. 'I saw friends get blown up, and then – then I accidentally killed an innocent woman.'

She stares at me for a moment and despite myself I feel a tiny surge of triumph that, for the first time, she's lost for words. Then she says, 'I'm sorry.' When I don't answer, she carries on. 'But you can't do this. People will miss you. You'll hurt people.'

I want to laugh. 'There's no one to miss me,' I say. 'Mum left years ago, my dad's not around any more either, and my friends just think I'm a burden sleeping on their sofas. They'll all be better off if I'm not here.'

'I won't be.'

'What?'

She holds her hands out towards me. 'I won't be better off if you throw yourself off this bridge, not now. You'll traumatise me for the rest of my life if you don't let me save you.'

'I know. That's why I stopped.' This stranger in front of me is the only reason I have for living right now.

'Oh. Does that mean you're going to try again as soon as I'm gone?' She looks dismayed.

Am I? Do I really still want to do it? I think about the actual act of falling from the bridge into the icy water below and, for the first time in months, it doesn't feel like a better alternative than trying to live. 'No,' I say, honestly.

'Why should I believe you?'

'You shouldn't. But I won't. The moment's gone now.' I hesitate. 'So what happened to you tonight? Why are you dressed like that?'

She glances down at herself and shrugs. 'I was at a work party.'

'And?'

'And what?'

'And why are you here, trying to save a suicidal man's life, instead of still having fun at the party?'

'It doesn't matter.'

'Tell me.' I find I really do want to know, if only to take my mind off my own problems.

'I found my boyfriend shagging someone else.'

'Ouch.'

'He's also my boss, which means I don't have a job any more.'

'Why not?'

'Why do you think? He's humiliated me. I can't go back there.'

'You should. Why should you lose your job because he's behaved like an arsehole?'

'Wait, are *you* giving *me* advice now?'

'It does seem that way, yes.' I feel my lips tugging into a semblance of a smile for the first time in what must be months. A gust of wind buffets the bridge and I see her shiver. 'Here, have this.' I shrug my coat off and hand it to her, but she shakes her head.

'No, you keep it. I'll go home. You should too.'

Home. Where is that, exactly?

'You have somewhere to go, right?' she adds, as though reading my mind.

'Yes. I have somewhere to go.'

I want to make her stay, to sit and talk to this mysterious woman all night. The thought of her leaving me here, standing alone on this bridge, sends panic through my body. But I also know I have to let her leave – if only because she looks as though she's about to freeze to death. I want to ask her who she is. I have a sudden, over-whelming urge to make this woman part of my life – as something more than my saviour. I'm trying to think of the words to use, the right way to ask without scaring her off, when I realise a taxi has pulled up and she's climbing into the back and then she's disappearing off into the London night.

I've lost my chance.

She's gone.

2

13 DECEMBER 1991, 11.33 P.M.

Marianne

It's a cold, damp night, the kind that makes your hair frizz up like candyfloss. A band of fog hangs low over the Thames and gives the streetlights an ethereal, otherworldly glow, and dirty snow is gathered in piles along the edge of the path. As I walk – or rather, stumble – along the Southbank, indistinct figures glide towards me, their forms swathed in mist. It's a night for warm coats, woollen mittens and bobble hats.

It's definitely not a night for a mini dress, glitter and fairy wings, which is what I appear to be wearing. I'm absolutely freezing, more than a little bit drunk and, quite frankly, furious.

It's a Friday night – Friday 13, which should have been a sign – and as I make my way along the riverbank, away from the party, I stomp my feet, making my body reverberate with every step and my teeth rattle in my mouth. I pull my arms tighter around my waist and try to bring some semblance of warmth to my goose-pimpled skin, but the bitterness in the air makes it impossible. My lacy fingerless gloves aren't helping.

As I stomp, I replay the events of the night over and over in my mind. The images come in fits and starts, like a broken reel of film, the story interrupted just as it gets exciting. Except exciting isn't the word here. Depressing is probably a better one. Ridiculous. Pathetic. Humiliating.

I shiver again, my breath coming in puffs with every step. I shake my head to try to get rid of the memories, but they're insistent.

Robert disappearing for ages. Me wondering where he was.

The lights bouncing off the disco ball, making it hard to make out hidden figures in the shadows, shapes in the semi-darkness.

A dropped champagne glass, shards scattering.

A frantic search, my eyes glazed with too much booze and a film of tears.

A shout from the toilets, the bright light almost blinding after the darkness of the party.

A knock on the door, frantic whispers.

A door slowly opening, the looks of horror.

Robert. My boyfriend.

A woman. My friend.

Together.

I'd turned and run then, hadn't bothered to stop and listen to their pointless excuses. I should have known this would happen one day. A leopard never changes its spots, everyone told me that. I hadn't believed them, but now I know. But as I put more and more distance between me and the party, I've begun to realise I'm not even that angry about the betrayal. It's the predictability of it all that's making me so cross. An office party, a drunken fumble. It's a story as old as time – why should we be any different?

The lamps along the river are smudged and I realise it's tears that are blurring my vision. For God's sake, why am I crying? People stare at me as I walk, giving me pitying looks, worried glances. I know I must look ridiculous with the fairy wings still pinned to my back and tears streaming down my face, but I don't care. Let them stare.

I approach Waterloo Bridge from the south side and stop. Should I carry on along the river, or turn left here and head north across the water, back towards home? I hesitate a moment, weighing it up. Then, before I can change my mind, I turn and climb the filthy steps and start marching across the bridge, the swirling darkness of the water beneath my feet cheering me up. I stop and rest my arms on the freezing metal of the railings and lean over, as far as I dare, wondering what it would be like to just keep leaning, to lean until I reached tipping point, then past it, letting my feet lift from the ground and tumble head-first into the icy water. I wonder whether anyone would much care if I did. Whether Robert would care.

I stay there a moment longer, watching the lights of the city dance on the surface of the bottomless river, then right myself, pulling my bag back onto my shoulder roughly, adjusting my fairy wings. My halo bobs wildly above my head, but I can't be bothered to take it off, and I wonder briefly whether my make-up has smudged, leaving tracks in the glitter I'd plastered over my cheeks all those hours ago. I wipe my hands over my face, sigh, then turn towards the north of the city, ready to carry on. To my left, the river slides along threateningly, the line of trees along its edge nothing more than silhouettes, the buildings empty skeletons. To my right, headlights pass from time to time, tired city workers heading home, taxis full of drunk partygoers looking for somewhere to continue their night. I glance up at the imposing outline of Big Ben, its trustworthy clockface lit up like a beacon. It's after midnight. I need to find a taxi too. It's too cold to be standing here tonight, I'll catch my death.

I swivel my head, trying to make out the lights of an available black cab, but there's nothing. In fact, the bridge is strangely quiet tonight, just the odd car whooshing past, and then quiet again, as though the city is holding its breath. I take a deep breath myself, the cold air coating my windpipe, chilling my lungs, and let it out slowly, watching the mist of hot breath as it disappears into the frigid air.

And that's when I notice him. I catch the movement in the corner of my eye first, and assume it's just a ripple on the surface of the water. But then it happens again, and I slowly turn my head until my eyes focus on the man standing by the railings a few feet away. I watch as he hitches his foot up onto the top, and then swings his other leg over and lands on the other side. On the wrong side, on that tiny narrow ledge, hardly big enough to stand on. I glance around. Did anyone else just see, or am I imagining it? I look back, and step closer. He's still there, facing away from the bridge now, body turned towards the freezing river. He's gripping the cold metal with his hands, but his feet are balanced on the tiny ledge, and he's leaning outwards, over the water. If he lets go, just a tiny movement of his fingers, he'll tip right forward, and be swallowed up by the river below. I watch him a moment longer and then gasp as the realisation hits me.

That's exactly what he's about to do.

I can't believe it took me so long to realise, but maybe it's the alcohol dimming my mind.

I dart towards him, then stop. Startling him probably isn't the wisest course of action. I glance around again, hoping there might be someone else, a proper grown up; someone who isn't wearing fairy wings and has mascara smearing their cheeks. But there's no one. I'm in the middle of London, and I'm alone, with this man.

I shiver and take another couple of steps towards him. His skin is tinged blue with cold, and his face is sprinkled with stubble, hair cropped closely to his head. He's looking down at the water. It would only take a split second and then he'd be gone, and I'd be too late. I can't let him jump.

Without thinking, I grip the rails and pull myself over the top, landing on the tiny ledge next to him. Fear makes me light-headed, the city spinning round me, but I shuffle slowly closer until I'm near enough to touch him, unsure what to do next.

'Hello.' My voice sounds thin in the freezing air.

He turns his head quickly, his forehead pulled into a frown, his eyes haunted. He's still leaning forward, and his arms are starting to shake, with cold or fear I have no idea. I plough on, desperate to break the spell, to make him realise what he's doing, to try to stop him from doing it.

He looks at me for another second and then turns away, staring back down at the water again. I feel my heart begin to thump, fear flooding me. What am I doing? I'm no good Samaritan, I don't have a clue how to do this. It's ludicrous. Why do I even care?

I shuffle very slightly closer until I can see the goosebumps marking the exposed parts of his skin. He continues to stare out across the water, seemingly oblivious to my presence. I glance at his face; the unruly stubble that tiptoes its way across his chin, the dark, hooded eyes, the short, cropped hair. He's young, but he has the look of someone older, someone who has seen things no one should ever have to see. His eyes dart left and right, and his arms shake with the effort of holding himself up. I have to do something soon or it will be too late.

'Could you—' I cock my head towards the pavement, towards safety. 'Do you think you could come off there?'

He stares at me as though I've gone mad, and maybe he's right. Why am I being so calm? It must be the booze.

Or maybe he isn't English and actually has no idea what I'm saying. In which case, maybe action would be better than words.

'Can – can you just stand up straight?' I reach my arm out to grab his, but he snatches it away and swings wildly to the right, his whole body weight being held by just one arm now. I gasp as he hovers wildly over the water like a storm-damaged branch, and all I can do is wait and watch. I couldn't hold him now, even if I wanted to. Seconds pass, the clockface of Big Ben marking them out interminably above us like a taunt, while he decides what to do. I hold my breath as I watch him, the world stopping around us. And then, finally, he pulls himself round to face the railing, grips it with his left hand and leans on it.

'Thank you.' The word comes out as a whisper and it isn't what I'd meant to say, but I'm just so grateful that he didn't jump that I can't say anything else.

He shrugs, as though it doesn't matter either way whether he jumps or not, but I'm still holding my breath. I watch him and he hesitates, the cloud of his breath the only sign he's still here.

Then, excruciatingly slowly, he lifts his leg over the barrier, swings his other one round to join it. He drops down on to the pavement, then turns to help me back over too. A bus inches slowly along beside us as we collapse onto the pavement. Old snow seeps through my tights and my hands are numb, but I can't leave yet, not until I know he's going to be okay.

'Sorry,' he says, so quietly I wonder whether I've heard him properly. I turn to look at him and he's staring down at his hands.

'I—' I stop. I have no idea what to say. What if I say the wrong thing and he throws himself back over the railings and into the water? I clear my throat and shiver. 'Why?'

He shrugs again and I feel irritation bubble up.

'Look, I've had a pretty shit night too, as it happens, so I'd much rather not be sitting here freezing my arse off if you're not even going to talk to me.'

He looks shocked, but now the adrenaline has left my body, the fury is back, and this time I'm angry, not just at bloody Robert for humiliating me in front of everyone, but at this bloody man in front of me, who seems to think he's the only one in the world with problems. Selfish fuckers, the lot of them.

I push myself to standing and stamp my feet to try and get some feeling back. He stands too, and for the first time I notice how thin he is, his clothes hanging off him as though he's lost weight recently. Is he ill?

He steps towards me. 'I—' He stops, looks up at the sky as though he'll find answers there. You should be so lucky, I think. 'I'm sorry for scaring you. I'm just – I'm not very good at this.' He waves his hand back and forth between us. 'Talking.'

'I can see that.' I rub my upper arms vigorously, my fingers numb. 'So why were you trying to kill yourself?'

He stares at me a moment. 'There's nothing to live for,' he says, simply. His voice cracks at the end of the sentence and I wonder what's brought him here, to the edge.

'There's always something to live for if you look hard enough.' It's harsh but true.

He shakes his head. 'Not this time.'

'Oh, don't be so self-pitying. Nothing can be that bad that you need to throw yourself off a bridge.'

He looks down at the water again, as though thinking about what might have been.

'I killed someone.'

'What?'

'In Kuwait. I saw friends get blown up, and then I accidentally killed an innocent woman.'

I can't speak. Guilt floods through me at the pettiness of my own problems. I'd just discovered my boyfriend shagging my so-called mate in the toilets, which meant I no longer had a boyfriend or a job, and I thought it was the worst thing that could ever have happened.

Get a fucking grip, Marianne.

'I'm sorry.'

He shakes his head, dismissing my apology.

'But you can't do this. People will miss you. You'll hurt people.'

'There's no one to miss me. Mum left years ago, my dad's not around any more either, and my friends just think I'm a burden sleeping on their sofas. They'll all be better off if I'm not here.'

'I won't be.'

'What?'

I hold my hands out towards him. 'I won't be better off if you throw yourself off this bridge, not now. You'll traumatise me for the rest of my life if you don't let me save you.'

He nods. 'I know. That's why I stopped.'

'Oh.' Relief is followed quickly by another thought. 'Does that mean you're going to try again as soon as I'm gone?'

He stops for a moment, clearly thinking. Then he shakes his head. 'No.'

'Why should I believe you?'

'You shouldn't. But I won't. The moment's gone now.' A pause. 'So what happened to you tonight? Why are you dressed like a fairy?'

I glance down at myself. I must look ridiculous.

'I was at a work party.'

'And?'

'And what?'

'And why are you here, trying to save a suicidal man's life, instead of still having fun at the party?'

'It doesn't matter.'

'Tell me.'

I look up at him. He seems as though he really wants to know. If it takes his mind off killing himself, I'll say anything, so I tell him about finding Robert and Sandra together.

'Ouch.'

'It gets worse. He's also my boss, which means I don't have a job any more.'

'Why not?'

'Why do you think? He's humiliated me. I can't go back there.'

'You should. Why should you lose your job because he's behaved like an arsehole?'

'Wait, are *you* giving *me* advice now?'

To my amazement, he gives a small smile. 'It does seem that way, yes.'

A gust of wind almost knocks me off my feet. It's freezing and I shiver. He shrugs his coat off and hands it to me. 'Here, have this.' I shake my head.

'No, you keep it. I'll go home. You should too.'

He hangs his head.

'You have somewhere to go, right?' I can't leave him here with nowhere else to go. He doesn't answer for a second and I wait. Then, finally, he says, 'Yes. I have somewhere to go.'

I'm so cold, I'm numb to my bones. I don't think I can stand here much longer. Suddenly, there's a yellow light in my peripheral vision. It's a taxi, and I hail it and climb in the second it stops. My whole body is shaking, and my teeth are chattering the way I thought only happened in cartoons. It's not until the taxi pulls away and heads off across the bridge that I realise what I've done. I've just left this man standing there, and I have no idea whether he's going to try to jump again or go home, as he promised. What was I thinking?

My head is spinning with stale champagne and fear, and I'm

numb with cold, and as the taxi rattles towards home, I peer out of the back window before slumping back in my seat and closing my eyes.

I've just saved someone's life.

At least, I hope I have.

3

---

14 DECEMBER 1991, 3 A.M.

Ted

I can't stop thinking about the girl in the fairy outfit: my Fairy Girl. I keep picturing her face, peering like a pale moon through the back window of the taxi as it pulled away; while every part of me wanted to run after her, all I could actually do was stand and watch helplessly as it disappeared into the distance. I just didn't have the strength. I wish I had.

Something hard digs into my back and I wriggle to get comfortable on the lumpy sofa. The springs complain loudly. The flat is still freezing and the paper-thin blanket covering me is barely enough to keep the chill out. But I don't care about any of that because I'm alive.

What made me change my mind on that bridge? Was it the fact that I didn't want a witness? Was it the fact that Fairy Girl was right, it would have been a selfish thing to do? Or was it just because, as my father always insists, I can't do anything right? Whatever the reason, I'm glad. I think.

I hear the rumble of Danny's snores from the room next door, and wonder how long it would have taken for him to notice I wasn't coming back. Hours? Days? Weeks? And how long until he'd told the police? Long enough for my body to have disappeared forever, or would I have washed up somewhere in Essex, dumped on the riverbank like a bag of bones for some poor unsuspecting dog walker to find? I shiver at the thought and pull the blanket up to my chin.

I'd thought about Fairy Girl all the way home as the night bus engine rumbled beneath me. It was hard to hold a clear image of her face in my mind, but I could picture the fairy wings, the halo, the flash of blonde curls, the goosebumps on her arms. I wondered why she'd been sent to save me. Because that's what it felt like. As though I'd been saved.

I arrived back just two and a half hours after I'd left. It was hard to believe so little time had passed. Obviously nothing had changed here, but everything had changed for me. I hadn't given any thought to practicalities such as how I was going to get back into the flat – funnily enough, people don't tend to take keys with them when they're planning to throw themselves into the Thames. But luckily for me, Danny's a creature of habit and had left a spare key under the doormat, a burglar's dream if they ever wanted to stroll in and relieve him of his crappy old TV and ancient stereo system. Danny was home by the time I got back, a half-empty beer can resting on the coffee table and a kebab wrapper with a few remnants of unidentifiable meat the only signs he'd passed through the room since I left.

My eyes stare blindly at the swirls on the ceiling, the damp patch in the corner by the window, the stubborn brown outline where Danny sprayed beer at the ceiling a few weeks back, which won't come out, no matter how hard he scrubs it. I try to focus on the here and now, and not think about what might have been.

But it's impossible, and before I can stop it, snatches of memory tumble into my mind, flashes of the events that brought me to this sofa, in this city, right now. I think about what I said on the bridge, about having killed someone and not being able to live with it, and it's true. I have struggled with that. I see the woman's face over and over again, her expression as she realised what was about to happen, as she saw me aiming the gun, firing and the seconds before the bullet hit and she fell to the ground in front of her young son, those seconds which felt like hours, days, years. But what I didn't say – what I haven't told anyone – is that this is only the tip of the iceberg. There's so much more that I've spent the last nine months since I got home from Kuwait trying to block from my mind. The friends blown up, the hours spent waiting, anxiety sitting like a stone in the pit of my belly, ready for anything to happen at any moment. Ready for death to seek me out.

Then I'd killed an innocent woman, a mother to a young son, and it didn't matter how many times I told myself it was an accident, my father's words always sounded in my head. *Can't you do anything right, Ted?*

He was spot on. I couldn't do anything right.

And now here I was, back in London, sleeping on a mate's couch – and God only knows how long he'll be willing to put up with me – no job, no money, no prospects, no family. At least none to speak of, with Mum long gone and Dad living with his new wife in Spain. And so I'd given up. But then, like a vision from heaven, Fairy Girl had appeared, and everything had changed and now I'm still here. I just don't know why.

* * *

When I wake up again, my neck is stiff and my arms are like ice blocks on the outside of the blanket. The sky outside the curtainless window is a dull white, leeching colour from everything, making the sofa, the table, the carpet appear black and white in the dim light. I pull myself up to sitting and rub my face with my hands. There's a knot in my stomach that won't go away, and I sit for a moment, taking some deep breaths. I'm not meant to be here.

I hadn't planned for this day. Or the next, or the one after that, or all the days that now stretch out in front of me like a kite on a string, and the idea of having to fill them feels overwhelming.

I know I could still take the easy way out, but somehow it feels as if what happened last night happened for a reason. And throwing it away feels like betraying the woman who saved me.

There's no sign of Danny and I'm not in the mood for a hungover conversation about what a wild night he had, and how I really have to go out with him and the lads one night. He means well, and once upon a time I would have jumped at a night out with him, knocking back the pints and chatting up women. Of course, I'm grateful to him for letting me stay here for so long, but I just need some time this morning to process what's happened. To get used to the fact that I'm still here and to decide what I'm going to do about that.

I stand and my back cracks loudly, and the usual pain rips through my knee. I wait a few seconds for everything to settle, then head to the bathroom to freshen up.

When I emerge twenty minutes later, I'm surprised to find Danny sitting on the sofa, my blanket folded neatly to one side, two steaming mugs of coffee in front of him.

'Thought you'd probably need this,' he says, taking a loud slurp from his over-sized mug and nodding towards the other one on the coffee table.

'Thanks,' I say, slumping next to him and grabbing the cup

between my hands. The heat is almost unbearable against my palms.

'You're up early.'

'Banging headache.'

I nod. 'Good night?'

He drinks from his cup again and groans. 'I think I had a few too many. Good night, though, everyone was out.' I can feel him looking at me. 'You should have come.'

I take a sip of my scalding hot coffee instead of answering. He's remembered not to add milk this time and I'm grateful for the hit of unadulterated caffeine. 'Where did you go, anyway? You weren't here when I got home.'

'I just went for a walk.'

'In this weather? It's bloody freezing.'

'Yeah.' I force a smile.

'Thinking about Kuwait again?' I've told Danny some of what I went through, but not everything. For someone who on the surface appears to have all the emotional depth of an empty can of beer, he's been surprisingly sensitive about it. In fact, one of the reasons it was Danny I contacted when I got home was because he's always been more understanding than most of my friends. He doesn't ask inane questions either, rather just leaves me to get on with it, and lets me talk if I need to. I appreciate his surprising tact.

'Kind of.'

He nods and we both sit for a few minutes, drinking our coffee and not speaking, and for a second, I'm so overwhelmed by his kindness that I consider telling him what I'd planned to do last night. But then he stands up and slaps his thighs loudly.

'I'm going for a shit. You got any plans?'

I shake my head.

'Right, see you in a bit then.' He wanders off towards the bathroom and locks the door, leaving me the option of sitting listening to the sounds of his ablutions through the thin toilet door, or going out.

I take the empty cups through to the tiny kitchen and rinse them under the tap, leaving them upside down on the draining board. The flat might be small but it's surprisingly neat. Danny bought it a few years ago and has spent weeks of his spare time putting in a new kitchen to replace the half-rotted one that was here when he moved in, replacing all the wiring and making it feel like a home rather than a squat. He's always telling anyone who'll listen that when he makes his fortune, he's going to buy up half the houses in London and rent them out. I believe him, too. He's a grafter, Danny.

It makes me feel even more inferior, though. Years of hard work and Danny has a lovely little place to call his own in one of the most expensive cities in the world. He's only a couple of years older than me, and what have I got to show for my twenty-two years on this earth? A bag of clothes and a few bits and pieces Danny has let me store in his understairs cupboard. And some unbearable memories. Nothing more.

I throw my jacket on, pick up the set of keys I'd left on the table last night and shove them in my pocket. As I do, my fingers scrape the sharp edge of one of the rocks I'd filled my pockets with and I stop, floored for a minute.

Fuck. I was going to kill myself.

My heart feels heavy, and I leave the rocks where they are, feeling the weight of them in my rucksack too as I throw that over my shoulder. I'll get rid of them outside somewhere, I don't want Danny to ask any questions.

I leave the flat and minutes later I'm traipsing along the high street. It's busy for eight o'clock on a Saturday morning, and I wonder who all these people are who get up so early at the weekend. Shop workers, doctors, nurses, people still coming home from a night out, young mums with pushchairs looking harassed. Their life goes on in the same way every day. I envy them.

Crisp packets and chocolate bar wrappers swirl in the scrappy wind and I press on, head down. I'm not sure where I'm going, but I need time to think. I've spent a lot of time walking and thinking these last few months. Not that it's got me very far, but I need to try to process the events of the last few hours and this seems like the best way.

I didn't know this part of south London when I came to stay with Danny a few months ago, and although I'm familiar with the twists and turns of its streets now, it still doesn't feel like home.

Maybe that's why I find myself heading in the direction of the river. Although it's only a couple of miles away as the crow flies, it's a lot further along the side streets and main roads, and I'm glad of the distance and the chance to switch off.

Usually, when I walk, my mind is filled with the horrifying images that slide into it with alarming regularity – snapshots of my months in Kuwait, fighting a war I didn't understand against an enemy I had no beef with. I hadn't even wanted to join the army. It was just something I did to prove to my dad I could because despite everything, despite the fact he made it clear he'd prefer it if I wasn't around, I still wanted to make him proud of me. When I told him I was thinking of joining the army, it was the first time I'd seen that look of pride in his eyes that I'd always craved.

It was clear from the start, though, that I wasn't cut out for it. The other recruits all seemed to take it in their stride. The training was gruelling, and I dreaded my alarm going off every morning and having to get up and scrub everything clean and start a whole new day, terrified of what lay ahead.

It wasn't for me, but I couldn't let anyone know that, of course. As far as I knew, there were dozens of us who felt the same way, who were wondering how we'd ended up here in this hellhole existence and who wished more than anything we could go home and get a nice, normal job. But we all pretended everything was fine. I just kept thinking, if I could do three months, six months, a year, then maybe my dad would be proud of me. Maybe I'd make him happy at last.

Then we were sent to Kuwait and the worst few months of my life began. I shake my head to get rid of the memories, determined not to let them crowd my head again. I've given up too much of myself to that bloody war. I'm not giving it another single atom.

Instead, I force my thoughts forwards. It's the first time in a long time – since I got back to London, really – that I've thought about a future and it's hard to imagine what it might look like. But thanks to the events of last night – and thanks to the girl in the fairy wings – I feel as though there might actually be a chance of one now. I wish I could find her again and say thank you.

I can't stop thinking about her. About her pale face covered in glitter and the smudged make-up beneath her eyes where she'd been crying. About her sadness, and about how brave she was, climbing over the railings next to me. I honestly think if she hadn't have done that I would never have climbed back over the other side. But there was just something about her that made me realise that, maybe, there could be something worth living for.

I hurry my pace and a few minutes later I reach the river. The wind is stronger here, churning the water into angry peaks, and I watch as a barge chugs along, heading out of London and towards the flatlands of Essex and beyond. My hands are numb now and I shove them into my pockets and pull out a rock and heave it into the river, watching as it arcs outwards and then drops suddenly, creating barely a splash on the choppy surface. I pull out another one, and another, until my pockets are empty, and then I take my rucksack off my back and pull out the rocks from there and throw them into the river too. When they're all gone, it's not just the physical weight of the stones I'd been carrying that lifts, it's as though an emotional weight has been lifted from my shoulders too.

I turn away from the river and head towards the nearest bridge. I need to be back in north London, across the side of the water I'm familiar with. Then I have something I need to do.

* * *

To the girl in the fairy wings who helped me on Waterloo Bridge on Friday night. I'd like to find you, to say thank you. Please put an ad here if it's you. I'll look for your reply.

I read it through one more time. The message is a bit cryptic, but without her name, it's the best I can do. I just have to hope that if she reads it, she'll reply. I don't know what it was about her – apart from the fact that she saved my life – that's got under my skin so much, but I know if I don't at least try to find her, I won't be able to stop thinking about her. This advert in the Evening Standard's 'I Saw You' column is the only place I can think of to start my search.

I leave the newspaper office and head towards the Tube station. I haven't got much cash left and I weigh up whether to splash out on a Tube ride home or to walk back through the streets of the city again. It's a long way and the weather's turned even chillier, a squally rain zigzagging from the sky. The Tube is tempting, but in the end, I decide against it. The advert cost me enough, and I need to be careful with my money. I'm keen to give anything I have left at the end of the week to Danny. He never asks for anything, but I don't want to take the mick.

I set off across the river, trying not to look down at the dark, dangerous water. It takes me more than two hours to get back to Danny's flat, and by the time I arrive, the rain has turned to sleet and I'm frozen. I'm relieved to see the flat's empty and I take a hot shower to warm up my frozen limbs. By the time I'm done, Danny's home, and I can hear him clattering about in the kitchen.

'Oh.' I stop dead in the bathroom doorway, the air cool on my damp skin. There's a woman on the sofa. She turns and sees me, then stands and smiles shyly.

'All right?'

'Er, yeah, good thanks.' I can feel my T-shirt clinging to my damp skin, but I'm glad I at least pulled that on.

'I'm Danni.'

'Danni?'

Her cheeks turn red, and she smiles again. 'Yeah. The same name...' She waves her hand back and forth between herself and the vicinity of the kitchen. Just then, Danny walks back in, holding two mugs in his hands.

'Oh, all right, Ted, I see you've met Danni, then?' He grins and hands one of the mugs to Danni. 'Can you believe we've got the same name?'

'No.'

He glances at the towel wrapped round my waist.

'Sorry, mate, I didn't have time to warn you there was a woman about. At least you're decent.' He chuckles and sits on the sofa, looking like the cat that got the cream. 'Ted, this is Danni. Danni, this is my mate Ted. He's staying with me for a bit. He's a good'un, though, aren't ya, Ted?'

'I hope so.' I step towards Danni now and hold my hand out for her to shake. Her palm feels cool in mine. 'Lovely to meet you.'

'You too.' She shuffles over to sit next to Danny.

'We're just having a quick drink here, then we're off to the pictures.'

'Yeah, I wanted to see *The Addams Family* but Dan wants to see *Cape Fear*. Looks a bit scary for me.'

'Yeah.' I don't know what else to say. To be honest, I haven't got a clue what either of those films are. I haven't read the paper or kept up with anything since I got back. I haven't been able to bring myself to care.

'What're you up to tonight?'

'Me?' I shrug. 'Probably just watch a bit of TV.'

Danny nods. 'You should get out you know, have a bit of fun. Do you good.'

'Yeah, maybe.'

'Do you want to come with us?' Danni says. 'He'd be welcome, wouldn't he, Dan?'

'Yeah, course, mate. Come with us if you like.'

'No, no, don't be daft. I'm fine here.' I couldn't think of anything worse than trying to make small talk on someone else's date.

'Well, if you're sure. Just make sure you don't sit here every night. P'raps we'll go for a curry one night this week, whaddya reckon?'

'Sure. Sounds great.'

Satisfied, Danny stands and stretches. 'Right, shall we head off?'

Danni stands and smooths her skirt down and follows Danny to the front door. I wait until they're gone, then let out a huge puff of air. I know it's Danny's flat, but I'm glad of the peace and quiet.

After the events of the last twenty-four hours – of the last twenty-four months – I've got a lot to process. But the first question I need to answer is: what next?

4

14 DECEMBER 1991, 8 A.M.

Marianne

Fuck. My head.

I roll over and something crinkles. I turn my head as slowly as I can and spot the glittery tip of a fairy wing bent out of shape behind me.

Oh, *God.*

Memories of last night come flooding back, as welcome as syphilis. Bloody Robert in the loo with that stupid cow Sandra from accounts, his arse bashing backwards and forwards like some sort of bucking bronco. When he saw me, his face was red and sweaty and his hair, usually slicked back neatly even after sex, stuck out wildly around his face. His pupils were huge. Off his tits, no doubt, having snorted coke off the toilet seat he was currently banging away on.

He'd pulled away quickly, abandoning poor old Sandra, legs akimbo on the closed loo seat, his arms outstretched towards me.

As his skin had brushed mine, I'd pulled away. He made me want to vomit. I hadn't let him speak and I hadn't said a word either. I'd just turned and run from the party, and now here I was, no boyfriend and no job in just twenty-four hours.

I shake my head, trying to remember more about last night. And then, like a truck, it hits me.

The man on the bridge.

I sit up suddenly and the blood rushes from my head and I feel like I might be sick. I punch some life back into the pillow behind me and close my eyes, trying to stop the room from spinning. As everything settles, I return my attention to Bridge Man. God. I can't believe that really happened. I sift through my memory, trying to remember the exact sequence of events. I'd been walking away from the party. I'd still been pretty drunk, I know that, but I wasn't so drunk I didn't realise how absolutely Baltic it was. I'm not sure whether I'd been planning to walk all the way home or get a taxi but for some reason I'd decided to cross Waterloo Bridge. I'd been stomping along, fuming about bloody Robert and bloody Sandra, the image of them together in the party toilets going round and round my mind like a horror film. I'd been thinking about the fact I had no job any more, about how there was no way I could go back there now, when I'd seen him. Standing on the edge of the bridge, swaying about. And then I'd climbed over the barrier and stood next to him. *Jesus!* What was wrong with me? Who does that?

Had anyone seen us? We were in the middle of London. Surely someone must have noticed two people about to jump off the side of a bridge?

I think about how I'd got him to come back to the other side of the barrier, about talking to him, telling him about my terrible night, asking him why he wanted to kill himself. It was probably one of the only occasions in my life that my bluntness was useful.

We got to the point, and we got there quickly, before both of us froze to death.

I remember him standing up, and promising he wasn't going to hurt himself. And then I remember spotting a taxi, and getting into it and then... what then?

Surely I didn't just leave him there, standing right next to the place where he was about to jump?

I think back, scrabbling to piece together the hazy details. I'd asked him if he was still going to jump, and he'd said no. He was going home. And that was it? I'd believed him, just like that?

What was wrong with me?

I rub my eyes and swallow down a lump in my throat. I can taste stale champagne, but I don't know whether that's what's making me feel so sick or whether it's the thought that I could have left a suicidal man to get on with the job he'd already started. I squeeze my eyes shut, desperate to eke out any more details, any small look or word I might have forgotten that would give me a clue as to whether he meant his promise or whether he was just trying to fob me off. But there was nothing.

I roll over, press my face into the pillow and scream. When I'm done, the pain in my head is worse and I push myself to a sitting position and take a huge gulp of the dusty water from the glass next to my bed.

I press my feet into the carpet and pad across the room, listening for signs of life somewhere in the house. A floorboard creaks, but these floorboards are always creaking and squeaking at odd times of the day, often hours after someone has stepped on them, as though they're trying to scare me, so that tells me nothing. I don't hear the tell-tale sounds of Mum nattering on the phone, or Dad watching TV, or the kettle boiling, Dad humming tunelessly to the radio or, in fact, any of the other sounds that usually fill the house to let me know my parents are home. I think I'm safe.

I have a quick shower, pull some clothes on and run down the stairs. As I enter the kitchen, I see what I was hoping to find – Dad's usual stack of newspapers, already dog-eared from being read cover-to-cover, weighed down on the kitchen table by a half-drunk cup of coffee. He loves his newspapers, my dad; he devours news, pores over it like an over-eager student who's about to be tested on everything he's just read, and then tries it out on everyone he meets that day, testing out his opinions on the Poll Tax or the Gulf War like pairs of glasses, until he finds the ones that suit him best. I wonder what he'll decide he wants to discuss this evening as me and Mum roll our eyes above the overcooked fish and potatoes that Mum loves to serve on a Saturday night.

I make a cup of tea then sit down at the table and flick through the papers – last night's *Evening Standard*, today's *Times* and *Daily Mail*, as well as the *Hendon Times* and *Finchley Press*, my eyes flitting back and forth, up and down the columns, trying to catch a glimpse of a story about a man's body washing up in the Thames, or an appeal for a witness to someone jumping off the bridge. But there's nothing.

Realising it's probably far too early for anything to be reported anyway, I pick up the remote control and flick on the TV, hoping the local news might be tell me more. But when a quick scroll through Teletext reveals nothing, I turn it off again. I'm stumped now. I literally have no idea what to try next. There must be some way of finding out what happened to him. I wish I'd paid more attention and taken his name.

There's only one thing for it. I'll have to call Lance.

* * *

'Hang on, stop right there.' Lance's voice is shrill on the other end of the phone and I hold mine away from my ear for a moment.

'What?' I've only just started explaining to my best friend Lance – her actual name is Alison but she's always been Lance to me for as long as I can remember, thanks to her baby sister not being able to pronounce her name properly – what happened last night, but she's stopped me already.

'Tell me that bit again? Robert shagged someone else so *you're* losing your job?'

'Well, yeah. I can hardly go back there, can I?'

'But you've done nothing wrong.'

I know that. Lance knows that. Damn, even 'bloody Robert' as he shall now be forever known as, knows that. But none of that matters. Because Robert is the boss, and so he is untouchable. I, however, am just a lowly assistant.

'It's not just the fact I found him screwing someone else, although there is that of course,' I say now. 'But—' I stop. 'The thing is, I can't face everyone.'

'What do you mean?' Lance's pitch has reached new levels that only dogs can hear, and I flinch.

'Everyone in that place knew we were a couple. It was an open secret. Some of the bitchy women in that office said I only got the job because I slept my way into it.'

'So?'

'Well, they're right really, aren't they? I did only get the job because I was sleeping with Robert – it definitely wasn't because of my dazzling qualifications of three crap O Levels. And now – well, now I'm not sleeping with Robert, ergo, no job.'

'Three things. One, that's ridiculous. You've been doing that job for more than three years and you're good at it. Two, none of this is your fault.'

'And?'

'And what?'

'What's the third thing?'

'Oh, I was just questioning the use of the word ergo. It's not important.'

'Right.'

'By which you mean, *Lance, I've heard you but I'm still not going back to work*?'

'Pretty much.'

I hear her sigh on the other end of the call. She does that often, when she talks to me about Robert. But I haven't rung her to be reprimanded.

'Anyway, let me finish the story.'

'Go on.' I can hear a regular rasping noise and I realise she's filing her nails as she listens. I picture her, fiery red hair piled up on her head, face pack on, her poster of Brad Pitt in *Thelma and Louise* looming above her head, and I smile.

Then I tell her about the man on the bridge.

'Jeeez.'

'I know.'

'So you just left him?'

'Yeah. I was still pissed, and it was bloody freezing. I – I really thought he was okay, but in the cold light of day, I realise that's unlikely. I mean, he wasn't just standing there for the fun of it, was he?'

'I doubt it.'

'Shit, Lance, what am I going to do?'

'There's not much you can do, is there?'

'Is there no way to find him?'

A pause. 'Do you know his full name?'

'I don't even know his first name.'

'Do you know *anything* about him?'

I think for a minute, rub my eye. The world around me blurs when I re-open it. 'Only that he was in the Gulf War, and now he's home.' I stop a minute. 'I've looked in the papers this morning, but there's nothing.'

'They'll have been printed hours before midnight, you numpty,' she says. I can hear a sporadic sucking sound now and I know she's leaning out of her bedroom window, puffing away on a cigarette, blowing the smoke as far as she can so it doesn't drift back into her bedroom. She's still living at home too, although she's been looking at flats recently and thinks she's found somewhere in East Finchley. I'm still nowhere near that stage, and feel as though I never will be, destined to be stuck in my childhood bedroom for the rest of my life like an eternal teenager. I shudder.

'Okay, okay. Have you got any useful suggestions then?'

''Fraid not.'

'Great.'

Silence falls for a moment, and I sigh. 'I can't stop thinking about him, Lance. I'm really worried.'

'But why? You said yourself he got off the edge and seemed much better when you left him. It doesn't sound as though there was much else you could have done.'

'I know.'

'So why are you stressing about it? It's not like you at all.'

I shrug. I can't explain it, but the thought that the man from the bridge might have jumped after I left him has consumed me since I woke up. Lance is right, it's not like me to worry so much. I'm a firm believer that worrying about something doesn't change the outcome, so why bother. But this has shaken me. Something about him has got under my skin.

'So there's nothing in the news, which means he probably just went home and hasn't given it any more thought.'

I shake my head. 'No.'

'No what?'

'I can't explain it, Lance. He really was going to kill himself. He just seemed so sad and desperate. He said there wasn't any point being here any more, that he was a burden. I can't see how anything I said to him will have changed that. I didn't exactly give him a reason to stay alive, just banged on about my own problems.'

This time she sighs.

'Well, then, I don't know what to suggest, Annie. Maybe you just need to keep checking the papers every day, see if anything's reported. And if not, you'll just have to try to stop thinking about it.'

'Yeah, I know you're right.'

'But don't think this means I've forgotten about Robert.'

'Oh, God.'

'I won't let you quit your job over this. You love that job.'

'It was all right. But I'm not going back there.'

'You have to.'

'I don't and I'm not. I'm handing in my notice on Monday.'

'I'm not talking about this with you any more. You're being ridiculous. I'll ring you tomorrow when you've come to your senses.'

'I won't—' But she's gone, hung up without saying goodbye, the way she always does.

I hang my head in my hands. I knew she'd react like that. Lance is always on my side. She's fiercely loyal and would fight any battle on my behalf. The only thing is, I don't need her to. We've been friends since primary school and not once have I ever needed her to fight my corner. In fact, she's the sensitive one, the one who freaks out over boys, who spends hours analysing everything they've said, everything they've done, and what it might mean every time she goes on a date.

I don't do that. For me, things are black and white. A boy either likes you, or he doesn't. And if he doesn't, well then, screw him. You're either good at your job, or you're not, and if you're not, then you should leave. And this situation was crystal-clear to me too. I'd got this job because I was having a relationship with Robert. Yes, I thought he loved me. Yes, I thought I meant more to him than I clearly did. Yes, I'm heartbroken about it. But there's no pointing pretending things are anything other than they are.

It's pretty clear-cut. The only problem is, what do I do now?

5

16 DECEMBER 1991

Ted

I'm jolted awake by something, but I don't know what. I'm covered in sweat and I can't catch my breath. It takes me a minute to remember where I am – I'm in Danny's flat, I'm safe, nothing can hurt me here. But then I hear a noise again and realise that's what woke me up in the first place. There's a distant but urgent banging sound. It's rhythmical, then it stops, then just as I think it's over, it starts again.

I swing my legs round and stand slowly. I feel weak, the adrenaline having drained from my body now. The flat is freezing and I'm only wearing boxer shorts and a T-shirt, so I grab the blanket from the sofa, wrap it round me and shuffle towards the door like an old man and press my eye to the peep hole. The corridor bends round but I can't see anyone. The noise is still there, though, and then I hear a scream. I yank open the door and run outside but I can't work out where it's coming from and then, all of a sudden, everything goes quiet again. I stand stock still for a few moments, my heart thumping in my temple, waiting to see if anything else happens but all seems to be quiet, so I walk back to the flat. By the time I get there, Danny's at the front door, his hair like Worzel Gummidge, his cheeks red.

'Woss going on?'

I shrug. 'Don't know. I heard screaming but I can't see anything.'

We shuffle back inside together and Danny sits on the sofa where I was about to go back to sleep. I perch on the other end.

'You all right?'

'Yeah.'

He nods in the direction of the door. 'Think we should call the police?'

'Probably.'

He nods again, and stands, his pyjama bottoms baggy on his skinny legs, his pale torso thin and sinewy. I listen as he rings the police station and speaks to someone, and a few minutes later, he puts the phone down. 'Wanna cuppa? I'll never get back to sleep now.'

I glance at the clock. It's 4.45 a.m. Danny has to be up in less than two hours. 'Yeah, go on then.'

Minutes later, Danny returns and hands me a steaming West Ham football mug full almost to the brim of strong tea. 'Ta.' It's warming my hands and I take a tentative sip.

'Police coming?'

He nods. 'Yeah. They said they'd check it out. Better to be safe than sorry, eh?'

I nod and take another gulp of tea, scalding the back of my throat.

'What do you reckon it was?'

Danny shrugs. 'Dunno. I've heard it before though, a few times.

Loads of banging and shouting, then screaming. Just don't feel like the sort of thing you should ignore, do it?'

'No.'

There's a silence for a few minutes, then Danny says, 'Do you wake up a lot? Since, you know...'

I give a small nod. 'Yeah.'

'And do you – you know, have dreams about it?'

'Yeah. Some nights.' I shake my head. 'Most nights.'

He nods and studies his bare feet for a minute. 'Must be a nightmare.'

'Yeah. It can be.'

'You know—' He holds his mug in one hand and runs the index finger of the other round and round the rim of it. 'You know you can always talk to me, dontcha? I mean, I know I'm not the best at showing my feelings, but I do get it.' His face flushes red. 'I mean, they say you shouldn't bottle these things up, don't they? Cause they only get worse.'

'Yeah, they do.'

He nods again. 'So if you need to tell someone about it, I'm here, mate. Know what I mean?'

I feel tears prick the backs of my eyes and blink them away. 'Thanks, Danny. Appreciate it.'

'Yeah, well.' He stands and holds out his hand. 'Want another?'

I gulp back the remains of my tea and nod. 'Yeah, go on, then. Cheers.'

As I listen to him clattering about in the kitchen, I sink back into the cushion that serves as my pillow and sigh heavily. Good old Danny. He might be as bad at expressing his feelings as I am, but he's got a heart of gold. And somehow, even though I probably never will confide in him, will never reveal the true horror of my night terrors or admit to him just how close I came to ending it all, just knowing the offer is there makes everything seem a little bit less bleak. And for that I'm grateful.

* * *

It's still dark when Danny emerges from the shower. I'm lying on the sofa with my eyes closed and I hear him go into the kitchen, then the sound of Cornflakes tinkling into a bowl, followed by crunching.

'Where'd you meet Danni, then?'

'Christ, Ted, I nearly had a heart attack, thought you were asleep!'

I open my eyes. 'Sorry.'

He sits at the tiny table and shovels another spoonful of cereal into his mouth, chewing slowly.

'She's a mate's sister. Couple of years younger than me.' He looks up, swallows. 'She's all right.'

'She seemed lovely. Shame about the name, though.'

'Oh, God, don't. My mates are well taking the piss, keep saying we should get married so we can be Danny and Danni Fletcher.'

'Maybe you should.'

To my surprise, his face turns red.

'Wait, do you really like her that much?' I say, intrigued.

'Nah, course not. I've only known her a couple of months.' His face stays bright red.

'Okay.' I know not to push it, but it's clear Danny really does like her, and I'm pleased for him.

'Actually, she's coming round tonight. You don't mind, do you? Thought we'd have dinner an' that.'

'Course not. It's your flat.'

'I know, mate, but, well, you know you're welcome. I like having you here, gets boring being on me own every evening.'

'Thanks, Danny. I'll make myself scarce.'

'Where will you go?'

I shrug. 'Don't worry about me. I'll find something to do.'

He studies me for a minute, then nods. 'Thanks, Ted. Appreciate it.'

He drops his bowl in the sink, then shoves his feet into his shoes and grabs his keys. 'Right, better be off. See you later.'

'See ya, Dan.'

He leaves and I'm left in silence. I close my eyes and try, once again, to picture Fairy Girl. She's been drifting into my mind more and more often, and if I really concentrate, I can conjure up individual features, rather than her whole face. Her blonde curls that billowed in the breeze, her little snub nose, her blue eyes that flicked out at the corner. A tiny mole on the edge of her chin. This woman who saved me, who stopped me from throwing away the rest of my life, and I have no idea who she is or whether I'll ever see her again. Surely I will? Surely there's a reason it was her and not anyone else who came along that bridge at that moment?

The knot is still in my stomach, and I'm filled with the vast emptiness that's been with me since I left Kuwait, but since that night on the bridge – was it really only just over forty-eight hours ago? – I feel as though something has shifted in me. I can't explain it, not even to myself, but it feels as though now, I'm more sure than I have been in months – probably years – that I *have* got a future, and that it will be worth living.

Why can't you just do something right for once, Ted?

My dad's words flit into my mind, but this time I ignore them. It's up to me now. It's always been up to me. And I'm determined not to waste a single minute more of the second chance I've been given.

* * *

Later that evening, wrapped in hat, gloves and Danny's ancient duffle coat, I wander the streets. I looked at Danni in a different light when she arrived for their date this evening, knowing how much Danny likes her. She's a sweet girl, eager to please but no pushover, just what Danny needs. I hope it works out for them.

I'm keen to give them some proper space tonight, and had been planning to find somewhere else to stay, but I couldn't get hold of any of my other mates who all seem to have dropped off the edge of the earth recently, so I'll just have to stay out as long as possible before I head back to the flat. I can feel the tug of depression pulling at my coat tails again, and I know it's because I feel so alone and such a burden to everyone. I mean, who wants a grown man kipping on their sofa for weeks on end, moping around the flat all day?

Before I know it, I'm back by the river. I don't know what I'm hoping to find here, but I'm drawn back to Waterloo Bridge, to the point where I nearly jumped three nights before. I glance around and feel myself shiver. It's busier at this time of the evening, cars, motorbikes, lorries, buses all ploughing up and down the road from north to south, south to north, in pursuit of something, someone, somewhere. People scurry past too, heads down against the chill of the night air, and Christmas lights sparkle from so many windows, reflected back in the bottomless black of the water. I can feel my hands shake and I place them on the cold metal railing and look down to where I nearly jumped. I can't imagine doing it now. What had I been thinking? I turn and lean my back against the railings and look up and down the length of the bridge. I can deny it all I want, but what I'm really looking for is a flash of blonde hair, a sparkle of fairy wing, a hint of pink cheek. I'm looking for the girl in the fairy wings, even though I know she doesn't live anywhere near here as she got in a taxi and drove away.

I stay there as long as I can, until my hands are numb and I'm shaking with cold, then I head north to look for somewhere to eat. Somewhere warm but anonymous where I don't feel tragic sitting on my own. I head to Charing Cross Road and find a Chinese restaurant that serves steaming hot bowls of noodles, and sit and watch the world pass by outside the window. People with briefcases and rucksacks, carrier bags full of Christmas presents, rolls of wrapping paper; people dressed up for a night out, all cropped tops and chokers, skinny jeans and backcombed hair. It feels like a world I no longer understand.

Two hours later, the waiter is sweeping up around me and I know I can't stay any longer. If I walk back slowly, take the long way, hopefully Danny and Danni will either have finished their date or gone to bed and I won't disturb them. I'm hit by a pang of jealousy. Not of Danni, exactly, but of the intimacy they have, of the simple fact of having someone to love, someone to hold. I don't dare to imagine it's something I'll ever have, one day.

Who would have me?

* * *

It's another two days before I leave the flat again, and this time it's to buy a newspaper. Danny had brought the *Evening Standard* home from work with him on Monday and I saw my advert in there. I almost pointed it out to him, told him what had happened that night on the bridge. But at the last minute, I couldn't bear the pity I knew I'd see in his eyes, so I kept quiet and listened to him telling me about his day at work and about his date with Danni, which had gone well.

I know it's optimistic to think that not only would the girl who saved me have seen the advert but that she would already have replied – I had to wait a few days for mine to appear, after all – but I can't help myself. I won't be able to stop checking until I either hear from her or I think enough time has passed to reluctantly admit she's never going to get in touch.

There's a temporary respite from the icy wind today and I feel warm as I hurry along the road to the newsagent. It's cloudy, but every now and then a shard of pure white sunshine lights up the grubby pavement and it gives me a burst of hope. Maybe it's a sign.

I roll my eyes at my own ridiculousness. She wasn't really an angel. She was just a girl. She probably didn't think about me again once she left me. Maybe she'd had more to drink than I'd realised and she didn't even remember helping me. Why on earth did I think she'd ever reply to this message?

And yet. What else can I do? The urge to see her again is overwhelming.

I grab the *Standard*, pay for it and leave the shop. I'm flicking through the pages, looking for the 'I Saw You' section before I'm even out of the door. It's started to rain and spots appear on the pages, darkening and dampening the flimsy paper. Finally, I reach the page I'm looking for and my eyes scan quickly down the columns.

Nothing.

I knew there wouldn't be, but I still can't help the disappointment, like a brick in my belly. I'll just have to try again tomorrow, and the day after that, and the day after that.

I shove the paper into the inside pocket of my coat and scurry home. Danny's out when I get there and I'm glad. I don't feel like talking, but I don't have a room of my own to escape to, for peace and quiet. These moments, alone in the flat when Danny's at work or out with Danni, are the only times I get. And while inside my own head is not always the safest place for me to be, today, I'm happy to be alone with my thoughts.

6

16 DECEMBER 1991

Marianne

'Marianne!'

I turn my Walkman up louder. I can hear Mum calling me but, like a belligerent teenager, I'm not in the mood to listen to her. She probably only wants me to help fold the sheets or dry the dishes or some other mind-numbingly tedious household chore. It's not like I don't do anything to help. I more than pull my weight, but right now I'm busy.

'Marianne!'

I press my ear into the ironing board, spread my hair out as best I can, place a tea-towel over it and then press the iron over it, holding it for a few seconds. I can hear a hiss as the hair beneath heats up and I hope I haven't ironed a kink into it.

Bang bang bang bang.

'Marianne!'

Mum's outside the door now and I quickly stand up just as she opens it. She sees the iron hissing on the board beside me, and immediately clocks what I've been doing.

'Are you ironing your hair again, young lady?'

There's no point pretending I'm doing anything else. She's found me doing this loads of times, and I always promise not to do it again, but how else am I meant to straighten out my wild curls?

'Sorry.'

'Give it here.' She yanks the plug from the socket by the door and picks the iron up with the other hand. 'You're going to go bald if you carry on like this, I've warned you.'

'It's fine, Mum. I just like it straight sometimes.'

'Well, you ruin your hair all you like, but you're not doing it with my iron, do you understand?'

I sigh. I love my parents but I'm twenty years old, not ten. Christ, I need some space of my own – space where I can iron my hair into oblivion if I damn well wish. Mum chooses to ignore my silence.

'Didn't you hear me calling you?'

'No.'

'Robert's left you a message.'

'Oh.'

She studies my face. 'He sounded upset.'

I still don't react.

'You not going to call him back?'

'Maybe later.'

She screws her eyes up as though trying to get me into focus. 'Everything all right?'

'Yep, fine.' I haven't told Mum and Dad about what happened on Friday night. They've never particularly approved of Robert – *he's too old for you, he'll only break your heart, etc* – and this will only give them the chance to say I Told You So.

'Hmm. Okay.' She wraps the cord around the iron decisively.

'Anyway, can you pop and feed next door's cat?'

'Can't Dad do it?'

'He's gone for a walk and I'm cleaning the bathroom and I've asked you to go.' She shakes her head. 'Come on, Marianne, I don't ask you to do much round here. It's not too much to ask you to feed the cat before you go to work, is it?' She looks at her watch. 'In fact, aren't you going to be late? You don't look very ready.' She eyes my dressing gown disapprovingly.

'I've got the day off. Actually, the week off.' I smile inwardly at my own ingenuity. The office is closed over the holidays, so this gives me until the new year to worry about how to break the news to them about Robert and the fact I don't actually have a job any more. I'm not relishing that conversation.

'Oh, right. You never said.'

'No, it was last minute. I had some holiday to use up before the end of the year.'

Mum gives me the side-eye, as though studying an over-priced menu to see whether it's really worth the inflated prices. Then she turns and walks towards the stairs. 'Well, that's even more reason to help me out then.'

She disappears and I flop onto my bed, starfish-like, and gaze at the purple lampshade above my head. I hate that lampshade. I redecorated my room in a fit of teenage enthusiasm four years ago when everything had to be purple. Now, I've repainted the walls, but the curtains and lampshade remain. I want to rip them down and throw them out of the window, but I don't have the money to replace them, and I know Mum and Dad would disapprove of the frivolity.

My thoughts wander back to the man on the bridge. If he didn't jump off, where is he, what's he doing? I bet he's not lying on his childhood bed waiting for his mother to yell up the stairs any minute to remind him to feed a neighbour's cat. Although I don't suppose he'll be having the time of his life, either. I don't think that's how it works – suicidal one minute, full of the joys of spring the next. But I hope he is alive, and I hope he's glad about it.

All I know about depression is what I've seen happening to Aunty Evelyn, Mum's sister. She's never been suicidal, or not at least as far as I know, and most of the time you wouldn't know anything was wrong. But when the darkness descends, it's like a black veil has been drawn round her, and she's not visible any more from the outside, and she's explained that she can't see things clearly from the inside either. Mum spends days at a time looking after her, popping round and keeping an eye on her, and making sure she gets out of bed, gets dressed, eats. But it always passes, and then everything goes back to normal again. Until the next time.

I wonder whether that's what it's like for Bridge Man. I wonder whether he's always been depressed, or whether it was just since he got back from the war. I can't imagine what it must have been like out there, watching people get blown up and dying right in front of you. I can't imagine what it must do to a person. It's bad enough watching it on the telly.

I push myself up and shove some clothes on. I would go next door in my dressing gown but it's not worth the earache I know I'll get from Mum. People say Londoners don't really know their neighbours, but Mum knows almost everyone on our street, and seems to care about what most of them think as well. It makes for quite a tiring life sometimes.

* * *

Cat fed, I choose my proper outfit for the day – it doesn't matter that I'm not at work any more, I still need to dress well. I apply some thick black eyeliner, flick mascara on my lashes, and hurry out of the door before Mum can stop me. Lance has insisted on meeting me on her lunchbreak and even though I know I'm going to get the

Spanish Inquisition about Robert, anything's better than staying at home and being made to do 'jobs' by Mum. Besides, I've got to get it over and done with sooner or later, so I might as well get some lunch out of it.

Before I get on the bus, though, I need to make a phone call. I can't risk doing it from home in case Mum or Dad overhear, but if I don't ring in sick to work, someone from the office will call home and give the game away. I push open the door of the phone box at the end of the road, shove a couple of 20p coins into the slot and call the switchboard. As I wait to be put through to Robert's office, I pick at one of the postcards that's peeling off the noticeboard advertising some woman's services. The corner comes loose and I pull at it until you can't see her lacy bra any more. I feel like I've done her a favour, made her more decent.

The phone rings and rings and eventually clicks to answer phone. Relief floods through me at the thought that I don't have to actually speak to Robert. I listen to my own voice telling me that Robert's not there and to leave a message, then I wait for the beeps.

'It's Marianne. I'm not well – bad tummy – so I won't be in today. Sorry.' Then, before he can hear it's me and pick up the phone, I slam the receiver down, my heart hammering.

Minutes later, I jump on the bus and head to my favourite seat on the top deck, right at the front where I can see everything, and where I like to pretend it's me who's in charge of the bus. It's childish but I love it. I can see for miles from up here, especially when we pass the houses and shops rather than the towering blocks of flats and office blocks. I can make out the Post Office Tower in the distance and, as we get closer to town, Big Ben. A memory flashes through my mind from the other night, of the huge clock face towering over me as I was helping the man on the bridge, and I shiver as I think about what might have happened to him.

Finally, we reach the river, and I can see my old office across the other side. I hope I don't bump into anyone I know. I get off the bus, hauling my bag onto my shoulder. It's not as cold today and I'm warm in my duffle coat as I scurry towards Lance's office. She's standing outside as I approach, and she spots me and starts walking towards me. I always find it strange when I see her at work. She's a trainee accountant, so she spends her days in power suits, her wild red hair pinned back into a severe bun that makes her look like she's in her thirties rather than almost twenty-one. It's such a different look from the Lance I know – face packs, fags and bottles of Diamond White in her bedroom before a night out – that I find it hard to talk to her, as though she's an imposter who just so happens to look like a more polished version of my best friend.

She grabs my hand and drags me towards a pub. It's a new gastropub, all wooden floors, long tables and sparkling chrome. We order a glass of wine and a sandwich each at the bar, then head towards a quiet corner. I feel underdressed in my short satin dress and biker boots among all the power suits and shoulder pads.

'I guess this means you're not at work, then,' she says before I've even taken my coat off. I plonk myself down on the hard wooden bench and take a glug of wine then wipe my mouth with the back of my hand.

'Nope.'

She sighs and sips her drink more daintily.

'Your lipstick's smudged.'

Lance sighs again and swipes at her mouth. 'Never mind my lipstick. I can't believe you're actually going to let this happen.'

I shrug like a belligerent child, which is how I feel when my best friend is dressed like a proper grown up. I inhale deeply and pull myself together.

'I just can't go back, Lance. Don't you get it?'

She shakes her head and not a single hair moves on her head.

'Not really. This isn't your fault, you haven't done anything wrong. You shouldn't lose your job over it.'

I shrug again. 'It doesn't matter. I can't work with him any more.' I feel a single tear trickle down my cheek and I brush it away angrily. Lance's face softens and she reaches for my hands.

'Oh, Annie. Why are men such shits?'

'I dunno. I don't know why I'm surprised, though.'

'Because you love him? Loved, at least.'

'Did I, though? I mean, I thought I did. But I knew it was never going to last, really. How could it?'

'Doesn't matter. He's still a shit.'

'He is.'

'And now you've left your job, you're never going to get out of that house.'

Lance has been saving up to move out of her parents' place for the last two years, and on her salary she's nearly there. But even though I've been working for longer than her, my job as Robert's assistant didn't pay much. I'd been doing the job for three years and hadn't had a single pay rise. I'd asked Robert, and he'd promised he'd up my wages, but then he never mentioned it again. I guess that's the problem when you're sleeping with the boss.

'I will. I just need to find a new job.'

'Like what?'

'Dunno. It's not like I'm exactly qualified for anything, is it?'

I'd started the PA job when I was just seventeen, after I dropped out of college without finishing my A Levels. School work didn't come naturally to me, and the thought of spending another year slogging away at something I was crap at filled me with horror. Lance had tried to get me to find work in one of my beloved vintage clothes shops in Camden, but then a couple of weeks later I met Robert and, after a drunken night together at his flat, he'd offered me a job as his assistant. I hadn't hesitated. A job in the city, a job with prospects – and it wasn't as though I was exactly spoilt for choice. Of course, everyone there thought I'd only got the job because Robert and I were sleeping together – and they were right – but I didn't care. I'd assumed he'd always look after me, and up to now I'd always been protected from any redundancies, and any of the bad things that happened at work.

But I hadn't banked on him shagging someone else.

'Well, I've got an idea,' Lance says now. She takes her hands away as our sandwiches arrive. Half a baguette and a pile of chips fill the plate, and my belly rumbles.

'Go on,' I say, my mouth so full of bread and Brie I can hardly open it.

She pops a piece of tomato in her mouth and chews thoughtfully. Then she leans forward. 'I've got this friend at work.'

'Right.' I take another bite, wait for her to speak.

'It's just...'

'Spit it out.'

She sighs. 'I don't want you to think I'm interfering.'

'I won't.'

She puts her sandwich back on the plate and threads her fingers beneath her chin. 'Her flatmate works at *Vogue*, and she said she could put in a good word for you if you want.'

I nearly choke on a piece of lettuce. 'Me? At *Vogue*? What on earth for?'

Lance looks me in the eye. 'Why not?'

'But I don't know anything about writing for magazines.'

'Doesn't matter. Besides, you'll just start by helping out, you know, making tea and that.' She swallows. 'She says there's a job going as an editorial assistant and when I told her how much you love clothes, she said you should go for it.'

I shake my head.

'Seriously?'

'Seriously what?'

'You seriously think I stand a chance of getting a job at *Vogue*? I mean, look at me.' I gesture at my outfit, a weird mishmash of goth and utilitarian. I *do* love fashion, but I don't really know anything about it, not officially. I know what I like and I love buying things from second-hand shops and sewing bits to them to make them all my own; I love putting quirky outfits together too, but it's never been anything serious. Not something that could get me a job at a fashion bible like *Vogue*.

'I don't see why not,' she says.

'I'll tell you, then,' I say, counting on my fingers. 'One, I don't have any qualifications. Two, I don't know much about actual proper fashion. Three, we both know the job will go to someone called Araminta whose daddy went to school with the editor, and not an ordinary girl from Finchley who's never had an ambition in her life.' I shrug, and take another bite of my sandwich.

'Well, you won't stand a chance with that attitude.' She takes a sip of her wine and holds it in her mouth a second before swallowing. 'There is something else you'd be really good at, you know.'

'If you're going to say get a job in a shop in Camden, I'm thinking about it, okay?'

Lance shakes her head. 'No, nothing to do with fashion.'

'Well, what then?' I take a glug of my wine.

'You know you've always liked helping people?'

I think about the fuss I made this morning when Mum asked me to feed the neighbour's cat and grimace, but I know what Lance means. For whatever reason, people always seem to come to me for advice.

'Yeeessss?'

'Have you ever thought about becoming a counsellor?'

'A councillor?' I say, shocked. 'Like a politician?'

Lance laughs. 'No, you numpty, the other sort, the ones who

help people. You know, listen to people's problems and help them sort their heads out.'

'Oh. Right. No, I've never thought about that.' I imagine what Mum and Dad would say if I told them I was doing a job like that, about it not being a proper job, about it being for the sort of people who had more money than sense.

Lance ploughs on. 'Well, I have. You always know how to help me when I'm having a crisis – which let's face it, is often.' She grins. 'But it's not just me. Whenever anyone's upset or needs someone to talk to, who do they come to? Not me.'

I nod slowly. I suppose I *am* quite good at giving people advice. It's just not something I'd ever have considered being able to do as a job.

'Do you think that's a thing, then? I mean, it feels a bit – I dunno. American.'

Lance nods excitedly. 'It really is. Everyone's doing it these days. Half my office see a counsellor. It could be great for you. And I bet you could learn on the job, not have to go to college for years.' She's getting excited now, her words tumbling over each other, and I let her get carried away with her ambition for me – at least someone has some. As she talks, I think about the man on the bridge and the mindless waffle I'd spouted at him as he'd swung precariously above the Thames. I mean granted, I'd been drunk, but I couldn't for the life of me understand how anything I'd said that night had made him change his mind about jumping. But it had. At least, I hoped it had. So maybe she's right. I'm about to say as much to Lance, but before I have a chance, she downs her wine, shoves her bag on her shoulder and stands up, looking at her watch. 'Look, I'm really sorry, Annie, I've got to get back. I've got a meeting in fifteen minutes.'

'Oh, okay.' I glance at the dregs of wine in my glass. 'I'll just stay for another.'

Lance frowns at me. 'You sure?'

'Yeah, why not? It's not like I've got anywhere else to go, is it?'

Lance kisses me on the cheek and is gone in a whiff of Calvin Klein 'Eternity'.

I stay for another drink, and let thoughts of *Vogue*, of Robert, and of Bridge Man swirl around my mind. The huge glasses of wine mean that, half an hour later, I'm feeling soft around the edges. It's only 2.30 p.m., and I really don't want to go home yet, so I wander round the streets of Soho and China Town, browsing shop windows and even stopping for another glass of wine before deciding to head back. It's dark now and the streets are busy, post-work drinks already beginning, the buzz of London life at Christmas buoying my spirits. My head feels fuzzy from the entire bottle of wine I've drunk throughout the course of the afternoon, so I walk down towards the river, feeling the chill of the evening air clearing my head. Before I realise where I am, I'm standing at the steps of Waterloo Bridge. I climb them and stand at the end, on the northern side of the river this time, Big Ben on my right, the river flowing beneath me. Standing here now, at six o'clock in the evening, with the rush of people flowing round me, it's almost impossible to believe that, just three days ago, I'd seen a man almost throw himself off here, and no one else had noticed. Despite everything else going on at the moment, he has been in my head ever since that night, lurking in the corners of my mind. I've wondered how he is, and whether my actions saved him. I wish with all my heart I'd stayed, somehow got him home safe and sound. But who's to say even that would have been enough?

Without thinking about it, I start to walk towards the spot where I'd found him, and when I get there, I stop. I don't know what I'd expected – had a part of me thought he might be here, reliving that night himself? Why on earth would he? And yet I still find myself glancing round anyway, looking for glimpses of a tightly cropped head, flecks of a beard, a dark, scruffy coat. I stand there for a few minutes, my back to the railings that I'd swung from so dangerously the other night, and watch people pass by, wondering, wondering. I think I see him once and my heart stops, but when he turns round the face is unfamiliar, older. Then I pull myself upright and head back north, towards home, towards the bus stop, and away from this madness.

* * *

I get off the bus one stop before home and pop into the newsagent to get Dad his copy of the *Standard*. He can't usually be bothered to walk to get it every night, but I know he loves it, the stories more up to date than whatever he read earlier that day, in his morning papers.

I tuck it into my bag and minutes later I let myself in the front door. Mum's in the kitchen and there's a smell of mince cooking. Dad's making himself scarce in the living room, his pile of newspapers next to him. But he's not reading them, he's dozing, his glasses perched on the end of his nose, a gentle snore emanating in time to the rise and fall of his chest. This looks more promising than the kitchen, so I sneak in and flop into the armchair next to him and open the paper. I skim over the stories about pollution levels and a new female head of MI5, my mind still elsewhere. I'm looking for the 'I Saw You' section, the bit where people are looking for someone they locked eyes with on the Tube, or a girl's searching for the guy who bumped into her in Sainsburys in Brixton. It's a cute way of looking for love, and I enjoy the romance of it, the thought that somewhere out there, someone could be reading this page and realising someone is thinking about them and wants to find them.

I turn the page and there it is. I start to read the top one.

Are you the girl who dropped her rucksack on the No 19 bus on Thursday and gave me a cute smile as I picked it up for you?' You had red hair and a pink dress and—

'I didn't hear you come in.' I jump and close the paper.

'Hi, Mum. No, I just got here.'

'Where have you been all day?' She's wiping her hands on a tea-towel.

'I met Lance for lunch.'

'And?'

I shrug. 'Just wandered around.'

She gives a disapproving nod and throws the tea-towel at me. 'Well, put that paper down and come and give me a hand with dinner.'

'But—'

'Come on.'

I sigh and haul myself out of the chair. There's no point arguing, it's easier to just get it over with. So I close the paper, fold it in half and leave it on the arm of Dad's chair for him to find when he wakes up. I'm chopping carrots when Mum says, 'Oh, by the way Robert rang again. Did you not call him back?'

I freeze, the knife hovering in mid-air.

'Er, no. I was busy.'

I know Mum's studying me, but I refuse to meet her eye.

'He seemed to think you were off sick today.'

I scoop the carrot peel up and turn away to put it in the bin. 'He must have got confused.'

'Hmm.'

I know what that sound means – she doesn't believe me but knows she won't get anywhere by pushing me.

'Well, make sure you ring him back. I don't want him calling here all day and night trying to get hold of you.'

'I will.'

We work in silence for the next few minutes until, mercifully, Dad comes through to see how long dinner will be. I know I have to call Robert sooner or later. I just don't think I can face it yet.

*   *   *

It's not until later that evening, when Mum has gone for an early night and Dad is dozing in front of the snooker, that I get a chance to ring Robert. This is one of the things I really hate about still living at home at twenty years old – having to sneak around in order to have any kind of personal life. I creep into the hall and grab the handset from the side table, take my duffle coat from the hook, check my fags are in the pocket, then head to the back garden. The temperature has plummeted and the cold hits my exposed skin like a slap. I fumble with the buttons of my coat, close the door and head to the end of the garden to sit on the bench outside Dad's shed. It smells of motor oil and grease down at this end of the garden, the only place where Dad's allowed to spend time tinkering with his beloved motorbike parts. He doesn't ride a motorbike any more – those days are long gone, he says – but he still spends hours out here in his shed taking apart and reassembling engines and wheels. Mum and I both know it's mainly so he can get away from us for a while, but it suits us all.

I light my cigarette and suck in a lungful, blowing the smoke out into the cold air where it evaporates immediately. The phone reception isn't great out here, but it usually works just enough, so with trembling hands – mainly from the cold but partly because I don't really want to be making this call – I dial Robert's home number. He must have been standing next to the phone because he picks it up immediately.

'Marianne?'

'How did you know it was me?' I inhale again and watch the blown-out smoke curl around the side of the shed.

'I didn't really, but I'm glad it is.'

I don't answer. It's not me who needs to apologise, so I wait for him.

'Oh, God, Marianne, I'm so sorry about what happened at the party. I was stupid. I'd had too much to drink – I think it was the whisky – and I didn't know what I was doing. You have to forgive me. Will you forgive me? Say you will.'

I listen to his words and let them wash over me. I knew he'd beg for my forgiveness. It's what men like him do – act like an arse, then assume they'll be forgiven, and then eventually they do it all over again. I've seen it happen so many times, to me, to Lance, to all of my friends. I won't let it happen this time.

'I forgive you,' I say, crossing my legs and shivering as a blast of air whips round the corner, making the branches of the ancient hawthorn tree tremble.

'You do? Oh, thank you, Marianne. Does that mean you'll come back to work tomorrow?'

'Absolutely not.'

'But you just said—'

'I said I forgive you. As in, I don't bear a grudge. I didn't mean I want to work for you ever again, and I certainly don't want you anywhere near me.'

'But Marianne! I said I was sorry. What do you want me to do?'

I think about it for a minute. I know right now I could say I want him to give me a pay rise, to never cheat on me again, to tell me he loves me, and I know he'd do all of that and more. But I also know it's not what I want. A man like Robert, a man with power over the little people, will never change and I don't want to live like that for the rest of my life.

'Nothing. Just leave me alone.' My heart hammers against my

ribs as I wait for his reply. He doesn't say anything else for a moment, as though stunned into silence. I hold the phone to my ear with my now numb fingers until he does.

'But I've told Sandra not to come back in again. I thought – I thought we could work this out. You and me, we're worth more than this, aren't we?' His voice is wheedling now, and I wonder what I ever saw in him. My mind flicks, fleetingly, to Bridge Man, and the cut of his cheekbones, the flash of his dark eyes, and I shiver. He was so much more of a man than Robert will ever be, and I wish again that I'd taken his name, his phone number, anything so I could see him.

'You obviously didn't think so when you shagged Sandra in the toilets,' I reply.

'I said I was sorry about that.'

And suddenly, I don't want to do this any more. 'We're done,' I say. Then, before he can say anything else, I end the call. I stand for a moment, feet planted in the icy grass, trying to work out how I feel. A pang of sadness, definitely, but only the way you do when your favourite TV show comes to an end and you know you're going to miss the characters. But it's nothing more than that, I realise.

The overwhelming feeling, though, is one of relief. So much so that I can almost feel the pressure pouring off me like water from a shower, running down my arms, my torso, my legs and into the ground. I'm free.

7

13 MARCH 1992

Ted

I wake up and sweat pours off me, my whole body shakes. For a moment, I don't know where I am, the empty fields and destroyed towns of Kuwait in my mind's eye having evaporated in the cold morning air. A pale moon hovers above me and gradually it comes into a focus. A face. Whose face?

I sit up, and the moon moves with me, and all of a sudden, I know with absolute clarity where I am. No longer at war. No longer in danger. Safe. I'm on Danny's sofa. Danny's face is the moon in front of me. Adrenaline seeps away, leaving me weak.

The sofa sags beside me as Danny perches on the edge of it and waits as I pull air into my lungs. Slowly, bit by bit, my heartrate begins to return to something approaching normal. I stare at the carpet in front of me in the murky grey half-light.

'You okay, man?'

I nod, unable to meet his eye. 'Yeah.' I'm still breathless, my voice shaky.

'You were screaming. It was—' He stops, clearly not wanting to overstep the mark. 'Anyway. I just wanted to make sure you were all right.'

I look at him now, grateful that someone cares.

'Thanks, Dan.'

He nods, looks away again. We sit in silence for a moment. There's the odd bump and squeak from the flat above, and somewhere in the distance, five floors and God-knows-how-far away, tinny music floats from a car stereo and through the cracks between the wall and the window. It's surprisingly quiet for London, and I wonder what time it is. The glowing green numbers of the VCR tell me it's 2.34 a.m.

'Sorry to wake you up at this time of the night.'

He shakes his head. 'Don't worry. I just—' He rubs his eye and shuffles his body so he's facing me. I can tell he doesn't know how to say what he wants to say, so I wait for him to find the words, and eventually he does. 'You can tell me what's going on. If you want. I think – I reckon it could help.' He shrugs, awkward. 'You know, a problem shared is a problem halved and all that.' He drops his gaze to his hands.

I take a deep breath in and let it slowly out. We both listen to it in the motionless air.

'I have these dreams.' I pause and gather my thoughts. 'I wake up and think someone has been blown up, or shot, or we're running away from someone and I can't get away and they're getting closer and closer, only I don't know who it is I'm running from.' I inhale deeply. 'I hoped they'd fade over time but they're not. Nothing seems to help, it's just some nights they're worse and I—' I stop, my voice catching, and I realise my cheeks are wet.

'You've got to get help.'

'I know. I'm just not sure I can.'

Danny nods. 'Have you – do you think you're depressed? I mean, you know, properly, like?'

This could be the perfect moment to confess everything. To tell him how I almost ended it all three months ago, how I don't want to be a burden, how I don't really know what the point of being here is. To tell him about the girl on the bridge, and how I've become obsessed with her, how, when I'm not thinking about the war, I'm thinking about her. Trying to jigsaw together the wispy slivers of memory I have of her into something concrete, firm, until I think I'm going mad.

But something stops me. The truth is, Danny is the only person I've got. Dad's in Spain, living his fabulous new life with his new wife, and my mum hasn't been in my life since I was eight years old. A few people have let me kip on their sofa for a night or two at a time, but most have slipped quietly away. And I can't blame them. Who wants someone like me hanging around, bringing them down?

Danny has been the only one who's made me feel welcome. This man, who I'd only known for a few months before I went off to war, who's let me stay with him for months on end without ever asking anything of me, just accepts me for who and what I am – and I can't risk scaring him away. I need him.

'Yeah, a bit,' I say, instead of saying any of this out loud.

'A mate of mine at work, his girlfriend saw this counsellor after her mum died. He said it was amazing, the difference it made.'

My heart soars with affection for him. He's clearly been thinking about this, maybe even asking around.

'Yeah?'

'Want me to get her number? The counsellor I mean, not the girlfriend. Although...' He raises his eyebrows and gives me a wonky grin. 'Sorry, not the time.'

I smile back. 'It is the time. Thanks, Danny.'

'No worries. I just—' He stops. 'I saw what depression did to my dad. Mum always reckoned if he'd have got the help he needed, he would have been all right, in the end.'

'What happened to him?' Guilt floods through me that I've never talked to him about his family. Have I really been that self-centred?

'One of his mates got blown up down the mines. Saw his limbs flying all over the shop, you know—' He stops, realising what he's said, his face colouring. 'Anyway, he never talked about it, bottled it all up and it broke him, in the end. Ended up in a mental institute for a time, but he was never the same when he got back. I just reckon – well, I reckon you can sort yourself out, with the right help. Get yourself back on your feet. But you can't do it on ya own.'

It's rare that people surprise me, but tonight, Danny has. It also explains why he's been so happy to help me. Some people are just good, solid people. Salt of the earth. Danny is definitely one of them.

He stands, brushes imaginary crumbs from his pyjama bottoms and takes a step towards the kitchen.

'Wanna coffee?'

'Do you mind if I don't? I'll never get back to sleep.'

'Course not. See you in the morning, then.'

'Night, Danny. And thanks.'

'No worries, Ted.'

He creeps around in the kitchen and I drift off into what will hopefully be a dreamless sleep.

* * *

The only good thing about being in the army, for me, was the structure it provided. There was a purpose to every day – however awful and terrifying that purpose was – and I knew what was coming. At least most of the time. The worst thing since I got back has been the drifting from one day to the next with no sense of direction. To counter this, in the last few weeks, I've worked hard to get some semblance of a routine going. I've always been one for list-writing, and it's the technique I have gone back to now. I make one at the end of each day, ready for the following morning, and although things don't always go to plan, it's helping bring a sense of ease back to my life.

Today's goes something like this.

Morning:

Go to the barber's.

Buy milk, bread and cheese. And beers if enough cash left.

Ring Dad? (I probably won't do this but it makes me feel better to have the intention there.)

Go to the Job Centre.

Afternoon:

Do a couple of hours' labouring for Danny. (As well as a roof over my head, he's managed to give me a few hours here and there, cash-in-hand to keep me going and top up my meagre dole handouts.)

Danny finds my lists amusing, but I think he gets why I need to write them, so he never takes the piss too much. But I have found him adding things to the end occasionally. The other day was 'Buy Danny a brilliant present' and another time it said 'Get chippy chips for dinner'. I did it, of course, even though I knew he was only teasing. It's the least I can do.

The jobs they keep suggesting for me at the Job Centre are relentlessly depressing, and I'm not even being fussy. I would do most things if it meant I could find something to keep me busy and bring some cash to the table. But the thought of a few hours of cleaning here and there or night shifts in a factory just make me feel even worse than I already do. To make matters even worse, the two posts I did send my CV off for I didn't even get an interview for. Over-qualified, they said. Fuck's sake.

Always at the back of my mind, from the minute I wake up until the minute I lay my head on the pillow on Danny's lumpy sofa to go to sleep, is the girl from the bridge. I still haven't told Danny about her yet, clutching the secret of her to my chest like some sort of talisman.

She didn't reply to my ad in the *Standard*, and not knowing whether it was because she didn't see it or because she saw it and chose not to reply is hard. It's definitely not something I can fix with a list.

So, instead, I've started sketching. I was good at drawing as a boy, but I haven't done it for years. I bought myself a cheap sketchpad and a packet of pencils from the art supplies shop down the road, and I spend a few hours every day drawing. At first, they were awful, hulking great buildings resembling wonky rectangles, trees with spindly branches that looked like a child had drawn them. But as the days passed, I found my mojo again, and my drawings started to look half-decent.

Then one day, in the semi-darkness, when Danny was out with Danni and I had the flat to myself, I found myself sketching Fairy Girl's face. I'd spent so many hours trying to draw her in my mind, pulling together the fragments of her face that I could remember, snatching them out of the darkness of that freezing, terrible night, that it seemed only natural to start trying to capture them on paper. My first attempts were terrible, and I'd screw them up and throw them in the bin, start again, angrily. But then I'd capture something just right – the tilt of her head as she'd looked at me, the roundness of her lip as she'd asked me to get down from the edge of the bridge, the curl of her hair in the orange glow from the streetlamp, and I'd try again, adding one correct feature to another and another until, finally, I had it. At least, I had the image of who I thought she was.

I kept that one, tucked away between the covers of one of the books I bought at the second-hand bookshop. Just sketching her face has brought me some kind of release, helped me move on from that night. It's been a kind of therapy for me and now it's time to stop.

* * *

When I was small, about five or six years old, mornings were my favourite time of the day. Before Mum left, Dad always got up early for work, and I knew that, if I timed it right, he'd have time to make me a hot chocolate, and sit and chat with me at the tiny kitchen table before he had to leave, while he drank his own cup of sweet black coffee. He'd always spoon in three sugars, and I'd watch, mesmerised, as he slowly stirred it round and round, over and over, creating a whirl in the centre of the cup. As he stirred, he'd tell me stories about the people who worked at his office. It seemed like a magical place filled with funny characters, and every morning he had another story to tell that I'd lap up. I loved those times with Dad, they felt special, our little secret, just me and him.

But then one day when I was eight years old, everything changed. That morning, we both got up as usual. The house was quiet, quieter than it should have been and looking back I think we both knew something was wrong. By the time I'd finished my hot chocolate and Dad was ready to leave, Mum still wasn't downstairs, ready to take over so Dad could leave for work. So Dad had gone back upstairs, briefcase still in his hand, to see what was keeping her. He was gone some time and I heard no voices, so I just sat on my chair, frozen, until Dad came back down.

'She's gone, son,' he rasped. I'll never forget the look on his face, as though all of his thoughts had fallen out and left an empty hole.

Mum had left in the middle of the night when both of us were sleeping. Dad found a note propped up next to his pillow that he'd missed when he first got up. I never found out exactly what it said, but what he told me was that she needed to go away to 'find herself'. Whatever that meant. To an eight-year-old boy, it was devastating.

Mum leaving didn't just break me, it broke Dad, too. He couldn't – wouldn't – talk about her, at all. In fact, he wouldn't talk about anything. It felt as though I'd lost my mum and my dad in one fell swoop. As time went on, Dad drifted further and further away from me. He started going out more and more, leaving me to my own devices, until by the time I turned thirteen, I had a pretty good repertoire of one-person meals down to a tee (particularly if they involved tins of tuna), and could get a wash on without any help. Dad still paid the bills, fixed things, gave me money when I needed new school shoes, but essentially, he was no longer a father. He barely noticed whatever I tried to do to please him. He was a broken man, and, I soon realised, a raging alcoholic. And the alcohol turned him cruel.

Sadly, I've inherited the reliance on alcohol to numb pain. I know I'm not alone, but it doesn't make it any easier to know it's common. As I'm tipping the whisky down my throat, I know it's not doing me any good, but it's so hard to stop.

Danny's right. His dad should have got help, and my dad should have got help. And, unless I want to end up like them, my life defined by tragedy, I need to get help too.

I owe it to Danny.

I owe it to myself.

And yet this morning, as I watch the peaceful sunrise, the orange glow slowly spreading across the rooftops of the city until the whole sky is lit up like a fairground, I don't want to tackle the first thing on my list: ringing my GP. Danny had offered me the number of his mate's counsellor, but there's no way I can afford to pay private prices, so the NHS has to be my first port of call.

Sadly, though, the GP makes me feel as though I'm talking to a brick wall when I finally pluck up the courage to go to see him.

'I can give you some anti-depressants,' he says, grabbing a prescription pad from next to him on the desk. I'd struggled to explain to him the darkness of the feelings I sometimes had, how bad it had got that night just before Christmas. If I could just explain, so he can understand, maybe he could take it all away. But somehow the right words don't come.

I take the prescription with me, but even as I'm shoving it in my pocket, I know I'm not going to use it. Drugs aren't what I need. I need a brain reset.

Which is why, in the end, I ask Danny for the counsellor's number after all.

'Well done, mate,' he says, as he hands me a torn envelope with a London number scribbled on the back. 'I'm proud of you. And I'll lend you the cash to pay for it, you know, if you need it.'

I want to cry, but instead I just smile weakly and mumble a thank you.

It still takes me another week to muster up the courage to ring the number, and even then, I slam the phone down several times before I actually speak.

'Hello, is this Lynne?' I have a picture of Lynne in my mind already, a tall, athletic woman with short curly hair and a decent collection of cardigans. I imagine she lives alone with her dog, although I have no idea why. Her voice, when she answers, takes me by surprise with its low pitch.

'Speaking. How may I help?'

I pause for what feels like minutes, the line between us

humming with static, but she doesn't say anything until eventually I do.

'I think I need to come and see you.'

'That's wonderful.' Her voice is warm and gentle, and I already feel more at ease. 'Let me just take a few details.'

I give her my name and Danny's address, and we agree to meet the following week. As I put the phone down, a sense of pride floods through me. Maybe, just maybe, I can find a way to live with the memories and get on with my life again.

As I climb beneath the thin blanket on Danny's sofa that night, I realise that today is the first time for weeks that I haven't thought about the girl from the bridge.

Maybe I can do this alone after all. Maybe I really am enough.

8

13 MARCH 1992

Marianne

I breathe in deeply and close my eyes. Markets have a distinctive smell, a mix of mothballs and fabric conditioner, and something else, a unique, musty undertone that you never smell anywhere else. And I love it.

I haven't been to Camden market for ages. I used to come every week, but since I left my job, I haven't been able to afford my weekly splurge so have had to stay away. I still don't have a new job, but I needed to get out of the house, to come somewhere where I feel like myself for an afternoon. Besides, I can afford something cheap, and I'm a canny shopper.

I walk past the stalls selling handmade silver jewellery and hand-painted headscarves, tie-dyed dungarees and light-up deely-boppers. There's a stall in here that I love, and I'm dying to see what new stuff has come in since I last ventured here.

Suki sees me before I get there and waves maniacally at me.

'Marianne, I thought you'd abandoned me!' she cries, rushing round to the front of her stall and embracing me tightly.

'I'd never do that,' I laugh as she pulls away. She looks me up and down and I squirm. Suki's long hair is completely grey, but today it's shot through with purple and green stripes; the colours vary according to her mood. It's piled messily on top of her head and backcombed into a huge beehive at the front. Silver bracelets jangle on her slim wrist, and today's choice of a long, flowing dress hangs off her, sweeping the floor majestically. She looks incredible.

'You look like you're in need of some serious Suki therapy,' she says, ushering me round to the back of her stall. 'And I've got just the thing.'

'Oh, I—' I stop. I'm about to tell her I can't afford to buy anything today, but then I see what she's pulling out of the seemingly chaotic pile of garments behind her and I gasp.

'Ta-da!' she says, holding up a slightly shabby-looking deep green velvet jacket with a couple of buttons missing and a dubious-looking stain near the pocket. 'I know it doesn't look much, but it just screamed *Marianne* at me and I thought you could make it into something special, with your skills.' She's looking at me expectantly and I break into a smile.

'It's fabulous, Suki. I just – I can't really afford it at the moment.'

'Oh, I don't want any money for it.' She shoves it into my arms before I can object.

'You can't just give it to me, you're running a business here,' I say.

'That may be so, but I'm doing well enough to give my friend a present. And I kept it aside for you anyway, so you'd be insulting me if you didn't take it.' She crosses her arms over her chest, her bangles jangling loudly.

'Oh. Well, in that case, thank you. But it's too kind of you. I only really came to say hello. But I promise to make it fabulous, okay?'

'I have absolutely no doubt about that, my angel.' She turns and picks up a cup. 'Now, will you have a cup of tea with me before you flit off? I'm not very busy and it would be wonderful to catch up.'

'I'd love to,' I say, making myself at home on one of Suki's patchwork chairs. With the soundtrack of the market around me, I spend the next half an hour telling my friend all about the events of the last few weeks. It feels good to talk about it.

As I'm leaving, she presses something else into my palm. I open it up to find a tarnished silver four leaf clover. 'Now I know you think this is all nonsense, but trust me here, okay?'

I nod dubiously.

'This is a lucky charm. It's meant to bring happiness and peace to your life, but most of all, it's for success.'

'Mm hmm.'

'Oh, Marianne, always such a cynic. Well, do an old woman a favour and just take it, eh? You might not believe it will do you any good, but it can't do you any harm either, can it?'

'Thank you, Suki.' Despite my doubts, I'm grateful for her kindness.

She kisses my forehead, and as I turn to leave once again, she shouts, 'Don't stay away so long this time!' at me and I blow her a kiss which she pretends to catch. As I clutch my new jacket on the bus home, I'm buzzing with happiness. There's something about Suki that always cheers me up, no matter how bad I'm feeling. But as the bus rumbles on, northbound, my thoughts return to the argument I'd had with Mum earlier that morning.

'It's all well and good sending all these applications to magazines for some pie-in-the-sky job you don't even know exists, but you need to get out there and bring in a wage while you're doing it,' she'd said. It wasn't the first time. She found out that I'd quit my job – although I didn't tell her all the details of why – in the new year when I couldn't keep it from her and Dad any longer.

Ever since, she's been making little digs and 'helpful' suggestions about what I should be doing with my life, leaving the *Standard* open on the jobs pages, that sort of thing. The trouble is, neither her nor Dad have ever had any ambition. For them, like all their friends and the people they spend their time with, going to work is about nothing more than earning money. It's about getting up, doing a day's work and coming home again. It's not about job satisfaction, or doing something you love, or that makes you feel happy. Those ideas are alien concepts and that's how I've been brought up too.

But now, for the first time, I'm beginning to realise there's more to life than sticking with a job you hate. I was never very good at school, and when I started A Levels at college, it didn't take me long to realise it wasn't for me. But now? Well, I listen to Mum complaining about her cleaning job and Dad about his job as a postman, and at the same time, my own mind is buzzing with possibilities.

I've been thinking about Lance's words a lot since the day we met for lunch. I have been sending out endless letters to fashion magazines asking for some work experience and getting no response, but what I haven't told her, or anyone else, is that I've also been thinking seriously about whether I *could* be a counsellor after all.

It's not something I'd ever thought about before. People like me don't do jobs like that. You have to be brainy, do well at school, go to university. But something about Lance's words that day triggered something in me. She was right, I *did* love to help people. I did like listening to people's problems. It was always me that friends had turned to at school if they were having boyfriend problems or a family crisis, and somehow, I seemed to know what to say to help them. Or if I didn't, then I simply listened to them, and often that was enough. I *had* managed to help Bridge Man get off the bridge, hadn't I? The more I think about it, the more I'm convinced not everyone could have done that.

So a few days ago, I'd spoken to a lady called Lynne who was a friend of a friend and who worked as a counsellor, and, after several back and forth phone calls made from the phone box round the corner so Mum and Dad couldn't earwig, I'd made an appointment to go and have a chat with her.

* * *

The next day, I wait until Mum and Dad have both left for work before I get up. I know they mean well but I don't feel like answering any questions about my plans for the day. When I hear the front door close firmly for the second time, I climb out of bed and head for a shower. I'm equal parts nervous and excited. I haven't told anyone about the meeting, not even Lance. After all, I might get laughed out of there. It's not as though I've got anything to offer, and I don't have any qualifications apart from three below-average O Levels. But the more I've thought about it, the more sure I am I want to give it a go.

I pick up the carefully curated outfit I'd laid out last night, and put it together piece by piece. Trousers and frilled white shirt on, hair in an intricate up-do, I slip the restored and revitalised velvet jacket on and check myself in the mirror one last time. I'd spent a good couple of hours on my sewing machine in my room changing the buttons, taking in and making small adjustments to the jacket Suki had given me, and now it looks like it's been made just for me. I love it.

I pick up my bag and head out. The route into town is so familiar I could walk it with my eyes closed, but today I'm not heading straight into the city centre. The rooms where Lynne is based are in Kentish Town, just north of Camden.

Forty minutes later, I ring the bell outside the converted house where Lynne's office is and am being buzzed in. I feel a flutter of excitement in my belly as I walk up to the first floor and push the glass door open. The woman behind the counter looks up and gives me a huge smile and immediately I relax. Her hair is dyed bright orange and backcombed like Cyndi Lauper ten years ago, and she has crimson lipstick on her teeth. She looks like my kind of person, and I smile back brightly.

'Hello, how can I help you?'

I step up to the counter. 'Hi. I'm here to see Lynne.' The confidence in my voice belies the nerves in my belly.

'Oh, you must be Marianne. Lynne's expecting you. Take a seat over there and I'll give her a ring.'

While I wait, I study the reception room. It's clearly been decorated with some thought. After all, people who come here don't want to feel they've come to some corporate meeting where they have to prove themselves. The décor here does exactly the opposite – you almost feel like you're at home. I'm sitting on a cream sofa with stripy cushions against a warm terracotta wall. There are vases of flowers and pot plants dotted around and a pile of magazines on the coffee table. The top one has a picture of Sharon Stone on the cover. A jug of water sits on a side table and I'm just about to pour myself a glass when a door opens and a tall woman with short dark hair dressed head-to-toe in loose-fitting linen wafts towards me with her hand out.

'Marianne,' she says, her voice deep and gravelly.

I stand and shake her hand which is firm in mine. 'Lovely to meet you.'

'You too.' She takes her hand away and studies me for a moment and I wonder what she sees when she looks at me. Does she see someone who's spent hours over-thinking what to wear to this meeting? Or, as I suspect, is she searching for something else in my face, something deeper?

Whatever it is, she's clearly soon satisfied as she turns on her heel and strides back into the room from which she came and indicates I should follow her.

'Could we have a pot of tea in here, please, Heidi?' she calls to Cyndi Lauper as she disappears, and then she closes the door behind her and we sit facing each other from opposite armchairs.

I'm relieved when she speaks first.

'So, do you want to ask me any questions about being a counsellor?'

I like the directness of the question. Directness I can deal with. It's beating about the bush I can't stand. I sit up straight, muster my confidence. It's not like me to be lost for words, and I won't let it happen now.

'Yes, please.'

'Fire away.'

I'd prepared a few questions before I got here, but now it doesn't feel right to pull out a piece of paper and start reading from it. Instead, I say the first thing that comes into my head.

'Is it hard?'

She tips her head to the side while she thinks. Her cheekbones are incredible, giving her face a strong, handsome structure.

'Hard, yes. But it's also the most satisfying job I've ever done. Scratch that. It's not really a job. It's—' I really hope she doesn't say it's her 'calling' because I won't be able to resist rolling my eyes – 'necessary.'

'Oh.'

'You seem surprised.' She leans forward, her hands making shapes in the air as she speaks. 'The thing is, this isn't the job I thought I would do when I was a grown up. I always thought I'd be a writer – well, a poet, actually. But I wasn't that good, and after a few failed attempts at making it, I decided I needed to find something I *was* really good at. And this is it.' She holds her hands out, palms upwards as though presenting something. 'I'm assuming you're at the same sort of place?'

'Exactly the same. Apart from the writing bit.'

Like any counsellor worth their salt, she doesn't talk to fill a silence, and so when she doesn't reply, I speak again, and this time I tell her the whole sorry story about never having any ambitions, never thinking I could achieve anything, and about the admin job that I only got because I was sleeping with the boss.

'The thing is, I was actually quite good at that job,' I say. 'But I knew it wasn't something I'd do forever. And then there's the clothes making. I love fashion, but I don't think it's something I could do as a job. I think it would spoil it for me, in a way. Do you know what I mean?'

She nods but continues to say nothing.

'So here I am. My best friend Lance – Alison – actually suggested it. I don't think I'd ever have thought of it myself. But she pointed out how much I like helping people, how I always listen to her whenever she's got problems, and help her solve them.'

She nods, just as Heidi comes in with a teapot and two cups on a tray and leaves it on the table. The conversation pauses for a moment as Lynne pours tea. 'Milk?' she holds up the tiny white jug and I nod. I wait while she takes a sip then puts her cup down carefully.

'When someone comes to me for counselling, they think they want me to give them the answers to their problems. But, actually, what they really want, and really need, is for me to steer them in the right direction so they can solve the problem themselves. That's what's so amazing, because most of the time, that's exactly what happens, given enough time.'

I nod, unsure what to say.

'So, do you think it's something you'd like to try?'

'I think so.'

'Good. I think you'll be good at it.'

'Really?'

'Yep. After all these years, I get a pretty good sense of people early on. I'm fairly certain you're not just considering this out of desperation, but because you really think it's something you might be good at.'

'Yes, I really do.'

'Good.' She claps her hands together and I jump. 'So, the good news is, I've been considering taking someone on for a while, so I'm in a position to offer you a sort of apprenticeship. Of course, you'll have to do a trial for a month or so, make sure you're cut out for it, and you won't be with any clients for quite some time, but I think it could work. I've never done anything like this before so we'll have to work out the rest of the details, but I thought maybe you could do a couple of days a week and study for your qualification the rest of the time. I've had a quick look into it, and I believe there's a part-time course that takes a couple of years, and you can work at the same time. It would be perfect. What do you think?'

'Oh!'

I stare at her for a moment, overwhelmed. I've never had someone believe in me this much, and I'm not quite sure what to do with it. On one hand, it feels too much too soon. But then on the other hand, it feels amazing to have someone else make decisions for me, and to make me finally get on with something.

I find myself nodding and saying, 'I think it sounds great, thank you,' and how I find myself, just half an hour later, heading off to speak to someone recommended by Lynne about enrolling in a psychotherapy and counselling diploma the following September.

* * *

When I get home, the answer phone is flashing. I press play and listen to the message as I untie the laces of my boots.

'Marianne, it's Robert.' My heart plummets. 'Please ring me. I know you won't forgive me, but I miss you. I don't want it to end like this.' A pause, then the beep to indicate the message has ended.

I press delete instantly. He's rung a couple of times since I told him to leave me alone, always leaving the same messages. I haven't rung him back and I have no intention of doing so. As time has passed, I've discovered I don't actually care what he has to say. I miss my job more than I miss him.

In fact, I've found that, rather than thinking about Robert all the time and regretting what happened between us, my mind has been on something – or rather, someone – else entirely. I still can't stop thinking about the man on the bridge. At first, I told myself it was just because I was worried about him, was concerned I hadn't done a good enough job of saving him. But as time has gone on and he continues to occupy my thoughts, I know there must be more to it than that. I can barely even picture him – let's face it, there was a bit more to think about that night. But something about him seems to have stuck in my mind, like a fly to a sticky trap, and won't let go.

With a sigh, I sling my boots in the understairs cupboard, then gather up my bags and head to my room to pore over the information I've been given about training to become a counsellor. I wonder how much of my decision to do this is linked to what happened with Bridge Man. Quite a lot, I suspect, and for that I guess I should thank him. I just wish I had a way of finding him and letting him know how much he's changed my life already.

9

JUNE 1992

Ted

Some habits are hard to break, even if you know they're not doing you any good. Whenever I do something new, or go somewhere different, I wonder whether my parents would approve. I don't know why I do it, it's not as though either of them have even been around to encourage me. But it has become a habit formed over the years that is proving difficult to break.

Not that we're not trying, Lynne and me. But the problem is, I still have the nagging voice of my father in the back of my mind every time I visit her, and it's proving to be a big barrier to my progress.

What do you need to talk to someone for?

Just man up and get on with it.

Over thinker, that's your problem.

Too sensitive by half.

He might have had some outdated attitudes, but Dad also had some redeeming qualities. In fact, if I think about him before Mum left, I remember him as a kind father, if a little distant. But after the age of about eight, all I recall is disapproval or, worse, disinterest in anything I had to say or do, and yet still I have an overwhelming urge to do something to please him.

Lynne and I are getting somewhere, though. We've talked a bit about my childhood, although we are yet to get to the nitty gritty of what's causing my nightmares. Today, Lynne surprises me with an unexpected topic.

'So tell me more about this girl who saved your life,' Lynne says, watching me with her steely grey eyes. When I first arrived, she was nothing like the image I'd had in my mind. She was as tall as I had guessed but she is younger than I'd imagined, and rounder, and definitely doesn't wear comfy cardigans. Instead, she has a selection of plain linen tops and trousers that she wears on rotation, and piles of chunky jewellery round her neck, her wrists and even in her ears. Her hair is jet black and short, and she has the most amazing cheekbones.

I meet her gaze now, not knowing where to start. All I've told her so far in the two months since I've been seeing her is that I'd planned to jump from the bridge but that a girl stopped me. I'm not sure why she wants to focus on this, but I trust her enough now to tell her what happened that night on Waterloo Bridge.

When I've finished, Lynne's studying me. I'm not sure where to look so I focus my gaze on a bunch of yellow flowers in a vase on the side table. Daffodils? Tulips? God knows, I have no idea about flowers.

The silence in the room grows louder until, to my ears, it becomes almost deafening. I'm about to speak, just to say something, anything, to fill the silence, when Lynne beats me to it.

'And why do you think this has taken on such a significance to you?'

I stare down at my feet. My trainers are battered, and there's a small hole in the fabric of the toe. I look up and meet her gaze.

I could be snarky. I could say it's significant because I've never been suicidal before, or I've never had someone save my life before. But I know what she's asking me, and she knows I know.

'Because she cared enough.'

Four words, but it feels as if they weigh a tonne, and now they're out of my mouth I am lighter, all of a sudden.

Lynne nods.

'Go on.'

'Since my mum left, I've never felt as though I mattered enough, to anyone.' I take a deep breath. 'I obviously didn't matter to my mum, otherwise she would have stayed. But after she went, I stopped mattering to my dad, too. He'd always undermined me, even when I was young, although I don't think he meant to. But once Mum had gone, he didn't even care enough to do that. He wouldn't have noticed whether I was there or not.'

I stop. Am I being unfair? Maybe. There were times when Dad was proud of me, but he was meagre with praise, and quick to put me down, until I truly believed nothing I did was right. But when your mum's made it clear she doesn't want you any more, you need more from your dad, it's as simple as that. And my dad didn't step up.

'I joined the army to please him, because he likes people who are real men's men, you know, even though I knew the army wasn't right for me. I tried to stick it out, but it was worse than I'd ever thought it would be. But all I could think about, as I cried myself to sleep every night, was how pathetic I was, and that no wonder my parents wanted nothing to do with me.'

Lynne nods again and leans forward.

'And since then? Since the army?'

I shrug. 'There's been no one.'

'What about your flatmate?'

'Danny? He's not really a flatmate. He's a good mate who's let me stay. But it's his flat and he can boot me out any time he wants.'

'But he's been there for you, you've been important enough to him for him to offer you a bed?'

I nod, acquiescing. 'He's been good to me. I've been lucky.'

'So tell me about your suicide attempt.'

This is the thing I like about Lynne. When she wants to make a point, she goes straight there. We haven't talked about this yet, it hasn't been the right time. But now we're here, I want to tell her the truth.

'I just thought it would be easier all round.'

'Easier?'

'For everyone. Danny, Dad – I don't know, the taxpayer, whoever.' I shrug, feeling agitated. 'I just felt like I was a burden on all of them, and if I wasn't around any more, it would make life simpler for everyone. It's not as though there was anyone to miss me.'

Lynne says nothing.

'I'd fully intended on jumping off that bridge. I nearly did it. But when the girl climbed over the barrier next to me and begged me to stop, something clicked in me. It was as though I could suddenly see clearly that maybe there could be something worth living for. Or I should at least try to find something.'

'Understood.' She pauses. 'But why her? Why this girl? What is it about her that's made such an impression on you?'

That's a good point. Would the outcome have been the same if someone else had seen me that night, or is it just because it was this particular woman? I haven't yet admitted to Lynne how much I've been thinking about Fairy Girl over the last few months. How much she's filled my mind, replacing some of the bad thoughts, giving me slivers of hope. But she must have picked up on it from the few times I have mentioned her.

'I don't know. She—' I pause, unsure how to explain it. 'There was just something really honest and open about her. Something – special.' I feel my face flushing.

'In what way?'

'She seemed like she really, really cared. Like it really mattered to her whether I jumped off the bridge or not.' I stop, shrug. 'I have no idea whether that's the case, but I – she...' I rub my face with my hands. The truth is, I've been obsessing over someone I only met for a few moments, and whose face I can barely even picture any more. I've imagined seeing her on the streets several times but it's never her – I don't even know whether I'd pick her out in a line-up.

Except something tells me I would.

'I've tried to find her.'

Lynne waits.

'I put an ad in the paper. I even went back to the bridge, although I didn't really expect to find her there. I just – I wish there was a way I could track her down. To say thank you.'

'And anything else?'

'What do you mean?'

'Is there any other reason you want to find her?'

'To say thanks but also to tell her I'm okay.' I can see Lynne knows I'm not telling her the whole truth, but how can I? How can I admit that Fairy Girl has infiltrated my thoughts so much that I've thought about her almost every day for the last six months?

'But right now, she's your reason for living?'

Lynne's hit the nail on the head. Thanking the girl on the bridge, whose name I don't even know, has become a reason for carrying on.

'Yes.'

Lynne waits a few moments, then says, 'I think we should leave it there for today. You've done well.'

I smile, pleased with the praise. I'm not convinced it's true, but I do feel as though I made some sort of breakthrough today. Who knows how much it matters that this stranger is my main reason for living right now, but at least I've acknowledged it and that's got to be a start.

I stand and Lynne shows me out of the room. As we enter the reception area, I hear voices, someone saying, 'See you tomorrow!' then a figure whooshes past me. I look up in time to spot a flash of blonde hair turning the corner at the bottom of the stairs and I stop for a second, breathless.

Was that...?

Can it be...?

Fairy Girl?

I shake the thought free from my head. I've imagined seeing her plenty of times before, and it's never her. Why on earth would she be here?

'Ted, are you all right?'

Heidi, whose previously orange hair is a strange shade of purple today, is watching me with concern, and her voice snaps me out of my reverie. The woman has gone now, and I hear the outside door slam closed.

'Yes, sorry, I'm fine.' I turn back to Lynne and smile. 'I just thought I saw someone I know.'

Lynne gives me a knowing look and sticks out her hand.

'Until next week?'

'Next week.'

As quickly as I can without making it look as though I'm hurrying, I run down the stairs and am out on the street in seconds. The sun is bright, and I squint as I exit the cool darkness of the building. Among the usual hectic Londoners buzzing around like worker bees, others mill about in the sunshine, shirtless men, women in shorts and bikini tops, as though we're in the middle of St Tropez, not a slightly down-at-heel street in north London. I stand on my tiptoes and look right, then left, then right again, like a meerkat, as a bus rumbles past pumping out fumes, desperately trying to catch sight of a flash of blonde curls in the sunlight. But there's nothing, no one. Whoever she was, she's gone.

10

JUNE 1992

Marianne

'Thank you so much.' I hold out my hand. Angela, the woman in the chair in front of me, presses her damp palm against mine, and dabs a tissue under her already red eyes. I give her a smile and wait while she gathers her bag and her dignity. This was her first meeting, to see whether counselling was right for her – it's something Lynne insists on, adamant she doesn't want to take on anyone she doesn't believe she can help. Not that I can imagine there is anyone out there who wouldn't be helped by Lynne. She's like a miracle worker. Some days, I watch her while she's talking to someone, trying to get them to dig deep to the real root of their problem, and I'm in awe. I also worry there's no way I'll ever be as good as her but, as she says, baby steps. For now, at least I know I'm watching and learning from the best.

Angela finally stands, clutching her handbag into her side like a shield.

'Thank you for seeing me today,' she says now, her voice still shaky. Her head's bowed, and her shoulders are hunched over. She's a woman who needs Lynne's help if ever I saw one. I hope she takes her on.

'It's my pleasure,' I say, standing by the door.

She steps towards me, and I open the door into the reception area.

'I'll let you know when Lynne can see you. Do you want to speak to Heidi to let her know the best way to get in touch with you?'

Something I've learned since I've been training with Lynne is that, often, the people who come here for help don't want their partners to know about it. Sometimes it's because they're the reason they're here in the first place. Other times it's more complicated, they feel like they're a failure for admitting they need help. And so we always ask how we should contact them, rather than just ringing home numbers or writing to home addresses.

I head to the kitchen while Heidi helps Angela. I don't have a space of my own here yet, so I leave my coat and bag on the rack in the tiny kitchen. But despite my reservations, I've loved my first few weeks under Lynne's wing. I've learned so much, and for the first time in my life, I think I've found something I'm really good at. I'm truly starting to believe this might be something I could make a career out of. Even Mum's impressed when I tell her about my day – she's stopped leaving the job pages of the local paper open on the table every evening, although I'm sure that won't last forever. But thinking of Mum drags my mind back to the terrible conversation we had last night.

'I'm so proud of you, love,' she'd said, as I stirred a slightly dodgy-looking stew I'd made. I might be handy on the sewing machine, but I can't cook to save my life. I ignored her grimace as she peered into the pot.

'Thanks, Mum,' I said.

'Have you put any salt in that?'

'No.'

'Here, let me just...' She reached into the cupboard and threw in a handful of salt, a few pinches of pepper and a stock cube. Then she grabbed the wooden spoon from me and gave it a stir, and licked the end of the spoon. 'That's better. Got a bit of flavour now. Doesn't take much.' I bit my tongue, determined not to start a fight.

'Right. Well, it's ready now, where's Dad?'

'I'll go and get him.'

I served the dinner and it was as we were sitting down to eat the still-bland plate of food that I saw Mum give Dad a look. He shook his head.

'What?' I said, looking between them.

'What do you mean, what?' Mum looked all wide-eyed and innocent, while Dad just carried on shovelling stew into his mouth mechanically and pretending he hadn't noticed anything.

'What was that look you just gave Dad?'

'Look? I don't know what you mean.'

Dad put his spoon down. 'Oh, come on, love, she's not stupid. We might as well tell her.'

'Tell me what?' I paused my knife in mid-air, my breath held.

Dad let out a huge sigh. 'I'm having to cut my hours down.'

I stared at him. Dad was a postman, and although it was just a job to him, he was the most loyal employee you've ever met, never took a day off sick, rarely took holiday. I couldn't imagine anything that would make him take time off. Unless...

'Why? What's happened?'

Dad raised his eyes from his bowl and looked at me. 'I've not been feeling very well and – well, the doctor told me I need to start taking it a bit easier.'

'Doctor? When did you go to see a doctor?' My voice was getting higher and higher, but I couldn't help it.

'Your dad was just feeling tired and achy a lot,' Mum said pushing a piece of lamb round her plate. Dad looked relieved not to have to say any more. 'He kept getting breathless too, and that's when I told him, *Patrick, you have to go and get yourself looked at.*' She looked up at him then, and I saw her eyes shimmer with tears.

Dad took over again. 'Turns out I've got a bit of a dodgy ticker,' he said. 'Doctor told me I've got to get rid of some of this—' he rubbed his pot belly affectionately – 'and start taking things a bit easier.'

'But—' I didn't know what to say. 'You never told me any of this.'

'No, we didn't want to worry you, love, not if there was nothing to worry about. And it's fine, really it is. I'll be fine as long as I do what I'm told.'

'That'll be the day,' Mum said, and Dad gave her a sheepish grin.

'So what does this mean? Do you need me to find somewhere else to live, give you a bit of space?'

'Gosh, no, we don't need to be that drastic. It'll be helpful having you around the place, to be honest.' Mum looked at Dad again and I waited. 'It's just – well, what with Dad not working as many hours, I'm having to take some more work on and – well, we could do with you helping out a bit too.' She flushed and fiddled with her fork.

'Oh! Of course.' The truth was I hadn't really known what to say. I knew that, with their jobs, money had always been tight, but they were my mum and dad, and I never thought of them as having problems. At least, not like this. I felt ashamed of myself.

Now, as I grab my bag, I think about how to broach the subject of money with Lynne. I'm still training, and have a long way to go. But being here twenty hours a week means I don't have time for much else. If she can't afford to give me a bit more, I'm going to have to find a part-time job elsewhere. But I'll do whatever it takes. I'm twenty years old, for goodness' sake. It's time to step up and be the adult I've resisted being for so long.

As I'm leaving, Lynne is coming out of her room with her last client of the day. I'm not in the mood to talk to her about money right now, so I don't wait to say goodbye, and instead hurry towards the stairs with a quick 'See you later!' over my shoulder to Heidi.

'Bye!' she calls after me as I gallop down the stairs, shrugging my cardigan on as I go. I can hear voices in reception – Lynne and the deeper tones of a man – but I don't glance back as I round the corner of the stairs. I head out into the busy street, the sun warm on my skin as I walk south, away from home, towards Camden. I'm going to ask round all the clothes shops, see whether there are any part-time jobs going, pop and see if Suki can help, or knows anyone who can. If I have to find something else, it might as well be something I enjoy.

Just then, the bus pulls up beside me and I jump on, swipe my travelcard, and climb up to the top deck and sit right at the front where I can see the world go by. As the bus roars away from the kerb, and my mind is filled with thoughts of Mum and Dad, I see a man standing on the pavement outside the office I've just left, and my heart flips over. He looks familiar, and it takes me a second to realise why. Is it—? Could it be—? I twist round in my seat to get a better look, but he's disappeared behind a group of girls in skimpy denim shorts and cropped tops, and even when I press my forehead against the grimy window, I can barely make him out any more. Then we turn the corner and he's gone.

I slump back in my seat, a frown on my face, my heart thumping in my temples, and wonder.

Did I *really* just see the man from the bridge?

11

DECEMBER 1992

Ted

I step back from the wall and admire my handiwork. Even though I'm twenty-three years old, I've never put a shelf up before and I'm pathetically pleased with myself.

I'd had to borrow the tools from Danny, of course – in fact, he'd even offered to do it for me. But I've taken enough from him over the last few months. Besides, I have to learn to do these things for myself sooner or later.

I'm finally in my own flat. I still have to pinch myself to really believe it, especially when I think back to where I was this time last year. Alone, desperate, suicidal.

And while I still struggle, support from Lynne and Danny means I finally feel strong enough to get back on my own two feet and try and make a life for myself at last.

Now here I am. The flat's only tiny – this is London, after all. You'd have to be a millionaire to afford to buy a house on this street, the rent's steep enough. But thanks to Danny helping me out with some work – I just carry bricks and do all the tedious jobs but I don't care, I'm just grateful to be earning some money at last – I can finally afford to pay my own way, and I moved into this place three weeks ago. Man, it feels good to have my own space.

I look around the room. It's pretty empty. Apart from the – slightly wonky, now I look at it again – shelf I've just put up, there's an old sofa bed I bought second-hand from Loot, which I covered in an old blanket to disguise the stains, a couple of wooden chairs that I might get round to painting one day, a small folding dining table I found in the local junk shop, and a TV on the floor. I still need to get a TV stand for it, and there are no curtains at the windows yet, but it's starting to come together, and just being here, on my own, knowing nobody is about to come in and disturb me, feels wonderful. I'm still waiting for BT to connect my phone, so for now I'm blissfully uncontactable.

I walk into the tiny galley kitchen and fill the kettle with water. Then I think better of it and pull a beer from the fridge. I know I need to try harder to curb my drinking, but I also need to take it one step at a time. I've already cut down on the whisky, but for now beer is taking its place by helping to numb my senses a little, dampening down the thoughts that spin unchecked through my mind every evening without it.

I head back to the living room and plonk my can on the table and open the folder that's been sitting there waiting for me since I got back earlier. I only had a half day at work today, so I'd headed to the library this afternoon to start my research.

I pull the sheets from the folder and take a sip from my can.

Training to become a doctor.

Even the words give me a shiver of excitement. I've been racking my brains over the last few months, trying to work out what I want to do with the rest of the life I've been gifted. I owe it to the girl on the bridge and myself to do something good with it and not just drift along and let it pass me by. Otherwise, why else did I get a second chance?

I think about Fairy Girl now. I've talked about her a lot with Lynne, and I often wonder whether she can sense that someone out there is talking about her. I wonder too whether she ever thinks about the man she saved on the bridge that night.

It took me a while to realise how fixated I'd become on finding her. It had seemed like the most important thing in the world, somehow. I'd created a sort of separate area in my mind that was entirely occupied by her, and my obsession had become unhealthy. Lynne helped me to see that, but she never made me feel like I was being judged for it. In fact, she made me understand why Fairy Girl had become so important to me. It was as though she was the bridge – excuse the pun – between my old life and my new life. As though she underpinned my whole existence from now on as a result of saving me.

Now, although I still believe I owe her my life and would love to see her again, I no longer find myself thinking about her endlessly. Just occasionally in the middle of the night when I wake up after one of my slowly diminishing nightmares. And the times when I think I spot her on the street – which, admittedly happens most days, although even that's happening less and less.

'It's okay to think about her,' Lynne said to me one day. 'It's perfectly natural. But do you think it's healthy to idolise her?'

Idolise felt like a strong word. But maybe she was right. I finally realised I owed it to us both to not only move on, but to do something good with my life. Something that would make a difference. That would be the best way of thanking her for what she did for me.

And so here I am, considering training to become a doctor.

'Don't you have to study for, like, ten years or summat to do that?' Danny had said when I'd told him my idea.

'I think it's a bit less than that, Dan. I just think it would be good to give something back. You know, after everything.'

'Fair dos.'

I'd told him, eventually, about how low I'd got, about what I'd tried to do that night. He'd been shocked but, as expected, entirely practical about the whole thing.

'Fuckin' 'ell, Ted.'

I'd nodded. 'I know.'

He shook his head. 'Jeez, why didn't ya tell me? I could've helped you, you know. Been here more, looked after you.'

'That's why I didn't. I already felt like I was a burden. I couldn't ask anything more of you.'

'But I didn't do anything, mate. I just let you kip on my sofa.'

'Dan, listen to me. You did more than you ever needed to.' I shook my head. 'Fuck, mate, you did more than my bloody parents have for the last fifteen years.'

'Have you heard from your dad?'

'Not for a few weeks. Wouldn't tell him anyway.'

He'd been silent for a few minutes. I didn't try and explain it to him any more. If you've never felt that low, that desperate, it's impossible to understand it.

'Are ya—' he stopped. 'Will you...'

'Will I do it again?'

He nodded.

'No.'

'Right.'

'I promise, Dan.'

'I know.' He coughed. 'So what stopped you?'

I hadn't planned on telling him about the girl with the fairy wings. I already felt mad enough that she'd become such a huge part of my life even though I'd met her for all of twenty minutes. But I found myself telling him about her, and about how I'd tried to find her; the newspaper ad, the visits to the Southbank to see if I could bump into her again, the times I've followed random women on the street only to discover they're not her when they turn round and give me a frightened glare. My desperation to find the girl who had saved me.

'What for?' Danny said.

I shrugged. 'To say thanks?'

'Oh, right. Nothing else?'

'I guess... there was just something about her. Something special. Something – different.'

'Right.' He chewed a loose piece of nail and looked me in the eye.

'You know you've got to stop looking for her now, right? Otherwise it'll drive you mental.'

And there, in a few succinct words, was the simple fact of the matter. I'll give him this, he's astute, that Danny, even if it's not immediately obvious. He's wasted as a builder.

So that was the day I decided to start getting on with it. And now here I am, reading about how to become a doctor. I think maybe I've already gone mad.

* * *

I never make promises I can't keep, but sometimes, I believe it's okay to stretch the parameters of them a little. Which is why I try and ignore the pang of guilt at the promises I made to both Danny and Lynne as I walk out of the framing shop with a picture under my arm, wrapped in brown paper. I feel like a thief, as though everyone is watching me, waiting to catch me out.

When I get back to the flat, I place the picture on the table while I fetch a beer from the fridge. I need Dutch courage for this. Taking a deep swig, I place the can carefully on the table, far enough away from the package, and stand for a moment, staring at the inanimate object in front of me. My heart thumps in my temples.

Get a fucking grip, Ted.

Carefully, I peel the tape off the back, and open the flaps of the folded paper, bit by bit. Finally, as all the sections are revealed, I relax. I was right. This is a good picture.

It's my sketch, the one I hid inside the covers of a book while I was still living with Danny. It's simple, just a few black lines, but I smile as my eyes trace the outline of a cheekbone, of lips. Of curls. And of fairy wings.

I might have promised to stop trying to draw Fairy Girl. And I have.

But I didn't promise I wouldn't ever look at the picture I kept.

I grab the hammer I'd been using earlier to put the shelf up, find a nail and hammer it into the wall. And then I hang the picture above the table, where I can see it from everywhere in the room.

It's just a picture. Nobody will ever know who it's meant to be, or even that I drew it. But it will help me to never forget that night, and how close I came to losing everything and how I have this woman to thank for saving me.

12

DECEMBER 1992

Marianne

Since Dad had to stop working so many hours, my life has become ridiculously busy. While Dad gets under Mum's feet at home and potters about with his motorbikes in the shed, I'm trying to fit in my counselling coursework, my twenty hours a week with Lynne, as well as working in a clothes shop in Camden on weekends and a couple of evenings every week. It feels like I have no time for anyone or anything else.

Lance isn't impressed.

'Come on, you need time to have a bit of fun,' she said yesterday, when I told her I couldn't come to the pub tonight.

'I know. But I'm working till nine and I'm always knackered after that.'

'Excuses, excuses.'

I was determined not to give in. I might have been contributing more financially to Mum and Dad these days, but with Dad's heart problems, I still felt I needed to be around more often to help out.

'Don't be daft,' Mum said when she overheard me telling Lance that. 'You go.'

Which is why I now find myself heading reluctantly to the World's End pub to meet Lance and a few others.

I walk through the doors and the smoke hits my lungs immediately, and my eyes sting. It should be an awful smell, but actually I love it. It reminds me of home, my dad puffing on his endless cigarettes. The music thumps loudly in the background, Manic Street Preachers, and I make my way to our usual table, as far away as possible from the entrance.

'Annie!' Lance shouts as she spots me approach and I sigh inwardly as she throws her arms around me. Everyone's clearly been here for several hours already, and I'm at least three drinks behind even the most sober person. I have two choices. Stay for a quick drink then make my excuses and go home to bed. Tempting, given how exhausted I am. Or play catch-up and spend the night dancing with my friends. Despite the hangover I know it'll leave me with, now I'm here, I feel like having fun.

I head to the bar. I'm not exactly flush these days, but I can at least afford to buy myself a few drinks. I order two pints of snakebite – well, saves me queuing twice – and am turning to head back to the table with my hands full when I crash into a man who's striding past.

'Oh, God, I'm so sorry,' he says as cider drips down my forearm to my elbows and forms a puddle on the already sticky floor.

'Don't worry about it,' I say, taking a sip from each of my drinks so they're not so full.

'Let me get you another.'

'No, it's fine.' I glance over to the corner where Lance is waiting, and make a move to walk over there. But before I do I glance up and stop, suddenly.

'Oh!'

He looks puzzled as I stare at him, open-mouthed. Suddenly I'm not in that pub in Camden any more; instead, I'm back to this time last year, standing on a freezing cold bridge in a pair of fairy wings, telling a man I've never met before why he shouldn't jump off a bridge. The man in question is watching me, his forehead creased in puzzlement.

'Are you okay?'

Then, as quickly as it disappeared, the pub comes back into focus – the thump of the music, the chatter of voices, the smell of stale beer. And I realise. It's not him. I shake my head.

'Yes, sorry. I just – I thought you were someone else.'

He grins. 'I'm glad I'm not. You didn't look too happy to see the poor bloke.' He touches my elbow. 'Anyway, sorry again about the drinks.'

'No problem,' I mutter. I stand and watch him move across the bar. I don't know what made me think he was Bridge Man. Now I look at him again he looks quite different. He's bigger built, for a start, and shorter. But there must have been something in his face that made me stop so suddenly and my heart start to thump hard against my rib cage.

It's not the first time. Over the last few months, since the day I thought I saw him outside Lynne's offices, I've mistakenly imagined I've seen Bridge Man several times – once was at work again, the back of someone's head as they were leaving – and each time, as I've realised it's not him, or they've disappeared, I've felt my stomach drop with disappointment.

'Maybe you're just looking for proof he's still alive,' Lance said the first time I told her about one of my 'sightings'.

'Probably,' I agreed. But I also believe there's more to it than that. Finding Bridge Man again has become a bit of a secret infatuation that I haven't even dared admit to Lance, because I know how crazy it sounds. I mean, what would I achieve if I did see him again?

'Annie, why're you just standing there?' Lance's voice pierces my thoughts and I jump.

'Sorry. Coming.' I flash her a smile, and follow her back to the corner where our friends are already in various states of drunkenness. I see Gary and Chris gesturing at each other in the corner, and Katy and Nicky dancing next to them, beer splashing over the tops of their glasses as they bounce maniacally to the music.

'Who was that bloke?' Lance has to shout to make herself heard over the rhythmic thump of The Prodigy.

'Which bloke?'

'The one you were staring at just now.'

'Oh, no one.' Lance looks as if she's about to say something else, but then the moment passes. Normally she wouldn't let me get away with that, she'd quiz me for more if she thought there was a mere hint of interest in someone other than Robert, but with several vodkas in her, she's oblivious. She's been desperate for me to move on and find someone else, but the truth is I'm quite happy by myself for now. After meeting Robert so young, it feels like the right time to be single, despite Lance's efforts to set me up with various friends and colleagues.

I smile as the song changes and Lance jumps in the air and laughs. I quickly down most of a pint and feel the rush to the head that always comes when I drink too quickly. I throw back the last few mouthfuls of my drink and enjoy the beginnings of drunkenness settle over me. I need this tonight, I realise, more than I'd thought. I need to let go, lose myself and forget about the man on the bridge.

13

OCTOBER 1993

Ted

BEEP BEEP BEEP BEEP BEEP BEEP BEEP—

I slam my hand onto the top of the alarm clock and drag myself up to sitting. Five a.m. It's still dark outside, not even the birds have mustered the energy to make any sound yet. All I can hear through the single pane of glass is the occasional rumble of tyres, the sound of shutters being lifted somewhere along the street and, inside the building, the gentle hum of a radio above me. But even in the middle of the city, life hasn't really got going at this ungodly hour.

I groan and pull myself to standing and walk, robotically, into the shower. I'm soon wide awake, the cool water pummelling some sense into my head and waking my body up for the day ahead.

As I blearily make a pot of coffee, I stand and look out of the tiny kitchen window onto the flat roof outside, and all the rooftops beyond that, and think about the day ahead.

I never thought life as a trainee doctor was going to be easy. But sometimes, when I'm heaving myself out of bed for yet another early start after crawling into bed barely six hours earlier, I do wonder if I'm up to this.

My days are split between the lecture hall, where I have to regularly pinch myself awake when I feel my eyes drifting shut, the library, and the hospital. I've only just started shadowing the doctors at UCLH, and although it's exciting, it does mean my hours are even longer. But then, I tell myself, I might as well make the most of my life. I almost didn't have one. I drag my thoughts back to the here and now before they drift off again, tip the dregs of my coffee down the sink and hurry back to the bedroom to get dressed. I've got three hours in college this morning, then I've got a five-hour shift shadowing Mr Alexander, an A&E consultant, this afternoon. The first time I did a shift with him was the most overwhelming experience of my life, even more so than my first day in Kuwait. Then, we were shielded from the action most of the time, only being dragged in to battle when the commander said so. But in A&E, the pace is something else. There is no let-up, and someone always wants you, thinks they should be your priority, when you're trying to attend to another patient in even greater need. I felt like a lamb to the slaughter as I raced around, wanting to help everyone and being no help at all in my panic. Now, two months on, I know what to expect, and even though it's exhausting and I feel like I can barely lift one foot in front of the other by the end of a shift, it's also thrilling and satisfying.

'I think you're mad,' Danny had said when I told him how hard it was over a couple of pints in his local last week.

'You're probably right,' I'd agreed.

'Are you sure it's what you want, Ted?' I knew what he meant – he was worried my anxiety would come back, and with it, my excessive drinking.

'I need to, Dan.'

'Because of what happened, you mean?'

I nodded. 'Yeah. I just feel like I should do something meaningful. You know, now I've been given the chance.'

He nodded. 'Well, good luck to you, mate. Wish I 'ad the brains you've got.'

'Cheers, Danny.'

We sat in comfortable silence for a moment. It's one of the things I appreciate about Danny, his ability to know when a subject doesn't need discussing any further.

'Anyway, tell me more about the wedding.'

Danny and Danni had quickly become serious and, just a year after they met, Danny had asked her to marry him.

'Oh, God, I dunno. Danni's doing it all, I'm trying to stay out of the way, you know what women are like. All *do you want blue napkins or cream? Do you think we should have roses or lilies?* Christ on a bike, I don't know. I just want to get married to her, know what I mean?'

'I do mate, I do. So are you managing to stay out of all the planning?'

Danny looked sheepish. 'Well, there is one thing I've got to plan myself.' I watched him spin a beer mat round and round, like a nervous twitch. 'I just—' He stopped, then looked up at me. 'Listen mate, you don't have to say yes if you don't want to, I know you've got all sorts of stuff going on, but I wondered – well, me and Danni wondered – if you wanted to be my best man?'

'Oh!'

'You don't want to. That's all right, I just thought I'd ask but there's no pressure mate, none at all.'

'I'd love to be.'

'Oh. Oh, well, great.' Danny gave me a grin and held his hand out. 'Well, cheers. I'm really chuffed.'

'Me too.' And I was. More than I could let on. Danny had been so kind to me, but I'd never have dreamed he thought enough of me to want me to be his best man.

'Are you sure, though? I mean, you don't have anyone else you'd rather ask? Chris, or Si, or…'

He shook his head. 'Nah. I mean they're great an' that but I just think…' he shrugged. 'Well, you know. We've lived together, haven't we, mate? You know more about me than even me mum does these days.'

I didn't reply and Danny looked worried. 'You sure you're all right about it? Don't do it if you think it's going to be too much.'

I shook my head, feeling tears prick my eyes. 'No, I'd love to be. I just—' I swallowed. 'I don't want to be soppy, but I can't believe you've asked me, to be honest. No one's ever asked me to do anything like this before. It means the world.'

'That's all right. I mean we're mates, aren't we? And that's who you need by your side on a day like that, otherwise it's totally taken over by crazy women.' Danny grinned. 'Besides, you might get off with one of the bridesmaids – that's what best men are meant to do isn't it?'

'Yeah, I guess so.' I didn't have the heart to tell him that hooking up with a random woman at his wedding was the last thing I wanted to do. For now, I'd just enjoy the honour of being his best man.

* * *

The day is as hectic as expected. In fact, by the time it gets to 5 p.m. and almost time to leave, I'm watching Mr Alexander treat a patient who'd been brought into A&E with severe chest pains. I don't mind, we never usually get off on time anyway, but I know we've still got at least two patients to see.

I watch as Mr Alexander gently feels all around the site of the patient's pain, and I make notes as he asks questions I would never have thought of to try to work out the exact nature of the injury. Some days, I feel as though I'm nailing this being a doctor thing, and other times, I feel like I'm never going to match up to the experts I'm shadowing. It's all a matter of experience, I suppose.

'Okay, well, let me just speak to the nurse,' Mr Alexander says, turning away and gathering up his notes. He turns to me and is about to say something when a shrill beeping pierces the hush of the cubicle. He pulls his bleeper from the pocket of his white coat. 'We have to go – I'll be back shortly,' he says, hurrying out of the room. I give the patient a weak, apologetic smile. Sometimes it feels as though, after years of doing this job, the doctors and consultants forget that they're dealing with real people – people who are frightened they might die, and who need reassurance. But I understand why. Quite apart from the lack of time, if they got too involved with every patient, they'd be an emotional wreck. I still have a long way to go on that score.

I follow Mr Alexander, hurrying to keep up as he strides through the double doors and along the corridor.

'I've got an emergency brain haemorrhage,' he says, filling me in as I frantically scribble notes.

'But what about the heart attack patient in cubicle three?'

He glances at me, harassed.

'Don't worry, someone else will deal with him. Could you just go and let the doctor in charge know, then you can get off.'

'Are you sure?'

He gives an abrupt nod. 'Yes. There's not much you can do here anyway. Just go and sort it. See you tomorrow.'

I feel like a dismissed child as he strides off down the corridor and I'm left alone at the doors of A&E. I head back inside and go and find the doctor in charge, and tell him about Mr Alexander being called away to an emergency. He grunts. 'Oh, great, and a heart attack isn't an emergency?'

I bristle but say nothing. I know it's just the stress of the job, so I try not to take it personally. But it is hard knowing you're letting someone down, even if it's not your fault.

I wait until he's gone to find someone else to deal with his patient. For a moment, I consider going in there myself just to ask some preliminary questions, take some notes for the doctor. I can imagine the patient's fear as he waits in his side room, not sure what's going on; I can picture his wife clutching his hand, his kids standing round him, wondering whether he's going to die before someone arrives to help. You read about hospital overcrowding all the time, and they're not wrong. It's an absolute shambles sometimes, the emergency department totally incapable of taking any more patients, almost at bursting point constantly. But thanks to the dedication of the people who work here, stories of people waiting eight hours on a trolley in the corridor are few and far between.

I hover for a moment longer, trying to decide what to do. The room's just there, I can even hear voices, the family reassuring him he'll be fine, that someone will be there soon. A woman pops her head out of the room. She's in her mid-fifties, her hair pale and frizzy, cut above her shoulders, and I feel a pang of sympathy for what she's going through. But it's totally against the rules for me to go in there unaccompanied – I'm not qualified, so I decide against it. But I keep thinking about that poor man, as I'm taking my uniform off in the changing room; as I jump on the bus and head home, and as I microwave a ready meal for dinner that night, eating it on the sofa in front of *Eastenders*. I even find myself thinking about him as I drop off into an exhausted sleep later that night. I vow to check up on him, if I can, when I get there tomorrow.

14

OCTOBER 1993

Marianne

'Marianne! Oh, thank God you're home,' Mum says as I step into the house. She's flushed and her hair has frizzed round her head like a lion's mane. Has she been drinking?

'What's happened?' I say, throwing my bag down and following her to the kitchen. She doesn't answer but stops dead in the doorway and points.

'It's your dad,' she says. Her voice wobbles and I realise how frightened she is. Nothing fazes Mum normally.

Then I see my dad, on the kitchen floor. He's flat on his back, his eyes open. For one awful minute, I think he's dead, but as I get closer, I can see his chest rising and falling, but he's ghostly pale, and he's clutching his left upper arm.

'What happened?' I crouch down beside him.

'I went upstairs to put the sheets on the bed and when I came

down, I just found him here,' Mum says. Her voice is high pitched
and her hands flutter round her like butterflies.

'Have you called an ambulance?'

'Not yet. I should, shouldn't I?'

I stand. 'No, you stay here with Dad, I'll ring.'

It takes just minutes for the ambulance to arrive, and as the
paramedics come inside, I notice Mum visibly relax. Someone else
is in charge now, everything will be all right.

'I told him he was trying to do too much, all this bloomin'
gardening and DIY he was attempting,' she says, as the paramedics
lift Dad onto a stretcher.

'You know he won't listen,' I say.

'But that was the whole point of him stopping work, to rest.' She
shakes her head. 'I wish he wasn't so stubborn.'

I suppress a smile. Mum's the most stubborn person I know,
although she'd disagree, of course. I don't say that having Mum fussing
over him twenty-four hours a day was probably one of the reasons Dad
had been trying to keep himself busy. There's only so much patience a
man can have, even someone as even-tempered as my dad.

The paramedics begin to manoeuvre the stretcher out of the
kitchen and towards the front door.

'Are you both coming with us?' one says, and I look at Mum
questioningly.

'Will you come with me, love? I'm not sure I can do it on my
own.'

I'm meant to be working at the shop later, my shift starts in a
couple of hours, but Mum looks so frightened I can't leave her.

'Of course.'

As she fusses around collecting her bag and coat, I ring work
and explain what's happened, and then climb into the ambulance.
Dad's got some colour back in his cheeks already and the oxygen

mask is strapped firmly to his face. I can't sit next to him so instead I take a seat beside Mum and hold her hand. Her face is drawn and she's staring at Dad as though he's a precious artefact. I suppose, after more than thirty years together, he is.

'Will he be all right?' Mum asks the paramedic who's checking Dad's vital statistics.

'I promise we'll do everything we can,' he replies, I notice not actually answering the question. I can see Mum is itching to ask more, but I squeeze her hand and shake my head. 'Let them do their job, Mum, they know what they're doing,' I reassure her.

'All right, love.' Mum's hands look frail in mine and for the first time ever, I wonder how I didn't notice that she'd got middle-aged. Mum and Dad were young when they met, only in their early twenties. In their wedding photos, Mum looks like a teenager, even though she's twenty-three. But it was several years before she got pregnant, and although she never talks about it, I get the impression that by the time I came along they'd both given up hope of ever having a child. Mum was thirty-four when I was born, Dad thirty-six: normal for these times, but seen as old to be first-time parents back then. But now, even though she's still only in her late fifties, she looks suddenly older, drawn, the skin on her hands thinner than I remember, her veins more prominent. I shake the thought from my mind and look over at Dad. His still-thick hair clings to his forehead, and his face is chalky-white and clammy. His eyes are closed now, but his breathing is steady, the oxygen mask fogging up and clearing in time with his breathing. The paramedic checks something on a screen next to him and I take some deep breathes and try to relax. He's going to be fine. Everything's going to be fine.

We sit in silence until we arrive at the hospital fifteen minutes later. Mum and I clamber out and wait in the strobe of the blue light for Dad to be unloaded, and then we follow them into the warmth of the hospital.

I'm expecting a team of nurses and doctors to rush out and meet us at the hospital doors, like they do on *Casualty*. But instead, Dad's wheeled into a side room in the A&E department, and then we're left alone to wait for the doctor.

'What if something happens?' I say.

'It won't,' the paramedic says kindly. 'He's stable now, he'll be fine until he's seen.' He places his hand on my shoulder. 'The doctor won't be long.'

'Okay.' My voice is weak as I watch them leave, wishing they'd stay, and then it's just the three of us, me and Mum hovering aimlessly at the foot of Dad's bed.

'Sorry about the drama, love,' Dad says, his voice wheezy. Mum steps forwards and clutches his hand.

'Don't try and speak,' she says.

Dad gives a weak smile.

'Shall I go and see how long they're going to be?' I say.

'No, Marianne, I don't think we should make a fuss. They're busy, they'll be here as soon as they can.'

I hesitate for a moment, caught between wanting to do as Mum says and wanting to get someone in here as quickly as I can in case Dad's heart stops beating. But I know I'm being dramatic, and I know Mum's right. They wouldn't have left us here if they thought Dad was in any immediate danger. We'll just have to wait, like everyone else.

The room we're in is small, but at least it's private. Outside is full of life – the calm, centred voices of the doctors and nurses mingling with the louder, more frantic voices of patients and their families. I know how they feel, I think, as I pull a chair from the corner of the room and make Mum sit down. From here, we can still hear the ambulance sirens as they arrive, as well as the smack of footsteps on the cheap lino, the beep of machines and the rumble of beds being moved around the wards.

The minutes crawl by. The plastic clock above the door tick-tick-ticks, marking them out like a metronome, and after a while I can't stand it any longer.

'I'm going to go and get a drink, do you want anything?' I say, the plastic chair screeching across the cheap lino floor.

'No thanks, love.'

I leave the room to go in search of a vending machine or a café. I'm amazed at how busy it is at this time on a Thursday afternoon. Most of the chairs in the waiting area are full, and a couple of trolleys sit outside rooms, the patients on them in various states of distress and pain. There are people on crutches, people with cuts and bruises, and others whose pain you can only discern from the looks on their faces. I wonder whether the fact that Dad's been given his own little room means his case is more serious, or whether it's just luck.

I locate a vending machine and stick some coins in to get two cans of Coke and a packet of Monster Munch, then make my way back to Dad's room. As I pass a row of cubicles, I hear the shrill bleep of a pager, and a voice saying, 'We have to go – I'll be back shortly.' Then two men in white coats emerge from behind the curtain and charge off through the double doors in the other direction and I wonder what emergency has come up, and whether whoever is in such dire need will make it.

I get back to Dad's room and Mum's still holding Dad's hand. His eyes are closed now.

'Oh, there you are, love,' Mum says.

'I got you a Coke anyway,' I say, handing her the cool can.

'Thanks.'

'Any change?'

She shakes her head. 'He's just been sleeping.'

I watch her study Dad's face and my heart breaks a little.

'Dad is going to be okay, isn't he?' I hate sounding like such a child but sometimes you just need the reassurance of your parents.

'He has to be, Marianne. I can't be without him.'

I take a drink and wipe my mouth. 'Shall I go and find someone?'

She shakes her head and stands, then pokes her head out of the door and looks up and down the corridor before coming back inside.

'There doesn't seem to be anyone around, apart from a young man in a white coat who looks as though he's just left school,' she says. 'Hopefully the doctor won't be too long now.'

I look to see who she's talking about, but all I can make out is the back of his white coat as the young doctor strides away towards some other emergency.

So I sit down and wait, once more, and pray help doesn't come too late.

15

DECEMBER 1996

Ted

I don't want to go tonight. Scratch that. I don't want to go out any night, because after a long day at the hospital, I'm so utterly exhausted I just want to crawl into bed and close my eyes for as many hours as my next shift will allow. But I promised Danny I'd be there, and I refuse to let him down. It's his friend Jonno's thirtieth birthday, and they've hired out a pub and have a DJ and everything.

'It'll be a great night, promise you'll come,' Danny had said when he told me about it a couple of weeks ago. 'And some of Danni's single mates will be there too, so...' He nudged me in the ribs and grinned.

I rolled my eyes.

'Dan, how many times do I have to tell you I'm not interested in meeting someone? I mean, when would I even have time to see them?'

He'd nodded knowingly. 'Ah, that's just because you've not met the right woman yet. Anyway, there's nothing wrong with having a bit of fun, and at least you might stop thinking you're going to meet that flippin' Fairy Girl. Promise you'll come?'

I'd sighed and agreed. Since he and Danni had tied the knot a couple of years ago, Danny seemed to think everyone should be as loved up as they were. He didn't believe me when I said I really wasn't looking for someone, seeming to be under the impression that I was still obsessed with the girl from the bridge. I did still think about her from time to time, but no more than is strictly healthy. Danny was right, I just hadn't met the right girl yet to take my mind off her.

Now I find myself downing a strong black coffee and jumping into a black cab to Islington to make sure I'm not late for a party I don't really want to go to for someone I've only met a handful of times.

We pull up outside the pub and I pay the cabbie. The windows of The Bull are steamed up, and I can hear the steady beat of 'Born Slippy' by Underworld pumping through the closed doors. It looks like it's already busy and I take a deep breath as I enter.

There are not many people here that I know, and it takes me a few minutes to locate Danny and Danni towards the back of the room. They're standing with a group of people I don't recognise and, despite my job where I meet new people all the time, somehow it's different in social situations. I feel uncomfortable and ill at ease trying to make small talk.

'Heeey!' Danny spots me and chucks his arms round me. 'Here he is, the main man,' he shouts, close to my ear.

'All right, Dan? Hi, Danni.' I give her a brief hug. She's good for Danny, and I've grown to like her even more over the years since they've been together. She's got her head screwed on, that one.

'Hey, Ted. All right?' She pulls back and looks at me, her head tilted to one side like she's trying to read me.

'Yeah, yeah, good. Just had a busy day.'

She nods and says no more, but I know she gets it. She knows that one way I cope with all the anxiety and stress that still lingers from my time in Kuwait is to throw myself into my work. But I suspect she also knows that it doesn't mean it's gone away and that, sometimes, I'd just prefer to be at home, alone.

'I'm glad you're here.'

'Me too.'

She rubs my arm and reaches behind her for a bottle. 'Do you want some of this? It's a bit warm, but it's wet.'

'Yeah, go on then, ta.' I grab a clean glass from the table and she pours me a full glass of white wine. I take a swig and feel the warmth radiate from my belly, along my limbs and up to my head. Slowly, with each gulp, I start to unwind.

I see Danni watching me and put the glass down deliberately. She knows about my drinking problem, and although it's not as bad as it used to be, I know she worries about me going back to the days when whisky was the only thing that got me through.

'That's better,' I say, giving her a reassuring smile.

'So,' she says, placing her hand gently on my forearm. 'Save any lives today?'

I think about the teenage boy who'd suffered several broken bones in his leg and a cracked rib in a road traffic accident, who was lucky not to have smashed his skull open. I think about the little girl who'd fallen off the roundabout and come in with concussion, and the middle-aged man who'd been having searing headaches but hadn't wanted to worry anyone but was in fact having a brain haemorrhage. I still wasn't fully qualified, of course, so in the end the responsibility was someone else's, but the gravity of our work never left me, and it was hard to shake it off and pretend it hadn't affected me.

'Loads,' I say instead. 'Proper hero, me.'

'Good old Ted,' she says. She glances round then moves a bit closer. 'Did Danny tell you about my friend he wants you to meet?'

'He did, although he said it was you who wanted me to meet her.'

She rolls her eyes. 'He's been on at me for ages. He seems to think we need to do something to help find you a woman.' She smiles, her eyes sparkling. 'I told him you were perfectly happy on your own, but he doesn't believe me.'

'I told him the same thing. I think he hopes I'll meet someone as amazing as you, but I never will.'

She flushes and takes a delicate sip of her wine, then puts the glass down on the table and grabs my hand. 'Well, to get Danny off my back, will you let me introduce you to Sam? And if you don't like her, at least he might shut up about it for a while.'

'Go on, then,' I say, grabbing my wine glass in my spare hand and letting myself be dragged across the crowded room, slipping between hot, drunken bodies, trying not to spill my drink. Then Danni stops and I bump into her back. 'Sorry.'

She pushes me slightly forward and says, 'Sam, this is Ted, who I told you about.' She turns to me. 'Ted, this is my friend Sam. We work together and she's really lovely.'

I always scoff at those moments in films where two people meet and the room around them fades away and all they can see is each other, but as I lay my eyes on Sam for the first time, I do feel as though the room has quietened down a bit, and all I want to do is talk to her. Her dark hair hangs in curls, her eyes are huge, and her lips are painted a bright red. She's got a Betty Boop sexiness and I can hardly take my eyes off her. She holds her hand out.

'Hello, Ted.'

'Oh, hi.' I shake her hand and try not to think about how nice it feels. God, what is wrong with me?

'So, how do you know Danni?' Sam moves slightly closer to me so I can hear her over the pounding DJ, and I can feel the warmth of her breath on my cheek.

'I've been friends with Danny – boy Danny – for years. I was living with him when they met. How about you?'

'Me and Danni have known each other years too, we lived on the same street. Our parents were friends. She hasn't changed a bit.' She smiles and places her lips round a straw. There's something about Sam I feel drawn to.

'So what do you do?' she says now.

'I'm a doctor. Well, a trainee doctor, still got a year to go.'

'Oh, I'm a paediatric nurse. Maybe that's why Danni thought we'd get on – we get it, you know what I mean?'

'Maybe.' I take a nervous sip of wine and look round the room, not sure what to say next. Luckily, Sam's much more adept than me at small talk, and as she quizzes me about my job, about my life and about anything and everything in between, I feel myself begin to relax. In fact, I actually begin to enjoy myself, and am glad I made the effort to come. Not that I'll tell Danny that, of course.

I don't know how much time passes before I feel a hand clamp my shoulder and turn to find Danny standing behind me.

'All right, mate?' he says, flashing me a huge grin. He's clearly sunk several more pints since I last saw him and, although he can hold his drink, he's swaying a bit. He looks from me to Sam and back again and winks. *Oh, God.*

'All right, Sam?' He hangs off my shoulder. 'Told ya you'd like our Teddy, didn't I? 'E might be a bit quiet, but he's all right once you get him going. Got a heart of gold, he has. Heart of gold.' Then, before anyone can say another word, he spots someone across the other side of the room and lurches off to say hello. I turn back to Sam.

She looks serious and I wonder whether Danny's arrival has broken the spell and put her off completely. Not that we'd got very far, but I was feeling quite confident that she might like me. And I knew I liked her.

'Shall we go somewhere more quiet?' she says.

'Oh, yes—' and before I can say any more she's grabbed my hand and we're walking quickly towards the back doors. The fire door is propped open and one of the barmaids is having a cheeky fag, so Sam drags me into the bitter winter air and out of sight of the doors. And then, before I can say anything, Sam turns around and presses her body against me and her lips against mine and I open my mouth to welcome her. She tastes of wine and salt and something else, something sweet. It's the first kiss I've had in years, and I let myself sink into it.

Eventually she pulls away and looks up at me, her huge brown eyes boring into me.

'Sorry, I've been wanting to do that for ages,' she says, her voice a whisper. I can still feel her pelvis against mine and I press myself a bit closer.

'I'm glad,' I say, putting my hand on the back of her neck and pulling her in for another kiss.

She pulls away again, breathless. 'Can we go somewhere else?'

'Back to mine?'

She nods, and turns and drags me towards the street to flag down a black cab. And for the first time in as long as I can remember, I'm not thinking about work, or Fairy Girl, or anything else apart from what's happening right here, right now.

* * *

I must have forgotten to close the curtains because when I wake up the grey light is filtering through the grimy window and pooling on the bed. I open my eyes and see a fan of dark hair across the pillow next to me, pink lips pursed, and the curve of a breast where the duvet has slipped off. As if she can sense me watching her, Sam wakes up and smiles at me.

'Hey, you,' she says sleepily. I plant a gentle kiss on her lips and she presses herself into me again. I pull away.

'I've got to get up.'

She opens her eyes fully and sits up, pulling the duvet across her. 'Really?'

'Really. Sorry. Work...'

I pad across the bedroom towards the bathroom and climb into the shower, letting the warm water run down me, and I think about last night. Sam and I had come back to my flat, and for the first time in years, I'd spent the night with a woman. I don't know whether Danny had known we'd get on that well, or whether it was just luck, but there was something about Sam I was drawn to. She was sexy, but it was more than that. She was warm and funny and hadn't asked anything of me that I didn't want to give. I can't quite believe how full of feelings I already am for someone I've only just met – it's so unlike me – but for now, I'm happy to go with it. Why not?

Suddenly, I jump as something drops onto my shoulder and my heart pounds as I turn to find Sam climbing into the shower beside me, completely naked. My body reacts instantly, and I pull her towards me and kiss her deeply.

'I'm not sure this is going to be quite as romantic as it always looks in the films, but let's give it a go,' she says.

I'm not going to argue with that...

* * *

It turns out Sam was right. Having sex in a shower isn't very sexy or romantic. In fact, it's pretty awkward, especially in a tiny shower cubicle like mine, where your elbows keep smacking the shower screen and your feet slip on the ceramic base every time you try to move. But as we climb out, we're still laughing, and I realise something. I feel happy.

We both dry off and get dressed quickly in my cold bedroom. The radiators are temperamental in here and I can never get it quite right.

'Coffee? Tea? Something to eat?'

'Tea and toast would be amazing,' she says, pulling the jumper she was wearing last night over her head. It's all I can do not to rip it off her again and I wonder if perhaps Sam really is the tonic I need to forget about my worries once and for all.

I go through to the kitchen and start pottering around, boiling the kettle and slicing bread. I can hear Sam in the living room and a contentment settles in the pit of my belly.

'Here you go.' I place a plate of buttered toast, a pot of jam and a cup of tea on the table.

'Thanks,' Sam says, picking up the mug and taking a sip. 'Who's that?' She gestures at my sketch of the girl on the bridge and my heart flips. I don't know whether to lie or tell the truth.

'No one. Just – someone I met.'

She studies it a moment. 'She's pretty.'

I nod.

'Did you know her for long?'

'No, she's just someone I knew once, that's all.' I shrug. 'I just like the drawing.'

She takes another sip of tea. 'You should. It's good.' She picks up a slice of toast and takes a huge bite, then grins. 'Maybe you can show me some of your other drawings sometime?' I grin back, grateful to her for understanding that I don't want to talk about it any more. But I decide, then and there, that if this relationship goes anywhere, then Fairy Girl will have to go. In fact, maybe it's time to say goodbye anyway. After last night, it's clear that, no matter what happens next, I'm ready to move on. I'm ready to leave the night on the bridge behind at last.

* * *

They say love can drive you mad – and the fact that Sam's convinced me to come ice-skating with her today would suggest they – whoever they are – are right.

'But I can't skate,' I'd said when she suggested it just a couple of days after we met.

'Have you ever tried?'

'Well, no, but it looks really hard.'

She'd laughed, her loud throaty laugh that I'd already grown to love, and said, 'Oh, Ted, you are funny.'

So reluctantly I ended up agreeing to give it a go, which is why I'm now here, at Alexandra Palace ice rink, strapping hulking great skates onto my feet and tottering across the floor like a lamb to the slaughter, Sam's grip firm against my palm.

'Just relax,' she says, as we reach the edge of the ice.

'I'm fine,' I lie.

'Is that why you've gone green?' She stretches up onto tiptoe and kisses my lips gently. 'Come on, Ted, I know you're brave really. Honestly, this will be fun.'

I give a small nod and hesitantly place my left foot onto the ice. It immediately slips out from under me, and I grab the handrail for dear life, pulling myself back up to upright again. My heart pounds and my hands are sweaty. Sam might think this is fun but it's not my idea of a good time. How am I ever meant to stand up on this?

For the next few minutes, Sam patiently coaxes me out onto the ice. And after several more minutes standing at the edge like a toy soldier, refusing to move a single muscle, she finally convinces me to hold her hand and skate away from the side. To my absolute astonishment, I'm staying upright. In fact, not only that, I'm managing to move.

'See, Ted, I told you you'd like it once you got going,' she says, skating in front of me and gliding backwards, holding both of my hands in her gloved one. Her cheeks glow and her eyes light up. She looks beautiful and, for the first time since we arrived, I find myself beginning to relax. Maybe this won't be so bad after all.

For the next few minutes – actually, it could be longer than that, but I'm not paying any attention – we skate slowly round the ice. We're never going to be Torvill and Dean – although Sam is surprisingly good and even manages a couple of spins – but I am moving and not falling over, and I'm happy with that. Besides, who could fail to be happy with Sam by their side? The ice rink was fairly quiet when we arrived, but it's filling up now, which makes it harder to skate when you're not very competent. I barely look up as I go, oblivious to the people around me, far too busy concentrating on the ground in front of me. And so, when I fall over, it's a shock. My backside hits the ice first and makes my teeth rattle in my head.

'Ow!'

Sam stops and turns to face me, a smile on her face. 'Oh Ted, are you all right?'

'Apart from bruising my arse cheeks and looking like a total fool, yes.' My bum is cold, my jeans doing little to protect my skin from the cold of the ice. 'Help me up?'

'Come on.' Sam plants her feet firmly and I push myself off the ice with one hand, holding one of her hands in my other one, and eventually, after my feet go out from under me a few times, I make it back up to standing.

'Can we go and get a drink now?'

'Yes, come on, I think you've been tortured enough,' Sam says, and we slowly glide to the edge and back to our seats to remove our boots.

'You did well,' she says as she unlaces her boots.

'If *well* means I managed to only fall over once.'

She smacks my thigh. 'Honestly, the first time I came I was all over the place, had to have one of those little plastic penguins to hold onto all the way round.'

'Why didn't I get offered one of those?'

'Because they're for children, Ted. They come up to your knees.' She grins. 'Besides, you had me. I was your penguin.' I look at her black hair and black jacket and jeans and laugh. 'Well, you're definitely dressed like one.'

Boots off, we hand them in and head towards the café when Sam stops.

'Actually, do you fancy a proper drink?'

'What are you suggesting?'

'Pub?'

I think for a minute. My drinking is a bit more under control at the moment, so pubs don't pose such a threat as they used to. I nod. 'Nothing like a bit of daytime drinking to make you feel like a teenager again.'

So we leave the ice rink behind us, and set off, hand in hand down the hill towards the pubs of Crouch End.

16

DECEMBER 1996

Marianne

Is there a moment in your life when you can pinpoint the exact minute something changed? When you know that the decision you made, right there and then, sent your life off in one direction, whereas if you'd have made a different decision in that moment, your life would have turned out very differently?

I think about this a lot. I often wonder what would have happened if I'd never found Robert and Sandra shagging that night at the party. Would I have carried on working for him, oblivious? Would I still be stuck in the same routine, doing the same job that gave me no satisfaction but paid the bills, and sleeping with the same man – a man who was never going to marry me or even make it official between us?

Would I ever have made the decision to start training to become a counsellor if I hadn't left the party and come across Bridge Man?

After all, knowing I managed to convince him not to jump was a big part of the reason I decided I could do this job in the first place.

It's quite exhausting, thinking like that all the time. Lance, for one, thinks I'm mad.

'You would always have done this job, Annie, you were born to help other people,' she says.

'Maybe,' I say, tugging my ice skate on with a grunt. This is another thing you need to know about Lance. She's always got some hare-brained scheme on the go, something new we need to try. There have been so many times that we've got ourselves into ridiculous scrapes thanks to one of Lance's 'brilliant ideas'. Like the time we went walking in the Lake District and she thought it would be a great idea to go 'off-piste'. *It'll be much more exciting, more authentic*, she said. More authentic than what I'm not sure, but it ended in us getting so utterly lost that we had to spend the night freezing cold and huddled under a hedge until the morning when some other intrepid, clearly more experienced walkers came along and rescued us.

This time she has me strapping on ice skates, even though I've got the balancing skills of a baby elephant and have never so much as stood on a roller skate.

'It'll be fun,' she said when she suggested it and I immediately shut the idea down. 'It'll get us in the Christmas mood.'

I wasn't entirely convinced I wanted to get in the Christmas mood. I'm exhausted from working long hours at the counselling centre five days a week and in the shop two evenings and one weekend day. I'm still trying to save a deposit for a flat. Even though Mum and Dad are happy to have me around – and it means I can help out with Dad when his heart is playing up – I desperately need my own space. The trouble is, as quickly as I'm saving, prices are rising. Quicker, usually. It feels as though I'll be trapped in my childhood bedroom forever.

I think back to the Christmas five years before, the year I'd walked in on Robert and Sandra, and saved Bridge Man's life. I still think about him from time to time, and wonder whether he's having a nice life. I hope he's happy. But it also makes me realise how much time has passed. That was five years ago now, and apart from my new career, not much has changed in my life.

'Come on,' Lance says now, taking my hand and tugging me up to a standing position, where I wobble for a few seconds before righting myself. Together we walk, flamingo-legged, towards the ice rink. I stop at the edge, gripping the side so tightly my knuckles turn white.

'I'm not doing it.'

Lance tugs at my sleeve like a small child denied an ice cream.

'Come on, don't be a baby.'

I shake my head. 'Nope. No way.' I point at the expanse of ice in front of us, where a few people are showing off a range of skill levels, from the semi-professional spinner right in front of me to the guy walk-skating like a constipated penguin in the middle of the rink, clutching the hand of a woman dressed all in black as though his life depended on it.

I sigh and place my skate tentatively onto the edge of the ice. Lance won't let me off the hook, so I may as well get it over with sooner rather than later. I cling to the side with white knuckles, my single skate sliding uncontrollably beneath me.

'This is impossible!'

'It's not, come on.' She takes my hand and slowly, slowly, I place my other skate on the ice. If I stand very straight and don't move a muscle, perhaps I can avoid falling over.

'You don't need to be scared. What's the worst that can happen?'

'I fall over, someone skates over my fingers and chops them all off like a slice of meat?'

'That's never happened in the history of ice-skating. Even if you do fall over, you might have a sore backside, but that's it.'

Before I realise what's happening, she's pulled me away from the side and I'm gliding, like a statue, across the ice.

'Move this foot, and push it forward. Like this.' She shows me but I can't seem to recreate the movement and feel myself tipping, my skate stuck in place while my body lurches forward. Lance yanks me back to standing at the last minute.

'See? Can't do it.'

'You've only just started. Come on, let's try again.'

After what feels like hours but turns out to be only fifteen minutes or so, I'm moving across the ice a little more freely. I wouldn't call it skating, but I'm not falling over, at least.

'See, it's fun once you get going, isn't it?' Lance glides along elegantly next to me and I grimace.

'It's all right.' I sniff. 'I might go and sit down for a minute, though. I think my foot's about to fall off.'

Lance rolls her eyes.

'All right, loser, I'll see you in a bit.'

Carefully, I slide across to the edge, side-step round to the exit and throw myself into the nearest plastic chair. I've never been so glad to sit down. I wasn't lying, my foot is killing me. Surely it can't be natural to hold it at such a weird angle for hours on end. I rub the part of my ankle I can reach, then peer across the ice to locate Lance. She's wearing a bright orange bobble hat, so it's not hard to spot her, and I watch for a few moments as she glides effortlessly round the rink, paying no attention to anyone else, but giving me a grin each time she passes. I stick my tongue out in reply.

I let my gaze roam and my eyes land on a couple holding hands, although I can't work out if they're being romantic or just trying to keep each other upright. I think it's the guy from before, who looked as though he was as bad as me. He doesn't look as though he's improved much. She's much shorter than him, and much more competent, and I smile as his legs seem to come from under him, flailing around like a giant Bambi. More than once, he nearly falls, only to be saved at the last minute. But then, finally, he smacks down hard on the rock-hard ice. I hear an 'ow', then a shout of laughter float through the air and I smile to myself as I watch him scrabble around, trying to stand up. It takes several attempts, but finally, he makes it. And then, as he turns to face me, I gasp.

It's him.

It's Bridge Man.

Frantically, I look round for Lance, but she's right across the other side of the rink. Not that it would help, because she's never seen him before. Pulse roaring in my ears, I look back at the man, but he's turned away, and is starting to skate towards the other side of the rink, clearly ready to call it a day.

Until now, I would have said that the memory of his face had faded so much that I couldn't be sure I'd even recognise him in a line-up. But now he's here, in front of me, I see it instantly. And although he's clearly with someone and he probably won't know what to say to me even if I do explain who I am, I have a desperate urge to go and say hello. To confirm that I did the right thing that night, and just to know that he's happy.

They've reached the edge now and he's unlacing his boots, laughing with the woman he's with. They definitely look happy.

I look round frantically. I have a few seconds to decide what to do before it's too late. I can try to walk awkwardly on my skates round to where they are and hope I make it in time before they leave. Or I can skate across the ice towards them. The only other option is to sit down and unlace my boots and walk round as quickly as I can. There's no way I'm skating, and I'm not sure I can actually walk in these things, so I have no choice but to sit back down and try to undo my boots. I'm in such a panic that my fingers keep getting caught and I almost scream in frustration. Finally, I get the first boot off and look up.

He's gone.

I'm too late.

I sit and stare at the empty space where he was a few seconds before. All this time, wondering, and now I've lost the only chance I'm ever likely to have.

I feel an unexpected sense of disappointment, a feeling like loss. Except I didn't have anything to lose.

'What's up?'

Lance is standing next to me, and I look up, puzzled.

'I was calling your name, didn't you hear me?'

'No.' I shake my head. 'Sorry. I—' I stop. Now she's here, I'm not sure whether to tell her what just happened. I know how much she disapproves of me talking about that night, thinks I became obsessed with what happened.

Lance sits down next to me. 'Seriously, Annie, you've gone really pale. Have you hurt yourself?'

I shake my head. 'No. Nothing like that.'

'Well, what is it, then? Has someone hurt you?' She looks round to see who's nearby.

'No.' I put my hand on her arm. 'It's nothing. I just – I thought I saw him.'

'Him?'

'You know. The man from the bridge.'

She doesn't reply straight away, but when she does, her voice drips with disapproval. 'I thought you'd forgotten all about him. You haven't mentioned him for ages.'

'I had,' I lie. 'But then he was just there, right in front of me.'

She widens her eyes. 'You didn't go up to him, did you?'

I look guilty. 'No.'

'Oh, God, you did, didn't you? What did you say? What happened?'

I shake my head. 'No, Lance, I didn't go up to him.' I point down at my feet. 'Not because I didn't want to, but because of these bloody things. He was right there, and I couldn't get them off fast enough. And then they were gone.'

'They?'

I give a sheepish look. 'Yeah. He was with someone. A woman. She looked pretty.'

'Well, good.'

'Good?'

'Yes.' She starts unlacing her own boots and kicks the first one onto the floor, then turns to me. 'I know you think there was some sort of spark between you two or something that night. But think about it, Annie. What would have happened if you had approached him just now and he hadn't known who you were? Or, worse, he had recognised you and hadn't wanted to speak to you because you brought back terrible memories? I mean, it's not as though you met in great circumstances for him, is it? I can't imagine anyone, ever, has fallen in love with someone when they've been about to end their life. It's just not a thing.'

'I didn't want him to fall in love with me, Lance, I just wanted to say hello.' My voice is curter than I intended.

'Sure, yes, but what *for*?'

'To – to know he's all right.' I shrug, unsure how to explain it. 'I dunno, I guess I just thought it might get the whole thing out of my system once and for all. But you're right. The best it could have been is awkward and humiliating.'

She places her hand on my arm. 'Annie, it was five years ago. Chances are his life has moved on a lot. I'm not sure he'd have thanked you. What if the woman he was with doesn't know that he tried to kill himself, and he had to try and explain how he knew you?' She shakes her head. 'Promise me you'll stop this?'

'Stop what?'

'Obsessing about him? I honestly thought you were over him, but clearly not. But you know he's all right now, so it's time to stop. Promise?'

I look down at my feet, where one is still ensconced in its ridiculous ice skate, the other in a slightly damp sock, and nod. Lance is right. Speaking to him wouldn't have done either of us any good.

But she is also right that I have to truly put it behind me now and not let what happened that night shape my life any more. I'm grateful for the nudge towards counselling it gave me, but it's over.

I'll never think about Bridge Man again.

17

Ted

'Absolutely swear to me that you won't change your mind at the last minute? I can't go on my own.'

'I swear.' I lean over and plant a kiss on Sam's nose. 'But you really do have to get going now or you'll be late for work.'

'Okay, okay.' She grins. 'See you tonight.' She stands, hooks her bag over her shoulder and leaves. I watch her from the front window for a moment and smile to myself. I still can't believe how bloody lucky I am to have met Sam. We've only known each other for six months and already I can't imagine not having her in my life. We spend almost every evening together when I'm not working late – or she isn't – and although she hasn't officially moved in, she spends more time at my flat than she does at her own, and most of her clothes have migrated to my wardrobe. It's a strange feeling, contentment. One I'm not used to. But it feels pretty good.

Tonight, though, I've promised to accompany her to a school reunion party she's promised to go to, and I really wish I hadn't.

'There's probably a reason why I don't see most of them any more, but I promised my friend I'd go and keep her company,' she'd said when she told me about it. 'She wants to show the lad she went out with all through sixth form and who dumped her at the leavers' party what he's missing.' She gave me a grin and ran her fingers through my now less-severe hair. 'And if you come, I can show them how handsome my boyfriend is.'

'Do I have to? You know what I'm like at these sorts of things. I'll probably just show you up.'

'You will not. They'll all be jealous of me, with you on my arm.'

'Oh, just a token hunk then, am I?'

'Yep,' she'd grinned, and smacked my bum. 'So does that mean you'll come?'

I'd sighed and promised to check my shifts and see what I could do. And even though I'd planned to tell a little white lie to get out of it, I'd found I couldn't in the end.

Sam's long gone by the time I turn to leave for work myself. As I do, my gaze catches on the picture of Fairy Girl I put up all those years ago when I first moved in, and my heart hitches. I don't really think about her much any more. At least, not in the way I used to. She's still there, in the back of my mind as someone important in my life, someone I'd love to see again, but I've accepted that I probably won't, and that it's for the best. She's parcelled away now in the abandoned attic of my memories.

I've never told Sam anything about Fairy Girl and, since the first night she stayed over, she's never asked about the picture again. But she must wonder who she is and why I still keep her picture hanging on my wall. After all, she's here most of the time, so she has to see it most days. I know I'd be curious. More than curious. But she never asks, and for that I'm grateful.

I'm aware that the picture should probably come down now things between me and Sam have got more serious. It's the respectful thing to do. So I reach across the table and unhook the frame from the wall. The paint is slightly darker where it's been hanging. I carry it through to the kitchen and rummage around in a drawer full of foil, clingfilm and random bits of bubble wrap and pull out a Sainsbury's carrier bag. It's a thick one, and I place the picture and frame inside it and fold it over, sellotaping the top firmly shut. Then I walk through to my bedroom and place it right at the back of the wardrobe, out of sight. I'm not ready to get rid of it completely, but I feel better now it's not hanging above me every time I eat my breakfast. Less guilty.

I take a quick shower and shove on some clothes, then pick up the bag that contains my clean uniform – I always wash it as soon as I get home, which makes it easier to rotate the two uniforms I have, and then fold the ironed one up and put it in my bag ready the night before. The military gave me some useful habits, at least. I give the empty space on the wall one last glance as I leave the flat and head off to work. I've got a long day ahead of me.

I hurry down the corridor towards the ICU, where I've been called to help out with a case of suspected meningitis. I know it's urgent and my heart hammers as it always does whenever I'm called for something potentially life-threatening. I may look calm outwardly – you have to, to give your patients the confidence that they're in good hands – but I'm always seething with nerves and anxiety about what I might find when I arrive, and at the realisation that someone else's life is in my hands. I'm not even quite fully qualified yet, but we're so short-staffed it's often left to me if a consultant can't get there on time.

I swipe my card and push through the doors and head to the nurses' station in the middle of ward. Then I'm flung head-first into trying to work out what's wrong with my patient, and why she's presenting signs of meningitis when tests are saying she doesn't seem to have it. Bloods are taken, monitors are attached, and she's put on a drip, and all the time my adrenaline is running high and I'm utterly absorbed in the task.

Finally, an hour and a half later, the patient is stable and it's safe to leave her under the watchful eye of the nurses, so I wash my hands and leave the Intensive Care Unit.

'Bye, Dr Green,' the head nurse calls.

'Bye, Sister,' I reply, patting her on the shoulder as I pass.

As I walk away from the ICU, a wave of exhaustion washes over me and I glance at my watch – and stop dead. It's already seven-thirty. I'm due at Sam's party in half an hour. Even if I go straight from here – which I can't, as I'm still in my uniform and I desperately need a shower and something to eat – I'll be at least an hour late. I sigh. I may as well go home and get ready properly. Sam will be cross, but I can't turn up like this.

I quickly change and bundle my dirty uniform into my bag, then head outside to jump on the bus. It's a sweltering evening and as I sit on the top deck, squashed against the window by an over-weight woman with about twenty shopping bags, I lean my fore-head against the dirty glass and watch the world go by. When the bus is chugging along, the people are blurry, whooshing past like smudges on canvas. But when we stop, I find myself studying faces, and hair, and I know what I'm doing, even though I don't like to admit it. After all these years, it's become a habit to search through crowds for Fairy Girl.

I pull my face away and sigh. Instead, I think about Sam. Looks-wise, she's the complete opposite to Fairy Girl. Dark, not blonde, tall and willowy, not petite and pale. Deliberate? Danny reckons so.

But whether it is or it isn't, the fact remains that, by thinking about Fairy Girl, and not telling Sam about her, I'm doing Sam a huge disservice and I know it has to stop.

The bus arrives at my stop and I squeeze past the woman next to me who clearly has no intention of getting out of my way. This is what I can't abide about public transport in this city. Nobody wants to give up even a tiny inch of space. I'd hate to see the germs flying around in the air from person to person. I shudder.

Back at my flat, I jump straight into the shower and wash off the dirt of the day. It's a tough job, being a junior doctor, but there's something satisfying about the utter exhaustion you feel at the end of the day. It would be impossible to explain it to someone who didn't work in a hospital, and I know countless colleagues who have separated from their wives or husbands because they simply haven't understood the long hours they have to work. But Sam's a nurse and she gets it. She understands that, sometimes, you just can't get away when you're supposed to – in fact, you rarely do – even if it means you miss important engagements.

I still don't think she'll be too pleased with me tonight, though. Sometimes, it's one let-down too many.

I step out of the shower and towel-dry my hair, pull on a clean shirt and jeans and grab my keys and wallet. Before I leave, I throw my uniform in the washing machine, grab the clean one from the radiator and place it on the table ready to be ironed before I leave for work tomorrow.

I glance at my watch. Ugh, just after nine. It's going to take me almost an hour to get there. I'm suddenly so overwhelmed with exhaustion I'm not sure I can face it, especially when I know I'll be in trouble whether I go or whether I don't. I hover for a moment, undecided. Surely Sam will understand if I explain I had to work late? Sure, she might be cross, but she'll get over it. It's only a party, and she didn't even want to go in the first place.

I hesitate a moment too long, and before I know it, I'm in the kitchen, on my hands and knees in front of the sink, reaching into the back of the cupboard. I grope blindly around the pipes and along the wall and then, finally, there it is. My fingers wrap around the cool glass and pull it out. My secret bottle of whisky. I smile.

Before I can change my mind, I grab a tumbler and pour myself a large slug of the amber liquid, put it to my lips and tip my head back and down the whole lot. A warmth floods through me, and I stand at the counter, staring out of the window at the flat roof, bottle in one hand, glass in the other, and I feel my whole body start to relax. That's better.

Even as I'm relaxing, I know this is wrong. But, after the day I've had, I can't bring myself to care.

I've told Sam about my drinking. About how, when I got back from Kuwait, the only thing that could comfort me was a bottle of whisky, and she understood. But I also promised her that, even though I was a lot better by the time I met her, I would always tell her if I felt the drink pulling me back again.

'I watched my father drink himself into an early grave, I don't want to watch you do the same,' she said. And so, having seen my dad lose himself to drink too, it hadn't been hard to promise her. I'd meant every word. I still did mean it. Yet I kept this bottle in the back of the cupboard, for emergencies. And I hadn't told her about it.

I won't tell her tonight, either. After all, I've only had the one. I have this under control.

I stare down at the bottle and glass in my hand. They have to go back into the cupboard now.

My knuckles are white as I grip the neck of the bottle, and my hand starts to shake.

Pull yourself together, you're tragic.

That's the other problem with drinking. It brings my father's voice to the forefront again, the critical voice I spend so much of my life trying to ignore.

Just one more. Just to get rid of the stresses of the day, I tell myself, as I pour another large tumblerful. This time I take it through to the living room and sit at the table, and sip it slowly. It burns my lips and my throat, and I enjoy the familiar buzz it brings. That's better. I should go and put the rest of this away now. Just finish this glass, and then leave, otherwise it won't be worth going at all.

I sit for a moment, staring at the space on the wall where Fairy Girl's picture had hung until this morning, and I wonder why it took me so long to get rid of it. My mind drifts back to that night, to flashes of her face, of the black water below me, to the sense of desperation and hopelessness I'd felt. I glance back down at the glass in my hand and it's empty. I don't remember drinking the rest of it, but my fuzzy head tells me I must have done.

I know I need to stop drinking before it gets out of control. I know I do. I don't want Sam and her friends to see me totally wasted.

I also know that, now I've started, it's going to be hard to stop.

I check the time again. Nine-thirty. I'm officially very late now. The party started an hour and a half ago and I haven't even left yet. Is there any point?

I pour another glass. I'll go after this one. I take a sip, and then nearly spill it all over the carpet as the phone peals out. I freeze, listen to it ring four times, and then the answer phone switches on. No one ever leaves a message apart from my father, and you can tell, when he does, he's relieved I haven't answered so he doesn't actually have to speak to me, but he's done his duty for another few months. But then, to my surprise, a voice cuts into my thoughts.

'Ted, it's me. Are you there?' Sam. 'I don't know what's happened to you but I hope you're all right.' A pause. 'Maybe you're

on your way here. I'll see you soon.' Then a long beep and the call
ends.

That's all it takes to flick the switch and pull me out of myself.
What on earth am I doing, sitting here getting wasted, when the
woman I'm lucky to have is waiting for me at a party I promised I'd
be at? It's as though I'm determined to throw away anything good I
have in my life.

I've still got time to salvage this.

I tip the rest of the whisky down my throat and feel my legs turn
to jelly as I stand. I walk across to the kitchen, shove the bottle into
its hiding place at the back of the cupboard, and stand, gripping the
sink. The room spins and I take a few deep breaths. I can do this. I'll
be fine by the time I get there.

Before I can change my mind and pull the bottle back out, I
grab my keys and wallet, and head out to the street. I'd been planning to take the Tube to the party but it's so late now that when I
spot the orange glow of a free black cab, I hail it and jump in. As we
stop-start our way through the traffic, my pounding heart slows,
and I rest my head on the back of the seat and close my eyes.

'All right, mate, we're here.'

I wake with a start and look around. Where am I? My heart
pounds as I try to orientate myself. Then I see the cab driver's face
peering at me through the glass partition, and I remember. I've
come to meet Sam.

'Oh right, thanks.' I wipe drool from my mouth and pull out a
twenty-pound note and hand it over. 'Keep the change.'

'Cheers, mate.'

I clamber out and stand in front of the old school, which is only
a few miles from the one I attended, but a whole world apart.
Where mine was all red brick and prissy uniforms, this was a
rougher, less salubrious choice where the uniform was nothing
more than black trousers or skirt and white shirt, and scruffy ties

worn at half-mast. This was where Sam had gone to school. I take a deep breath and walk across the playground, following the sound of 'Zombie' by the Cranberries. I'm near the door when I'm almost bundled over by a girl with long red hair falling through it. Hooked under her arm is another, smaller woman with a huge billowy skirt that looks a bit much for a north London school reunion, bright blonde hair barely visible beneath her friend's arm. She looks as though she'd be on the floor if it weren't for the fact she was being held up.

'Sorry,' the redhead says, glancing at me. 'Is that your cab?'

'Yes. I'm finished with it.'

'Thanks.'

I watch them hurry across the playground, the blonde girl groaning as though she's about to be sick, the redhead desperately bundling her friend into the cab. Miraculously, the driver lets them in, and they drive away. Despite my own fuzzy head, I feel sorry for her. She'll feel half-dead in the morning. Mind you, I might be half-dead too if I can't convince Sam to forgive me for being so late. And for being drunk.

I walk inside. The main lights in the hall are turned off, the room lit up by spotlights bouncing off a disco ball as though it's 1980 all over again. Pockets of people linger around the edges of the room, and there are a few couples dotted around the dance-floor, swaying. I cast my eyes around and then I spot Sam chatting to a small group of women in the corner. I make my way over.

'Hey, sorry I'm so late.' I put my arm on her waist and plant a kiss on her cheek. She jumps in fright and turns to me. She looks angry.

'Oh, you're here. I didn't think you were bothering.' Her voice is slurred, and I realise I'm safe. She's more drunk than me so she'll never notice I've been drinking. I think I've got away with it this time. I vow there won't be any more times after this. I hope I'm strong enough.

'Yeah, I'm sorry. Work, you know.'

We never give each other details about what's kept us at work late, it's just implicitly understood that it was unavoidable. And, of course, it was this evening. Except that I could have easily been here at least an hour earlier, even with the hold-up at work. I don't tell Sam that, of course. She looks furious enough already.

'You're very late.' She checks her watch and frowns. '*Very* late.'

'Sorry, love.' I stand awkwardly, my head spinning. I realise Sam isn't going to introduce me to her friends, so I turn to them and hold my hand out. 'Hi, I'm Ted.'

They both shake my hand, and introduce themselves as Amy and Sarah.

'Were you both at school with Sam?'

'I was,' says Amy or Sarah – my head's too fuzzy to remember, even though they've only just told me their names. 'Sarah just came with me to keep me company.'

'Lovely to meet you.'

I turn to Sam, who still has a face like thunder, and is tipping white wine down her throat like it's going out of fashion. I put my hand on her arm. 'Do you want another drink?'

She nods. 'Sarah? Amy?'

'Oh, please,' Amy says. 'White wine, please.'

I head to the bar, glad to be away from the heat of Sam's glare for a while, and order a bottle of wine and a pint of beer from the makeshift bar. 'Can I have a whisky as well, please?' I pay for the lot, then glance over my shoulder to make sure Sam's not watching before I throw the whisky down my throat and leave the glass on the counter. Then I head back with a tray balanced precariously with drinks and place it carefully down on the table next to them.

'Drinks, ladies,' I say, holding out the bottle and topping their glasses up. 'So, what did I miss?'

'Everything.' Disapproval drips from Sam's voice.

'Right, yeah. I got that.'

Sarah comes to my rescue. 'You just missed our other friend,' she says. 'There were three of us that used to hang out at school, and the other one, Alison, was here but her friend got really drunk and had to leave, so Alison took her home.'

I think about the two women I'd passed in the playground. 'Have they only just left? One blonde, one tall redhead?'

'That's them. Alison's the redhead. Sam was really excited about you meeting her, weren't you, Sam?'

'Yes, well, it's a bit late now.' She pulls herself up to her full height. 'But at least you've met Amy now.'

Amy smiles.

'So, Amy, tell me what Sam was like at school. Was she always getting into trouble?'

'Oh, no, she was a good girl, most of the time. Although I do remember the time she got the whole school a detention because someone had put muddy footprints all up the toilet walls and across the ceiling and nobody would own up to it, so everyone got kept behind.'

'But it was Sam?' I smile, imagining a young Sam finding her prank hilarious.

'Yep. She spent all lunchtime doing it.'

I grin, but Sam still has a face like thunder. 'Oh, come on Sammy, forgive me?' I say, squeezing her shoulder. 'It was just work, I'm really sorry.'

She looks up at me and I can see her face start to soften. Her eyes are heavy, her lashes caked with clumps of mascara.

'I spose.' She gulps back more wine, then waves her glass around in front of her. 'I just really wanted you to meet my friends. We had such fun, didn't we, Ames?'

Amy nods in agreement. I can't help thinking how much Sam moaned about coming here tonight, how she begged me to come because she was worried that all these people she hadn't seen for ten years were going to be 'boring as fuck' (her words). But now, suddenly, they seem to be best friends again, reunited under the blurry hug of cheap white wine.

'Are you all right?' I hear Amy's voice first, then I look at Sam, who's turned deathly pale. Actually, she's ever so slightly green.

'I think I'm gonna be sick.'

I grab her elbow and half-drag her towards the exit. The last thing she needs is to be seen throwing up in her old school hall. We make it to the playground and I steer her behind what might once have been bike sheds but now seems to be some sort of outside classroom. Just as we make it into the shadows, Sam throws up. She heaves a few more times and I hold her hair back, rubbing her back. Finally, the heaving stops and she stands, her face pale in the dark.

'Oh, God, I'm so sorry, Ted,' she groans. 'How embarrassing.' She glances towards the school. 'You won't tell anyone about this, will you?'

'Don't be daft,' I say, smoothing stray strands of hair back from her face. She smells of vomit. 'Have you got any chewing gum in that bag?'

'What? Oh yeah, maybe.' She rummages around and pulls out a packet of mint gum and pops a piece in her mouth. Then she takes my hand and leads me to a bench a few metres away and flops down. I sit beside her and hold her hand.

'I'm so sorry, Ted,' she says again.

'It's fine—'

She holds her hand up to stop me. 'I am, you know. I feel like a moron. I just – I know I said I didn't really like these people, but it turns out that, actually, I do still quite like Amy and Alison. They're good people. I just – I wanted you to meet them, and then when you didn't come I felt so stupid I just kept drinking and now...' She holds her hands up. 'Well, now this.'

'Honestly, it's fine. It doesn't matter. It's quite sweet, really.'

'Sweet?' She looks at me as if I've gone mad.

I shrug. 'Yeah, you know. You were missing me so much you had to drown your sorrows.'

'Oh, ha ha.' She slaps me on the thigh, then looks at me. 'What happened to you, though?'

'Just work. Suspected meningitis at the last minute, you know what it's like.'

She nods and I feel a pang of guilt at the white lie. She doesn't need to know I could have been here much earlier, and much more sober.

'Well, never mind. At least you got here in time to see me throwing my insides up onto my childhood playground.' She smiles weakly.

'And I wouldn't have wanted to miss that for the world.'

We sit for a few minutes, listening to the faint sounds of Chumbawumba floating through the door every time it swings open, and I can hear Sam breathing deeply next to me, trying to pull fresh air into her lungs. I wonder what's on her mind. I'm thinking about her, and how lucky I am to have her, and how I never want to let her down again.

'What are you thinking about?' I ask.

'Not vomiting.' She grins and I lean over and kiss her cheek.

'Do you want to go back in, or shall we go home?'

'Let's go home. I've got Amy's number, I'll ring and apologise in the morning.'

And so, hand in hand, we walk across the playground and make our unsteady way to the Tube station, and back to my flat.

18

JULY 1997

Marianne

I might sometimes find it hard being an adult, but I'm not sure I'd ever want to go back to the heartache and drama of a north London comprehensive in the 1980s. So when Lance asked me to come along with her to her school reunion, I was reluctant, to say the least.

'I'd always assumed I'd be going to this kind of thing with my husband or at least long-term boyfriend,' she'd said. 'I can't turn up on my own, I'll look like a right loser.'

'I don't get why you're going anyway. It's not like you've stayed in touch with any of these people, and you still live in the same city.'

She'd shrugged. 'Aren't you just a bit curious? You know, about the people you spent your whole childhood with?'

'Not really.'

'Well, I am. A nosy bugger. You know – is Philip still a computer geek, will Helen still be the biggest bitch I've ever met? Or do people grow up, become better people? Or worse.' She'd taken a huge puff on her cigarette, the smoke blowing into my face.

'You just want to make sure everyone sees how hot you look these days, don't you?'

She'd grinned then. 'Well, there is that.' Lance had spent most of her school days slightly overweight with a terrible perm. It wasn't until she left, age eighteen, that she'd transformed herself into a tall, willowy knock-'em-dead redhead with abs to die for. If I'd changed that much, I'd want to show everyone I used to know too.

'Go on then. I'll come. But I'm going to get drunk and embarrass you, because you know that's the only way I can get through these excruciating social occasions. You have been warned.'

'Sounds like a plan to me.'

I start getting myself dolled up to go and spend the evening drinking cheap warm wine in a school hall about twenty minutes from the school I went to and have avoided ever since, just so my best friend can show off. The things we do for the people we love.

My hair's currently bleached white-blonde, curled in a Marilyn Monroe style, and I have chosen a homemade dress with a tight fitted waist and billowy netted skirt. When I open the door to Lance, she gives a low whistle.

'Swit swoo, Annie, that dress is—' She kisses her fingers like a chef.

'Thanks. I decided if I'm being dragged along to a school party, I might as well make an entrance.'

'Just try not to vomit down it, you'll spoil the fabric.' She grins and I close the door behind me and follow her down the road towards the Tube station.

By the time we push open the door of the 1960s monstrosity of a school, I'm hot and sweaty and desperate for a drink.

'Ta-da!' Lance sweeps her hand round the room and grimaces. 'The site of many memories – some better than others.' She grabs my hand. 'Come on, let's go and powder our noses before we see anyone.'

After we've reapplied lip gloss and fluffed up our hair, Lance is ready to make her grand entrance. 'Just remember, nobody at this school ever called me Lance. It's Alison.' She frowns. 'Come to think of it, nobody else in the world calls me Lance any more except you.'

'It suits you better,' I say belligerently.

'And if anyone asks, I'm wildly successful and have a string of boyfriends. I just didn't want to bring them with me. Right?'

'Message received and understood.' I grin and high-five her.

'Right, let's go.' She grabs my hand again and pulls me back towards the hall. It's still light outside so the room isn't completely dark yet, making the disco lights that are flicking back and forth across the room hard to make out. The music is still fairly low, 'Bitter Sweet Symphony' by the Verve playing quietly to itself. There are quite a few people here already, and Lance scans the room, looking for familiar faces.

'Ooh, there's Amy,' she says, pointing across the room at a woman I vaguely recognise, then setting off towards her at a great pace. I follow behind, my heels rubbing on the backs of my vintage shoes.

For the next half an hour, we stand talking to Amy and her friend Sarah who, like me, has been dragged along for moral support. I now remember Amy being one of their group of three back in the day. In fact, I remember being jealous of them – Lance, Amy and another girl whose name I can't quite remember. Lance was my friend, and because we went to different secondary schools and only saw each other at the weekends and the odd homework-free weeknight, I'd felt they were trying to steal her away from me. I realise now how pathetic that was, of course, and yet there's still a nugget of irritation buried somewhere inside me when Amy talks about Lance – Alison – and her.

'I'm going to the bar. Shall I get wine?' I say.

'Wine would be great, thanks,' Lance says. 'I'll get the next bottle, thanks, Annie.'

I head to the makeshift bar and, surprised at how cheap the Chardonnay is, I buy two bottles and head back to the group. As I approach, I see another woman has joined them.

'Oh, here's Annie,' Lance says, turning to me. 'Annie, you remember Sam, don't you?'

I take in the other woman and realise that I do know her, at least I remember her as well as I remember Amy. Unlike Amy, who's small and slightly mousy-looking, Sam is stunning. She has glossy dark hair cut into a neat bob, and large lips painted in a bright red. She holds out her hand. 'So good to see you again.' Her smile is wide and I warm to her immediately.

'You too.'

'Sam was just explaining that her boyfriend is on his way, but he might be late,' Lance says as I plonk the two bottles of wine and some glasses down on the tiny table next to us.

'He's a doctor – well, almost,' Sam explains. 'He works long hours, but he promised me faithfully he'd be here tonight, so I'm hoping he'll make it.'

'Must be hard, going out with a doctor,' I say.

'It's not too bad. I'm a nurse so I get it.'

'Well, we might as well get stuck into this while we're waiting,' I say, pouring glasses of wine for everyone. 'Cheers!' I hold my glass up and everyone chinks.

I tune out of the conversation for a few minutes while the three of them are having a proper catch-up. I take the opportunity to people-watch, one of my favourite activities.

I'm surprised by how busy it is. I know it was quite a large school, but I always imagined these reunion things to be something people enthusiastically accepted an invitation to but never actually went on the night. It seems most people from this school were keen to see their old classmates again. I wonder how many just came to show off, like Lance.

I realise my glass is already empty, and quickly refill it. The wine's too warm, but I don't care. It's been ages since I got really drunk, and I'm in the mood tonight.

'Come on, Annie,' Lance says, interrupting my thoughts and grabbing my hand.

'What?'

She flicks her eyes upward and then I realise. 'Jump Around' by House of Pain has come on – the song we always have to dance to, no matter where we are. I slam my glass down and head onto the dance floor, and for the next four minutes Lance and I, joined by Amy, Sarah and Sam, pogo around the otherwise empty dancefloor, to the bemusement of everyone else.

Finally, the song comes to an end and I'm breathless, laughing as we make our way back to where our drinks are waiting. I down the rest of mine like it's water and pour another one. The bottle is already empty, so I open the next one.

'God, I'm knackered,' Sam laughs, her cheeks flushed. It makes her look even more pretty. I notice her check her watch and a tiny frown flits across her features.

'I'm sure he'll be here soon,' I say, smiling.

'What? Oh, right. Yeah, sorry.' She gives a sheepish grin. 'I'm not normally this possessive. I just really wanted him to come tonight, to meet some of my old friends. We haven't been together long, but he's amazing.'

I can tell she's smitten with this guy, and something in the tone of her voice gives me a pang. I've never felt that way about anyone, not really. I told myself I loved Robert, but deep down I knew I never really did. I just felt flattered that someone like him would look twice at someone like me. But since Robert, I hadn't met anyone special. I'd been on the odd date, at Lance's insistence, but they'd never gone anywhere and, until now, I hadn't really thought about it. In fact, the only time I've ever felt even a flutter of excitement about someone was when I met Bridge Man, and that didn't do me any good.

'Are you with anyone?' Sam asks, and I shake my head.

'No. I've got two jobs, I'm too busy to meet anyone.' I look round the room. 'I'm not sure there are many catches here this evening either.'

Sam grins. 'You're probably right.' She takes a gulp of her wine and I follow suit. 'So what do you do? You said you have two jobs?'

'I work part time in a vintage clothes shop, and I'm a counsellor by day.'

'That sounds tough. It must be a hard job?'

I nod. 'It is, but it can't be as hard as being a nurse.'

'Oh, I don't know. I just deal with people's injuries, physical things you can see, you know. That's easy. I can't imagine what it must be like to dig down deep inside someone's mind and try and get them to tell you what's making them unhappy.'

'Yeah, lots of people who come to see me are reluctant. They've been referred, or they don't really believe there's anything wrong with them. But it can be really rewarding.'

'So what made you decide to do that?'

'It was Alison's idea, really. I've always been a good listener, you know, it was always me our friends came to if they had boyfriend trouble or family problems, and somehow I always knew what to say.' I shrug. 'She just pointed out it could be right up my street.

And then—' I hesitate, wondering whether to tell her about Bridge Man. 'Then one night, a few years ago, I stopped someone from throwing themselves into the Thames, just by talking to them, and it made me realise maybe I could be quite good at this after all.'

Sam's eyes are wide. 'Wow, that's amazing. See, I couldn't do that. I would have panicked, looked for someone else to help. Unless there was a visible injury, I wouldn't have had a clue what to do.'

'Neither did I, really.' I shrug. 'It was just luck.'

'Well, it sounds like you're doing your perfect job.'

'I really am.'

We fall into silence for a moment, and I realise, as I watch the lights spinning round the now-dark room, that I'm already quite drunk. Oh well, in for a penny and all that. I grab the bottle, but it's empty.

'Let me go and get another one,' Sam says, and disappears, leaving me standing there alone. I turn to Lance. 'I think I'm quite pissed,' I say, grinning. She looks at me.

'Oh, Annie, maybe you should slow it down just a little bit? It's only nine o'clock.'

'All right, Mum.'

She grins. 'You and Sam seem to be getting on well.'

'Yeah, she's great. I remember her vaguely from before, but I didn't know her very well then.'

'Well, you never wanted to hang out with us much.'

'Course not. I was jealous.'

'What of?'

'You and them. I thought they were stealing you from me.'

'Did you? You wally.' She hugs me tightly and I can smell her perfume, the same one she's worn for the last ten years. The familiarity is comforting, and it brings tears to my eyes.

'What are you crying for?'

'Nothing. I'm just a bit drunk.' I look at her. 'But I do love you, you know.'

'I love you too, Annie. But slow down, all right?'

'Promise.'

Unfortunately, it soon becomes clear that it's a bit late for slowing down. The rest of the evening passes in a blur of faces, drinks and stories until, finally, I'm not sure I can even stand upright any more. I sneak off to the toilet, and slump onto the loo seat for a few minutes, holding my head in my hands. The cubicle spins round me and I take a few long, deep breaths. I'll be all right in a minute.

'Annie?' Lance's voice comes from the other side of the toilet door.

'In here.' I reach up and unlock it, and she pushes it open from the other side.

'Are you okay?'

I look up at her. 'No. I think I need to go home. I'm sorry, Lance.'

'Don't be daft. I've had enough anyway. Got to get up early in the morning. Come on, let's get you home.' I stand and she takes hold of my elbow and I stumble against the door frame.

'Sorry,' I mumble again, my words thick against my tongue. 'Iss the wine. Cheap wine.'

'Yeah, it's definitely the fact that wine is cheap, not that you've drunk three gallons of it.'

I lean against her heavily as she guides me from the bathroom, then she deposits me by the front door. Cool air seeps through and I breathe it in greedily.

'Wait here, I'll go and get our bags.'

Minutes later, she's back, and we stagger outside. I'm leaning against her so hard I'm amazed she can hold me up, but I'm grateful for it. I just need to get home and get to bed and sleep this off.

'Is that your taxi?' I hear Lance say to someone coming the

other way, and I hear a low voice in response, then we're heading towards the orange light, praying it doesn't leave before we get there. I hear a muffled conversation with the taxi driver then we're in the cab, I'm handed a carrier bag to throw up into if need be, and then we're off, home.

I vow never to drink again.

19

NOVEMBER 1998

Ted

Looking for a flat in London is utterly soul-destroying. Even with two salaries combined, everything we want is still so far out of reach we'd have to win the lottery to be able to afford it. To compound the issue, prices seem to be rising by the day.

The flat we're seeing today is the last one on our list and if we don't like this one, I don't know what we're going to do next. It's not exactly what I dreamed of when I asked Sam if she wanted to live together.

'We'll be able to afford a much bigger place,' I'd said, avoiding saying the thing I really meant, which was that I just wanted to be with her all the time.

'Oh, you old romantic,' she'd said, kissing me lightly on the end of my nose. I knew how lucky I was. Lots of women I'd met over the years had needed reassuring that I loved them constantly. But Sam never demands too much from me. She knows, despite my reticence and my reluctance to actually say what I mean, that I love her.

That's not to say we haven't had our difficulties getting here. Just a few days ago, Sam had seemed distant and withdrawn. I'd tried my hardest to ignore the issue, of course, but in the end Sam had cracked.

'You're clearly not going to ask me what's wrong, so I'm just going to have to tell you, aren't I?' she said as I chopped onions one evening. I'd turned to her, my eyes brimming with tears from the vegetables, knife poised.

'What?'

'Good grief, Ted. I couldn't have made it more obvious that I'm upset about something, but you'd prefer to go through the rest of our lives pretending everything is fine rather than talk about it, wouldn't you?'

I opened my mouth to object but closed it again before replying. She was right, after all. I had known there was something on her mind, but had been too chicken to confront it.

'Go on, then. What's wrong?' I said, turning back to my chopping.

I heard her inhale deeply and waited.

'It's you, Ted. This. The way you are.' I turned to see her standing, hand on one hip, the other arm gesturing round the room. She sighed heavily. 'I just – you're so detached, Ted. So – distant.'

I put the knife down and leaned against the worktop. My hands were damp and sticky, and I let them hang down by my sides.

'I don't know what you want me to say.'

'I don't know either. But I just – I worry. That this – me, you, us moving in together, making this commitment – that it's going to tip you over the edge, send you even further away from me.'

'But it's the opposite, Sam, surely?'

She shook her head, frustrated. 'For most people maybe. But

you, Ted, you're—' She stopped, her shoulders slumped. 'I don't know. I just feel as though the closer we get, the less I actually know you. The real you, I mean.' She tapped her finger against her forehead. 'What's going on in here.'

'But I always talk to you!'

'About some things, yes. But you must know you can be withdrawn sometimes, and that you've never ever talked to me about your time in the Gulf, or, or about your dad, or told me how you actually *feel* about anything.'

I swallowed. There was nothing I could say to defend myself because all of these things were true. 'But you know I love you, don't you?'

She hesitated and my heart flipped over. Was she going to say she didn't even know that?

'Yes, Ted, I know you love me. But I need more from you. I don't need you to tell me you love me every five minutes, but I need you to tell me things, to want to share things with me. Not push me away.'

I hadn't known what to say. I didn't know whether I could make that promise, whether I had it in me to change and become the person Sam wanted me to be. So instead I'd taken three steps across the kitchen towards her and wrapped my arms around her and not let go until I felt her body start to relax, and I knew we were all right again. For now, at least.

Now here we were, about to go and see yet another flat – so far, we'd seen twelve in various parts of north London, even going as far as Enfield in our desperation to find something that gave us what we need – and I was just hoping that any worries or doubts Sam had had disappeared.

'Are we asking too much?' I say, as I pull my trousers on. Sam's just out of the shower, wrapped in a towel, and my heart flips when I see her. God, I'm a lucky man.

'I don't think so.' She rubs her dark hair with another towel and drops it on the floor. That's one thing I don't love about her, her untidiness. I know if I don't pick that towel up, it could stay there for days. I don't know whether it's my military training or whether I've always been this way, but I like things neat and tidy. I reach down and pick the towel up before it starts to annoy me. Sam barely even notices. 'I mean, we want two bedrooms,' she says, counting on her fingers. 'We want something we can put our own stamp on, and we want some outside space, if possible.'

'I'd quite like something with neighbours that don't leave old mattresses and sofas piled in their front garden and have a rabid dog barking at all hours,' I say, thinking of the flat we'd seen a couple of days before. I step behind Sam, who's now sitting on a stool at the dressing table, studying her face in the mirror, and gently massage her shoulders. She gives a gentle groan and rolls her head back and I lean down and kiss her.

'Hmm, fuss pot,' she grins, watching me in the mirror now. 'How about something without mould in the corner of the bathroom or a railway line practically running through the back garden?'

'Let's hope this is the one. Otherwise, I'm officially giving up.'

'It will be perfect, I can feel it in my waters.' She swivels to face me. 'Anyway, we can't give up. We can't stay here for the rest of our lives.'

I feel my stomach clench in irritation. I love this flat. It's the flat that signalled the beginning of the rest of my life after moving out of Danny's place. It's the place where I found my new beginning, and left the pain of the past behind.

But of course she's right, as well. It's entirely unsuitable for us. It's too small, for starters, and hardly the sort of place we want to spend the rest of our lives in. Especially if we do have children.

Sam's mentioned it already. Not in a 'have children with me or

I'll leave you' way, but definitely in a way that made it clear she did want children one day.

What if I end up being like my father?

I shake the thought away. I'm nothing like him. I'm not vain and selfish, for a start. And I'd never neglect my child or put him down. No. I will definitely be a better father than he was, when the time comes. Not that that's saying much.

'I know. It's just so depressing.'

She grabs my hand. 'We'll find something. I know we will.'

* * *

The street looks promising from the moment we turn the corner. Tucked down a quiet corner of Haringey, it immediately feels a world away from the hectic high street just a few steps down the road. The houses are neat and tidy, set back slightly by small front gardens and fences or walls. I feel Sam's hand clench mine tightly and I squeeze hers back. Neither of us wants to tempt fate before we see this flat, but I know she likes what she's seeing.

'What number is it?' she says, peering over my shoulder at the estate agent's details.

'One hundred and one.'

We keep walking, heads swivelling to look for the right flat, and suddenly, we're there.

'Is he meeting us here?'

'Yes,' I say, as a very tall, very young man walks towards us, wearing a suit and holding out his hand in greeting.

'You must be Ted and Sam?' he says, shaking my hand limply.

I nod. 'Lovely to meet you.' He pulls a key out of his pocket and heads up the short path to the front door. 'You're going to love this place. I don't think it will hang around for long.'

I roll my eyes and Sam nudges me in the ribs. We've heard that line before, usually when they're desperate to get rid of somewhere. We follow him into the flat – and immediately I know this is the place I want to live. I glance at Sam, and she gives a tiny nod. She agrees. But we must play this cool.

The flat is on the ground floor, with a lovely living room, two small double bedrooms and a kitchen at the back. But it's the garden that does it for me. Patio doors stretch across the whole of the back of the room and open out onto a small but pretty patch of green. I step towards the glass.

'Is this just for this flat?'

The estate agent checks his details and nods. 'Yep, looks like it.'

I stand for a few moments, letting the details of this place sink in as Sam and James, as he's introduced himself, go and look at the other rooms in more detail. As I stand there, watching the plants get battered by the wind through the glass, memories flood my mind unexpectedly. Me and my father, in our garden in our home in Cricklewood. He's pushing me on the swing and I'm high in the air, laughing. Me and my father digging the flowerbeds together, him helping me plant the sunflower I'd chosen from the garden centre. Him and me lying on our backs on rugs when the sun had gone down, watching the stars twinkle in the light-polluted sky and feeling the damp of the grass seep through the blanket and through our clothes beneath me.

All of these memories evoke a feeling. An unfamiliar one, when it comes to memories of my father. Happiness. I usually forget that my father made me happy once, back when I was little, before my mother left. He'd been happy himself then. Not the bitter, critical, angry man he later became. These feelings surprise me, and for a moment I'm overwhelmed by the intensity of them, and I reach my hand out and lay it flat on the glass.

'Do you want to go out and have a look?' James says, and I jump. 'Oh, yes. Thanks.'

As he unlocks the door, Sam grabs my hand. 'Are you okay?'

I nod, unsure how to explain the memories that had just floored me. What was it about this small patch of land that had triggered them? It's not as though it looks anything like the garden I remember from my childhood.

We step out into the garden. A fence runs down the middle of it, and on the other side is a patch of lawn that needs a mow, and a few sorry looking flower pots. On our side, though, it's a riot of colour, roses climbing the walls on one side, a trellis with wisteria climbing along the back fence, and a stylish, sculpted seating area towards the back.

'This is your bit,' James says unnecessarily.

'It's gorgeous, isn't it?' Sam whispers and I nod.

'Lovely.' I turn and head back inside and James follows.

'We'll let you know,' I say, shaking his hand as we stand on the front step once more.

'Yes, do. But don't leave it too long. We've already got eight viewings lined up today. I wouldn't be surprised if it's gone by the end of the day.'

Now I've seen the flat, I believe him. This is somewhere I can picture me and Sam living together, and I can't imagine anyone could leave this place and not feel the same way.

As we head back towards the Tube station, we pass a woman in a bright red bobble hat, walking arm in arm with someone who must be her mum, in the opposite direction and clutching the same details as we have in our hands. I avert my gaze, and nudge Sam.

'We won't let them get it,' Sam says.

'You liked it too, then?'

'It was perfect,' she says.

We walk in silence for a moment, and then I feel a tug on my arm and Sam's pulling me through the door of a coffee shop.

'What are we doing?'

'I thought we should get to know our new neighbourhood,' she says.

'A bit presumptuous.'

'Maybe.' She heads towards a table near the back and sits. I sit opposite her and she grabs my hands. 'But, Ted, we have to get that flat. Don't we?'

I nod. 'We do.'

She grins. 'So we will.' She pulls her new mobile phone out of her pocket and pulls the estate agent's details towards her. 'Okay, what are we offering, then?'

Not for the first time, my heart swells with love for this fierce, decisive, determined woman I'm lucky to call my girlfriend.

* * *

It all happens quickly, in the end. We made our offer that day, and by the following morning, it was accepted.

I didn't like to think about that poor woman who went to see it after us, and who might have loved it as much as we did. All I could think about was how happy we were going to be in our new home. The start of a new future, together.

The people selling it were moving into a rented house, so the move was easy. So, just nine weeks later, it's moving day.

Even though we'd spent the previous evening packing boxes late into the night, there are still a few more things to sort out first thing in morning. At first, I didn't really understand why it took so long when I don't have much stuff, but as we packed more and more boxes, I realised how much Sam had infiltrated my life. Her clothes hung in my wardrobe, her toiletries filled my bathroom cabinet, and her favourite foods – endless cans of Diet Coke, packets of cashew nuts, paper-thin slices of expensive ham from the deli – were everywhere. It has almost happened by osmosis, it was so stealthy.

I walk through to the kitchen, where there's a pile of papers on the side ready to take out to the recycling. I casually flick through it to make sure Sam hasn't tried to chuck out something I might need, when I see it. I freeze and, slowly, I pull the crackly newspaper out from the middle of the pile. It's dated from seven years ago, and I know without opening it that it's the paper I ran the advert for Fairy Girl in. I don't know why I kept it all this time, but I hope Sam hasn't seen it – not that she'd have the faintest idea what it was.

I can hear her still clattering about in the bedroom, so I carefully open the crispy pages and flick to the 'I Saw You' section. And there it is.

To the girl in the fairy wings who helped me on Waterloo Bridge on Friday night. I'd like to find you, to say thank you. Please put an ad here if it's you. I'll look for your reply.

What had I been thinking? Had I really thought for one minute she might see this and come and find me? And then what? We'd fall madly in love? Live happily ever after?

The truth is, the whole thing had felt a bit like a fairytale, even at the time. I'd always felt that there *should* be a connection between me and the girl in the fairy wings; that, thanks to the circumstances in which we met, there had to be something up there in the universe that would bring us back together. And with nothing else to hold onto, I'd clung to that like a lifeboat, holding on for dear life for far longer than was healthy.

I see that now.

Yet there's still a part of me that can't help returning to thoughts of 'what if?'

'I can't believe you've got such old papers lying around.' Sam's voice behind me interrupts my thoughts and I close the page guiltily.

'Yeah. I know.'

'It's weird because it's so unlike you. Now, had it been me, I would have expected it.' She smiles and takes the pile from me. 'I'll go and shove them in the recycling bin.'

'No!' I grab them back more forcefully than I mean to, and she looks shocked. 'Sorry. I just mean, don't worry, you finish off in the bedroom, I'll take them.'

'Okay.' She steps back, gives me a funny look, and leaves the room. I swipe the newspaper from the top of the pile, fold it as small as I can and shove it into my jacket pocket, then take the rest out to the recycling bins.

When I get back, Sam's holding something in her hands and frowning. She turns to me and when I see what she's got, my heart stops.

'Isn't this the picture that used to be up there, over the table?'

I swallow. 'Yes.'

She looks back down at it.

'Right. So, why's it in the back of the wardrobe?'

I shrug, hoping for casual. 'Not sure. I must just have forgotten it was in there.' I picture the empty space on the wall above the table where we eat dinner together most evenings. Sam had asked me about the picture the morning after the party, and I'd told her I was bored of it and was going to replace it with something else. She'd just nodded at the time. But now she looks suspicious, as though she knows there's something I'm not telling her.

'Well, do you want to keep it?'

I don't know how to answer that. Yes, I want to keep it. But how can I keep something that makes me feel I'm betraying the woman I love? Because I do love her. It doesn't matter what residual thoughts and feelings I might have for the girl on the bridge.

I still haven't told Sam about my suicide attempt and now that so much time has passed, it doesn't look likely that I ever will, which means there will never be a good time to explain who this picture is of, and why it's important to me.

'I'll take it. See if it goes anywhere once we're settled in.' I take it from her and put it by the front door, ready to go into the van. Then I return to the bedroom, which is now just an empty shell, apart from a few boxes stacked in the corner.

I take in the tiny proportions; the familiar crack in the pale green paint in the corner by the window; the peeling paint on the window frames, the marks on the floor where my bed has stood for the last six years. Next to me, Sam stands up and brushes her jeans down, then she's in front of me, her arms around my neck, her forehead resting on mine.

'Are you going to miss this manky old flat?'

I nod.

'Me too, weirdly.'

I pull back and look at her. 'Really?'

'Yup. Even though it's tiny and not very nice and needs a total overhaul, it's the first place we met. Well, sort of. It's where we got to know each other, and fell in love, and – well, you know what I mean.' She blushes.

'I do. But we'll be happy in our new place. You know that, right?'

'I hope so.' She looks as though she wants to say something else, but then there's a knock at the door, and it's time to say goodbye to the place forever. It's time for a new beginning.

20

Marianne

'Come *on*, Mum.'

I stand on the doorstep, tapping my foot like a belligerent child. Finally, after years of saving, I'm ready to buy a flat of my own, and Mum's meant to be coming with me to see the fifth or sixth one on my list.

'You can't be too fussy,' she said, when I was sitting on the sofa a few nights before, poring over all the details I've collected from estate agents across north London. 'Beggars can't be choosers.'

'I know,' I'd snapped. I was cross with her for putting a downer on it, the same way she did with everything. But it turned out that, in this case, she was right. The places in my price range – even those just above my price range – were mostly dumps, in questionable areas, had dodgy neighbours, or damp problems. It was beginning to turn into a bit of a depressing process.

But this flat was looking more promising, and I was keen not to be late.

'The estate agent said there's been lots of interest in it,' I say, waving the details at her as she picks her way carefully down the stairs. For the first time, I notice she's getting older, and it pricks my heart. I've always taken her for granted – Dad too, until his heart attack. But now, with the prospect of leaving them behind at long last, I'm beginning to see their vulnerabilities, and realise they won't be around forever.

'Estate agents always say that, love, it's part of their sales patter.' Mum might be getting older, but it hasn't blunted her acerbic manner, I think, smiling. I wait impatiently as she checks her reflection in the hallway mirror and wipes lipstick off her teeth, then claps her hands together. 'Right, I'm ready.'

At last, I don't say.

'Thanks for coming with me,' I say instead, as we set off down the street. It's cold today, and windy, leaves and scraps of paper whipping around in gusts of wind. I tug my red bobble hat on and tuck my hair into it to stop it going wild.

'You look like a boy when you do that,' Mum says, and I roll my eyes. She doesn't change.

The bus journey from North Finchley to Haringey doesn't take long, and Mum seems pleased. 'I thought it was further than that,' she says, stepping off the bus and almost being blown away by a sudden gust. I link her arm through mine.

'See, it won't take long to get here. And a taxi's even quicker.'

'It wants to be, the amount those cabbies charge.'

'True,' I reply, not wanting to get into yet another argument about money. I just want her to come and see the flat with me, with no dramas.

We walk arm in arm along the street and I glance at the *A–Z* every now and then to make sure we're heading in the right direction.

'Shops are nice here,' Mum says, nodding at a small deli and a toy shop whose window is stuffed full of wooden toys. 'Bit different to the grocers on the corner by ours.'

I know Mum's loyal to the part of London where we live, but it's still hard to ignore the small note of bitterness in her voice. I know she wants me to find somewhere nearer, but I need to find my own feet.

'I don't know why you can't just go and have a look at those flats round the corner,' she'd said last night.

'She's already told you why,' Dad had interjected. I'd given him a grateful smile and he'd rolled his eyes.

'I know, Patrick, but she could at least take a look at them. They're brand new, and you get a lot more space for your money than you get in central London.'

'Haringey is hardly central London, Wendy. It's barely four miles away. There's not many people lucky enough to have their daughter living so close these days.'

'And the bus only takes about twenty minutes,' I'd added.

'All right, all right, you two, no need to gang up on me, it was only a suggestion.' Mum had started aggressively dusting the top of the TV then, her way of showing she knew she was wrong and so wasn't going to discuss it any further.

'Thanks, Dad,' I said, when she retreated to the kitchen a few minutes later.

'No problem, love. She'd have you living here forever, your Mum would. But you're twenty-seven now, it's about time you found a place of your own.' He'd put his newspaper down and looked at me long and hard. 'I'm proud of you, you know.'

'Are you?'

He nodded. 'You've worked bloody hard to save for this flat. It's not like we've been able to give you anything to help out, especially not since I've had to give up work.' He'd sighed. 'It's just as well this place was paid off before it happened, or we'd have been out on the street.'

'That would never have happened, Dad. I'd have made sure it didn't.' He'd smiled weakly. 'But are you sure you're happy for me to move out? I mean, it's a lot, with your heart and everything.'

Dad had made a good recovery, considering. But he'd never been able to return to his job as a postman, and had taken early retirement. He loved pottering around the garden and spent hours in the shed tinkering with his motorbikes. But he struggled with not being busy, the way he had been for his entire life. Some days, he seemed a bit lost.

'I'm grand,' he said. 'I just want you to get out there in the world and show 'em what you've got. You're much brighter than either me or your mum.'

'I don't think so, Dad,' I'd said, smiling. Dad had an amazing brain, able to retain any information you gave him for future reference. He was a whiz at pub quizzes, almost always walking away with the prize. He'd even been asked not to go back to a couple, because the locals had complained he ruined it for them.

'Pub quizzes are one thing, love. But you've got your head screwed on.' He'd looked down at the paper in in his lap, where the crossword was almost complete. His face was half in darkness, lit up from the other side by the electric fire next to his armchair. 'It's not as though me and your mum ever encouraged you to have much ambition. I wish we had.'

'If I can be half the person you are, Dad, that'll be good enough for me.'

I'd stood then and planted a kiss on the thinning hair of his head.

He'd wanted to come with us today, but Mum had told him to

stay at home and rest and, actually, it was nice to spend some time with her, out of the house when we weren't getting under each other's feet.

'Right, this is the street,' I say, turning right.

'Oh, it's a lovely road,' Mum says, as we walk along. She peers through people's windows as I squint at door numbers, trying to make out how far along we need to be. We pass a couple walking in the other direction and I notice them holding the same sheet of paper with the same house details on and my heart sinks. Oh no, that's not a good sign. I glance up at them to see if I can get any indication of what they thought of the place they've just seen, but the man has his head turned away, saying something in her ear, and then the moment's gone and they've passed us.

'Here we are,' I say, stopping outside the house, where a man in a cheap suit is waiting.

'Hello, you must be Marianne,' he says, stepping forward and holding out his hand. 'I'm James.'

'Hello,' I say. 'This is my mum, Wendy.' Mum shakes his hand and then we step inside. I know the instant I walk through the front door that this is the place I want to live.

* * *

I didn't get the flat. It was inevitable, really. It had been a few thousand pounds over my budget anyway, so when it went to a bidding war, I stood no chance. I hope whoever got it is happy there, because it truly was a lovely home for someone.

I found somewhere else, in the end. Slightly different area, on the first floor of a three-storey block. It's nice, it's in budget, and it's probably cheaper to look after than the other flat. I still can't help feeling jealous of whoever gets to live there, though. I wonder whether it was the couple we passed on the way there.

Being a first-time buyer with only a single bedroom's-worth of stuff to my name, it doesn't take me long to be ready to move and, just nine weeks later, I'm moving in.

'Is this all you've got?' Lance says as she climbs out of the car a few metres away from the front door.

I look down at the bags and boxes piled on the front path. Apart from my precious sewing machine and bundles of fabric, it does look a bit meagre for twenty-seven years of life.

'Apart from a bag of food Mum's insisting on giving me, pretty much.'

'Right, well, this won't take long then.' Lance bends down and picks up a box and I do the same and follow her to her Ford Focus.

'Thanks for this, Lance.'

'Don't be daft, I wouldn't miss it for the world.' She leans into the boot and produces a bottle with a flourish. 'Besides, I need to help you christen the place when we get there.'

'We might have to drink it out of the bottle, I'm not sure I've got any glasses.'

'You have, love, I wrapped a couple of mine in newspaper and popped them in the box marked *kitchen*,' Mum says, appearing behind me.

'Just as well one of you thinks ahead, eh?' Lance says, winking at Mum, who smiles happily. She loves Lance, has always considered her like another daughter ever since we were little girls playing with our Sindy dolls, right through the teenage years of boys and drunken nights out, and even now, as allegedly real grown-ups, Mum has a soft spot for my best friend.

'You don't have to gang up on me,' I say, pretending to sulk.

'You love it,' Lance says, hugging Mum and climbing into the driver's side.

'I'll come over tomorrow when I get back from work, all right, love?' Mum says, squeezing me tightly.

'Perfect,' I say, hugging her back.

Then I climb into the passenger seat, we pull away from the kerb and I watch Mum's retreating figure as we drive away from the house that's been my home for my whole life. I know I'm only moving a few miles across town, but it might as well be a whole world away. It feels like the start of something new.

It takes us half an hour to drive the short distance to Wood Green through the traffic, but when I pull up outside, my heart does a flip. It's a lovely block of flats, and I'm lucky.

'Let's get these boxes unpacked,' Lance says, heaving the heaviest one from the boot of the car. After a small battle with the lock, we step inside my brand-new home.

Light floods through the windows, and the living room feels bright and airy. The bedroom is large, and I'm thankful now that the previous owners agreed to leave me their double bed. I'm not sure I could face sleeping on the laminate floors for weeks until I got myself organised.

The only other furniture in here is an old futon and a shelf attached to the wall. But it already feels like home.

* * *

Two hours later and the boxes are inside, and the empty bottle of champagne is lying on its side on the floor, two empty tumblers next to it. I've been to the shop on the corner and bought another bottle and we're already halfway through that.

I tip my head back on the futon and sigh.

'I'm meant to be going to buy a few bits of furniture,' I say. 'I've got nowhere else to sit.'

'Ah, you can always go tomorrow. I'll come with you, we can go to Camden, load the car up.'

'Would you?' My heart lifts at the thought of browsing through my favourite market stalls for things to fill my flat with rather than heading to the huge IKEA round the North Circular for some generic tables and chairs.

'Course.'

I glance at her. I've been so preoccupied with the move recently, I realise I haven't asked her anything about what's going on with her. Including her fledgling relationship with the delicious Jeremy, who started as a junior at her accountancy firm a few weeks before.

'Are you not seeing Jeremy this weekend?'

She swigs her fizz, and shakes her head. 'Nope.'

I lean forward and look her in the eye.

'Alison, are you withholding from me?'

She knows I'm serious when I call her Alison and she looks at me and smiles. 'No, not really. There's just really not much to tell. We went on a few dates – as you know. He seemed lovely, but then it turned out he has a girlfriend, and they're moving in together, thank you very much.'

'*What*? Why haven't you told me about this?'

'It only happened a few days ago.'

'And?'

'And I thought you had enough on your mind, what with the move and everything.'

'Lance, you always tell me everything. I don't ever want that to change.'

She looks at me sheepishly. 'I know. Sorry. But, well, I've told you now.' She shrugs and polishes off her wine, leans forward and refills both of our glasses. 'Anyway, he's too young for me.'

'I thought he was the same age as you?'

'A year younger, actually. But no, I've decided I need someone older. Someone more mature, who can keep up with me, can afford to go the same places I like to go.' She shrugs. 'I need a sugar daddy.'

I grin. 'Well, there are plenty of older men where you work.'

'Ugh, not those fusty old gits. I want someone full of life, someone with life experience.'

'Where are you going to find him, then?'

'No idea.' She laughs and I join in. 'So, what about you?'

'What about me?'

'Feeling ready to go out there with me and try to find a man?'

I sigh. Lance is always on at me to find a man. She's always seeing someone, or thinking about seeing someone, has always been the same way. She's never quite understood how I can be content on my own.

'I'm all right,' I say.

'I knew you were going to say that.'

I shrug. 'Well, I am. I've got this place to sort out, I've got work, you, Mum and Dad to help out. I don't have time for anyone else.'

She shuffles round to face me, tucking her leg underneath her other one. Her face is serious.

'Oh, Annie, it would do you good. I know you like to be Little Miss Independent, but having a boyfriend doesn't make you any less so. It just gives you someone to have sex with. I mean snuggle up with.' She grins.

'I know. I just – I don't really need anyone.'

She peers at me, her forehead creased.

'What?'

'You're not... you're not still hung up on Robert, are you?'

'No! God, no. That was years ago. I couldn't care less about him.'

'Good. Good.' She continues to watch me.

'What?'

'And that other guy. The one from the bridge.'

My heart flips over as it always does when I think about him. 'What about him?'

'You're not still secretly holding out for him, are you?'

'Bridge Man? Don't be daft. I don't even know him.'

'No, I know that. But I also know what you're like. There was something about him that caught your imagination that night, and I know you've thought about him a lot over the years. But you know that he's more or less a figment of your imagination, don't you? I mean, he's real, but he's not a real person to you. You know nothing about him, apart from the fact he was desperate enough to want to end his life that night.'

'I'm not hung up on him.' My voice is sharp, and Lance holds her hands up in surrender.

'Okay, okay. I was just asking. I just – I don't want you to hold back from meeting someone else because you've got this daft idea that you might find him again one day. Life's not a Hollywood movie.'

'I'm not. I mean, that's not what I'm doing. I just haven't met anyone yet.'

She nods and doesn't reply for a moment.

'Okay then. Well, you're never going to meet anyone if you never go anywhere where there are any eligible men.' She stands, wobbles a bit and holds out her hand.

'Come on. Let's go out.'

'Where?'

'Just out. Go and research the local bars, see if there are any men out there worth getting to know.' She sweeps her hand round. 'It would be handy to meet someone who lives nearby. Practical.'

'I've got loads of unpacking to do.'

'Packing schmacking. Let's go and celebrate your new home, and get drunk. Come on, Annie.'

She plays hardball, Lance, always has. And so, knowing I won't

win this argument, I let myself be pulled up and dragged out of the
flat and along the road to the pub. Maybe Lance is right. Maybe I do
need to find someone. At least I can have fun looking.

Not for the first time, I'm grateful for my funny, crazy best
friend.

21

JUNE 2000

Ted

The flat is completely silent; no footsteps, no voices, no radio, no TV. Not even a tap dripping, radiator clunking or neighbour singing. I close my eyes and relish the peace for a moment, my body stretched out on the bed.

This is the first time in what feels like months that I've had any time to myself. It's the first time there's been any peace at all, and I want to enjoy every single second of it.

The last few months have been one big whirl of activity. People coming and going, phone calls all day long, one decision after another to make and not a single second to just take a deep breath and take stock. Today is my wedding day, and before it all goes crazy again, I'm just going to lie here and breathe slowly.

I think back over the last eighteen months since Sam and I moved into this flat. It was everything we'd hoped it would be, right from the day we got here. The flat welcomed us with open arms and, even though we barely had a stick of furniture to our names, we didn't care. I wriggle around, feeling the firmness of the mattress beneath me, remembering the days of sleeping curled up together on my cheap futon, the slats digging into my spine, leaving me tired and groggy for work the next morning. We spent our weekends painting walls, choosing furniture and putting up shelves and now, as I lie here, I open my eyes and look round with a feeling of amazement at how far I've come since my lowest moment.

More than eight years have passed since that night on the bridge, but I'll never take my happiness for granted again. It's been hard-won, and even now there are moments, snippets of time – often late at night – when I feel my mind slip back into darkness, when the blackest memories sneak in, and threaten to drag me back under again. But then I remember everything I've achieved since that day, the second chance I was given, and everything I have that's worth living for, and it pulls me back out again.

Things could have been so different, and I know I'll never forget that.

I'd proposed eight months before, and hadn't actually thought as far ahead as the wedding day. But Sam had been adamant she wanted a summer wedding and had ploughed full steam ahead into planning it.

'Are you sure you want such a huge fuss?' I'd said as she'd shown me yet another venue that, along with the catering, would have cost almost a year's wages.

'Don't you?' she'd said, her lower lip protruding.

'Well, no, not really. I just thought it could be small. You know, us, a few friends. Your family.' I hadn't mentioned my father and she knew not to suggest it. It was an unspoken agreement between us.

'Oh.'

'But why don't we meet somewhere in the middle?' I'd said,

desperate not to disappoint her. 'You know, a lovely venue, good food, all our friends? Something a bit more – us?'

She'd looked down at the brochure in her hand for a moment, and I'd thought she was going to cry. But then she raised her eyes and smiled. 'You're right. I'm getting carried away. This isn't us at all, is it?'

'Not really.' I'd laughed and then she'd started too, and before we knew it, we'd been hysterical, unable to control ourselves for at least five minutes. In the end, we'd agreed on something a bit more simple, a bit less formal and a bit more fun. And now the day is here.

My thoughts are interrupted by a banging at the door. I reluctantly peel myself off the bed and walk down the hallway.

'Here he is!' Danni squeals before the door is even fully open, and flings herself at me, wrapping her arms around my neck. I hug her back and throw Danny a grin over her shoulder as she pulls away.

'Oh, I never thought this day would come,' she says, placing her hands on my upper arms like an old aunt. 'I'm so excited!'

'Sorry, mate, she's been like this all morning,' Danny grins, stepping inside. His suit hangs over his arm, wrapped in plastic and he looks round for somewhere to place it before hanging it over the back of the sofa.

'Well, it's not every day your best friend marries one of my friends, is it? It *is* exciting.' Danni pretends to sulk but can't pull it off and is soon grinning like a Cheshire cat again. 'Anyway, I'm not staying long, I need to go and see your bride-to-be, I just wanted to give you a hug and say good luck today.'

'Thank you, Danni.'

'Right, you two. Make sure you keep track of time, and you won't leave Sam waiting, will you?'

'Course we won't.'

'I know you won't, Ted, it's this one I'm worried about. Timing isn't his strong point.' She jabs her fingers into Danny's arm, and he gives a sheepish grin.

'We'll be there, don't worry,' he says. She gives him a kiss, pecks me on the cheek, and is gone and climbing into her red Mini.

Danny turns to me.

'Right, just us, then.'

'Yep.'

'You look bloody terrified, Ted.'

'I am.' I walk towards the kitchen, motioning for him to follow me. 'I just never thought I'd ever be getting married.'

'I knew you would. She's great, Sam.'

'She really is.' *Too good for me*, I often think, but don't say out loud. I still struggle to understand what she sees in me, and what has made someone so content, so together as Sam want to be with someone like me. I've always known my inability to open up to her has been a problem, and I wasn't sure it was one we could overcome. Yet now here we are, and I'm still secretly waiting for it to all crumble around my ears.

I open the fridge and pull out a bottle of champagne. 'Sam's mum bought us this to drink tonight, but we've got gallons of the stuff already. Shall we have some? Steady our nerves?'

'It's only eleven o'clock, Ted.'

I glance at the clock, then shrug. 'It's my wedding day, you have to.'

'Go on then, I'll have some with ya. But just one.'

I pop the cork and pour us a glass each. I down mine in one and let out a huge burp. 'Sorry.' I wipe my mouth. 'I needed that.'

I let the familiar buzz of the first drink radiate through my body, feeling each bone, each muscle and each sinew relax as it does. I've missed this. After the night of Sam's reunion when the whisky-drinking got out of control, I've only had one more relapse, and then I vowed not to replace my secret stash. I've stuck to my word too, and only drink beer these days. That's not to say the whisky doesn't call to me sometimes, but so far I've resisted it. I'm proud of myself. I think of Lynne, my counsellor all those years ago, who I'd stopped seeing after a year, and wish I could tell her. I think she'd be proud of how far I've come too. Maybe I'll ring her once life has settled down again.

'Right, come on, Ted, let's get ready.'

Danny stands, a little more unsteady on his feet after champagne on an empty stomach.

'I think I need to eat first.'

'Good idea.' He heads to the fridge. 'You jump in the shower, I'll make some bacon rolls.'

I'm overcome by a sudden rush of love for this man. Despite his rough exterior, he has a heart of gold, and I honestly don't know what I'd have done without him over the last nine years. He's my best man today, but he's also my family. I'd sent Dad an invitation to the wedding, but I just received a card saying thanks for the invitation but he couldn't make it, and that was all I needed to know. So for me, Danny is everything.

'Thanks mate,' I say, the words utterly inadequate. But Danny hates a fuss, and I know he understands how important he is to me. Before I start to cry, I head to the bathroom to get myself ready.

* * *

Bacon rolls polished off, Danny and I are both suited and booted and ready to leave by one o'clock.

'What time is the taxi coming?' He checks his watch for the hundredth time.

'Two-fifteen. Make sure we're definitely there by three.'

'Great.' He lets out a puff of air. 'What are we going to do for the next hour, then?'

'Drink?'

'Ted, you can't. You've got the whole day to get through.'

'I know, I know, I was only kidding.' I hold my hands up in surrender, although the truth is I could kill for another drink now, to steady my nerves. I haven't been this terrified since I started my first shift as a junior doctor and was thrown head-first into A&E. My stomach's a knot and my heart is fluttering. I take a deep breath.

Then the phone rings. The phone never rings. In fact, the only people who have our home number are Sam's mum and stepdad, who hate these new-fangled mobile phones and refuse to call us on them, a load of random salespeople – and my father.

It can't be. Can it?

The thought of my dad makes my stomach clench even more and I stand frozen for a minute, unsure what to do. The last thing I need is for him to make me feel bad about something. I don't know whether he does it deliberately or if it's something he does unwittingly, but even now, as a fully-fledged adult with a grown-up job and an almost-wife, he manages to make me feel about three inches tall.

I think back to the time I was picked for the main part in a school play. I was never chosen for things like this – I was pretty shy, but the teacher had decided to give me a go. I was only ten years old. Mum had left two years before, and I'd struggled, retreated into myself. My teacher – Mrs Cowling – had spotted that, and had worked hard to bring me out of myself, to help bring my confidence back again.

If only my father had done the same.

'Dad, I've got the main part,' I'd told him excitedly that evening. He'd been at home when I got back that afternoon, with a glass of whisky in front of the TV, which was unusual as, even at that age, he often left me to fend for myself until he got back about seven or eight o'clock. I hadn't thought to find it strange that he was there, though.

He'd glanced at the slip of paper I'd been given with my name on, then looked away, back at the TV. I'd felt my stomach drop with disappointment but, determined not to give up, I held it out again. He batted it away.

'Fuck's sake, Ted, I'm watching this.'

'But—'

'But what? So you've got a part in a crappy little school play. Whoopee. Well done you. Now bugger off and let me watch this.'

I'd felt my face crumple but, determined not to let him see how much he'd upset me, I'd scooped the paper off the floor and run up to my bedroom and stayed there for the rest of the evening. He hadn't always been this way, I'd told myself. When Mum was here, he was much nicer. Gruff and grumpy, but not unkind. And even though he'd got worse and worse since she left, I still held onto the vain hope that, one day, he'd be my dad again. That one day, I'd manage to do something that would make him proud.

I never did, of course. At sixteen I left home, the second I was able. He moved to Spain when I was seventeen, and I've barely seen him since. But there is still a part of me that's clinging onto the hope that he might have changed his mind about the wedding and, somehow, made it over to congratulate me. To be there for me. To be proud of me for a change.

'Ted? You gonna answer that?'

I'm dragged back by Danny's voice, and I stare at him. The phone stops ringing, and I stand, rigid, fists clenched.

'You all right?'

I nod.

'You've gone really white, mate. Sit down.' He guides me to the sofa and I do as I'm told. My breathing is shallow and I make an effort to slow it down.

'What happened there, Ted? You looked really scared.'

I shake my head as if by doing so I'll shake the memories away. 'Nothing. I just thought—' I stop. 'I thought it might be my dad.'

Danny says nothing for a minute. He knows about my childhood, and he's never judged me about it.

'Why don't you find out? It'll show the last number that called.'

'I don't know if I want to. I mean, if it was him, I don't know if I want to do anything about it. But if it wasn't – I know it's pathetic, but I'll be disappointed.'

'You're not pathetic, Ted. It doesn't matter how crap he's been, he's still your dad.'

I shake my head. 'But he doesn't give a shit about me. Your dad's been there for me more than mine has these last few years. It's him I should be wanting to impress.'

'That's not how it works though is it, Ted? And you know that, right?'

I nod sadly. Beside me, Danny leans over to peer at the phone. I don't know whether to ask him what it says.

'Well?'

He nods. 'Spanish number.'

I nod, my feelings mixed. It was him. But he's still in Spain, which means he hasn't bothered to come.

'Want me to ring him back, say you were in the bath or summat?'

Do I? Do I want to speak to my father and risk him ruining the happiest day of my life? I know he won't give me what I want.

I shake my head.

'No. Not now.' I stand, shake my limbs loose. 'I'm having another drink. Want one?'

'Go on, then,' Danny relents, after a short pause. 'Just the one.'

* * *

The registry office is packed, and afterwards we head to our reception venue, a lovely old pub near Sam's parents' house in Finchley. It has a gorgeous beer garden and fairy lights are strung along the walls, and bunting and balloons hang from every conceivable pillar and post.

Sam looks stunning, almost ethereal. Her dark hair has been pinned up and her eyes sparkle. I'm not one for noticing make-up, but whatever she's done with it today, she looks bloody amazing and my heart swells with love for her.

As we make our way into the pub garden, I can feel the weight of her arm around my waist, and I grab her fingers and give them a squeeze.

'I love you, Ted,' she says.

'I love you too, Mrs Green.'

Although most of the guests are Sam's friends and family, there are a few familiar faces, and we spend the next hour greeting them one by one.

'This is Amy, my friend from school who you met at the reunion, remember?' Sam says, approaching one group of people.

'Yes, of course I remember, thanks for coming,' I say, shaking Amy's hand. She smiles back.

'And this is Alison, who you were meant to meet but arrived too late,' she says, giving me the side-eye as she turns towards a tall, attractive redhead. 'But the less said about that night the better, eh?'

'Ah, yes. Sorry about that. Lovely to meet you at last,' I say, grinning at Alison. Since that night, Sam's renewed her friendship with her old school friends, and although they only see each other once every few months for drinks, I know they were close at school.

'You too,' Alison says. Then she holds out her camera. 'Look, I know it's your special day, but would you mind taking a photo of us? We haven't had one together for years.'

'Course.' I take the camera from her and snap a picture of the three of them together.

'Now let me take one of you three,' Sam says, grabbing the camera before I can object and taking a snap.

'You will send me a copy of that, won't you?' Sam says, and Alison nods.

I grab my drink and we spend the rest of the afternoon and evening drinking too much wine, talking to people I've never met before, and laughing and dancing.

It's one of the happiest days of my life, and I'm sad when it's all over. But as we head back to our flat, which is where we'd both agreed we'd prefer to be over a hotel tonight before we fly off to Portugal for our honeymoon, a sense of contentment settles over me. I've never felt this happy before, so sure of my place in the world or so certain that I'm loved. Because, for the first time since my mother left, I know someone really does love me. And although I've never felt deserving of it, for today, at least, I'm happy to accept it.

As I sit cuddled up next to Sam, I can't help thinking about how far I've come since that day on the bridge, and about my unpaid debt to the mysterious woman who saved my life and occupied my thoughts for so many years. I have so much to thank her for.

22

JUNE 2000

Marianne

As I roll over, my stomach rolls over too, and my head starts to spin. Ugh. Too much wine. I peel my eyes open and quickly close them again. Bugger. Nick's here again.

I've woken up with Nick in my bed a few too many times over the last few weeks since we met in a pub down the road on one of Lance's many nights out. She's found a lovely man, of course, Tim, who's keeping her busy most nights at the moment. But I haven't found anyone special. Just Nick, who I know doesn't really fancy me and I don't really fancy him, but we keep ending up together because it's easy – he lives a few streets away, and it stops the long evenings from stretching on endlessly, alone with yet another ready meal and several episodes of *Ally McBeal*. I'd only rung him last night because Lance was at a wedding and I was bored. What is wrong with me?

I sit up and shake him awake. He groans and rolls over, his

morning breath curling out of his mouth and into my nose. I grimace.

'Time to go,' I hiss.

'What?' He rubs his eyes and looks at me. 'Already?'

'Yes, come on.' I poke him several more times in the shoulder.

'Can't I just stay here a bit longer? S'comfy.'

'No. Get up.' I give him another shove and he sits up grumpily.

'All right, God's sake.'

I honestly don't know why either of us bother with this. It's not as though the sex is that great. At the time, after several glasses of wine, it feels better than nothing. But afterwards it inevitably ends like this, with me desperate to get rid of him, and him getting cross with me.

'Let's not do this any more.' I pull the duvet up round my shoulders.

'Deal.' He climbs out of bed and I avert my gaze from his pale backside as he pulls his jeans back on and heads to the loo. 'You know, it might be nice if you at least waited for me to get dressed before you told me you never wanted to sleep with me again, just for once.'

'Yeah, all right. But it won't happen again, anyway, so it doesn't matter.'

'If you say so,' he says, flashing me a grin and locking himself in the tiny bathroom.

I throw myself back onto the pillow and let out a long sigh. I'm desperate for him to be gone before Lance gets here. I can't face getting the third degree about it again, and I know she'll want to know why I keep ending up in bed with someone I don't even like that much. I don't think I can face the lecture.

I listen to Nick moving around behind the bathroom door and feel my annoyance rising. What is he doing in there? Can't he just go home and have a shower?

Finally, he emerges, fully clothed. I glare at him as he picks his jumper off the floor. 'Don't worry, I'm going.' He pulls his jumper on. 'I'll see myself out.'

Finally, he's gone. My head's pounding and I'm already regretting the extra bottle of wine we bought at last orders, which means I'll probably waste most of today recovering. I'm just about to climb into the shower myself when the buzzer goes. Assuming it's Nick having forgotten something, I press the button.

'What?'

'Annie, it's me.'

'Oh, Lance. Hi.'

'Are you going to let me in, then?'

'Sure.' I buzz her in and seconds later she's at my front door. She looks tired, her hair dishevelled and her make-up smudged under her eyes.

'How was the wedding?' I ask as she shakes her jacket off and walks inside.

'It was all right.'

'And?'

She looks at me. 'And what?'

'What happened?'

'Oh, nothing. Tim went home early straight after the ceremony, didn't stay for much of the reception, and I spent most of the time feeling pissed off. I mean, he said it was because he didn't know anyone, but so what? You don't have to know people to enjoy yourself. And he knew me.' She throws herself onto the couch and curls her feet up beneath her, the way she always has.

'Not everyone is as good as you at talking to strangers,' I say.

'No, but it's not the point. He's always doing this. I'm not sure I can be arsed with it any more.'

'Do you want some coffee?'

'Please. Can you make it strong?'

As I make the coffee, I listen to Lance telling me about the rest of the wedding. It was her old school friend, Sam, the one she met for the first time in years at the reunion.

'She looked so beautiful,' she says as I hand her a steaming mug. 'Thanks.' She takes a sip and wraps her fingers round the cup, letting the steam curl round her face. 'She was so *happy*. I just can't imagine a man making me as happy as that.'

'Is that what this is all about?' I sit down next to her cradling my own mug.

She shrugs. 'Yeah, probably. It just made me realise that I've never been in love, at least not in the way she so clearly is. Her husband, Ted, he just seems so normal, and yet she's besotted.' She looks down at her coffee. 'I dunno, I guess it made me realise Tim's not The One, so what's the point.'

'Nick's definitely not The One either, if it makes you feel any better.' I smile sheepishly as she looks at me.

'Oh, God, you didn't? Not again?'

'I'm afraid so.'

'Oh, Annie, you've got to stop ringing that man!'

'I know, I know. That's definitely it this time.'

'You said that last time, and the time before that.'

'I know. But I really mean it this time. Especially now. I mean, what *is* the point, really, of wasting time with these men who don't mean anything to us?'

'You're right.' She sighs. 'I really thought Tim was The One, though.'

'And you say that every time.'

She laughs. 'Not every time. But you're right.' She takes a sip of her coffee and looks at me thoughtfully. 'You've been right all along, you know, Annie.'

'About what?'

'About not needing a man.'

'I only said *I* didn't need one. At least, not one I don't love. *You*, on the other hand, have always needed a man, ever since we were about eight years old.' I grin. 'Remember Greg, the boy you had that marriage ceremony with in the playground when we were about ten?'

'Oh God, yes! I loved him. I was deadly serious about that marriage, I'll have you know.'

'I know you were. And that's what I love about you, Lance. You throw yourself into any relationship, full tilt, and never really worry about whether it's right, or if he's The One. Unlike me, the cynical old git who never lets a man get near her.'

'You're not cynical, just more discerning than me, that's all. I admire you for it.'

I look at her, amazed. 'You do? I always thought you wanted me to be more like you and just live a little?'

'Well, yes, that's what I say. But really I'm a little bit jealous of how confident you are, not having a man. I don't really know why I feel the need to always be with someone. Why I'm always looking for the perfect fairytale ending when I could just be enjoying myself until the right person comes along.'

'I don't think you should try to change, Lance.'

'Don't you?'

'Nope. But I do think you should dump Tim.'

'Oh, don't worry, I'm planning to.'

We sit in silence for a few minutes, lost in our own thoughts. Mine are mostly about how I'm going to shake off Nick. He might not be the man of my dreams, but I'm pretty sure he has feelings in there somewhere.

'Ooh, do you want to see some photos?'

'Of the wedding?'

'Yes.' Lance rummages around in her bag and produces her

camera with a flourish. 'I didn't take many, but I want to show you Sam's dress. God, she looked amazing.'

She flicks a few buttons and the camera whirs to life. She passes it to me. 'Click this way.'

I take the camera and peer at the tiny screen on the back. There's Lance, looking as gorgeous as ever in a teal dress and towering heels. I recognise her friend Amy from the reunion. There's a photo of Amy and Sam. 'See?' Lance says. 'Just look at her.'

Sam's beauty is obvious even on the tiny image on the back of the camera, and she does look radiant. Perhaps Lance is right, and it is all down to the love of a good man. I flick through a few more pictures of people I don't know, and then there's one of Lance with Sam and Amy. It's the next one, though, that makes me stop in my tracks.

'Is this the groom?' I say, holding out the camera for Lance to see. She peers over.

'Yes, that's Ted.'

I squint at the tiny image for a moment longer, my heart pounding. 'Why, what's wrong?' she says.

'I just—' I stop, unsure. 'He looks really familiar.'

'Does he?' She peers at him again. 'I didn't recognise him. Maybe he just has one of those faces.'

I shake my head. 'No, it's more than that.' I look back at the grainy picture on the screen. 'I can't be certain but – he looks really like the man from the bridge.'

Lance pauses for a moment as though trying to work out what I'm talking about, and then she shakes her head.

'Don't be daft, it can't be him. That would be mad.'

'I know. I'm probably wrong. Maybe I know him from somewhere else.'

'You must do.' She looks at me for a moment. 'You've gone really pale, are you okay?'

'Yeah, fine.' But the truth is, whether Ted is the mysterious Bridge Man or not, seeing him has given me a jolt.

'I'm certain it's not him,' Lance says now. 'Sam's said he's lovely, works as a doctor.' She takes the camera from my hand gently. 'It's not him,' she says.

'I know.'

'But you're thinking about him again, aren't you?'

'A bit.'

'Oh, Annie. I thought you'd got over that a long time ago.'

'I did. I mean, I am over it. I just got a shock when I saw him, that's all. But even if it was him, why would it matter? He's married Sam, and you said yourself how in love they are.' I shrug. 'I guess it's just made me realise what I'm missing out on, being alone.'

'Well let's just agree neither of us are going to waste any more time on useless men, shall we?'

'Agreed.'

'Great.' She stands. 'Do you mind if I make another coffee? My head's banging.'

'Sure, help yourself.'

As she rustles around in the kitchen, I pick up her camera and take another look through the photos. There are only a couple more of Sam's Ted, and neither are very clear – one is side-on and in the other he's half-hidden behind someone else. But the more I look, the more certain I am that Lance is right. This isn't Bridge Man. It can't be.

So why has seeing him made me feel so strange all over again? What *is* it about that man, that night, that's grown to be a part of me for all these years, wrapping itself around my memories, my mind, until it feels as though he's part of my history, my story? When the truth is, he was nothing more than a walk-on part.

23

JULY 2001

Ted

God, I love the sunshine. I could honestly lie here all day long, just letting the sun roast my skin to a crisp. I can feel the tension seeping away from my shoulders and down through the sunbed and into the sand as I lie here. It's bliss. Then, all of a sudden, there's a stabbing sensation on my stomach and I sit up with a screech to find Sam standing over me, soaking wet, dripping freezing cold sea water all over me. She's grinning hysterically.

'Why the hell would you do that?' I cry, rubbing my belly.

'Sorry, I couldn't resist,' she says, her smile sliding away when she sees my face. 'God, Ted, it was only a joke, you don't have to be such a grump about it.'

'Not very funny, though, was it,' I grumble, then relent and hold my arms out and pull her onto the sunbed beside me. Her skin is cool against mine, and I pull her down towards me and kiss her deeply.

'God, you look sexy in that bikini,' I murmur and she slaps me and pulls away.

'Perv.'

'At least I'm perving over my own wife and not someone else's.'

'Fair point.' She stands and moves to her own sunbed in the shade. 'I don't know how you can lie there baking all day. It's unbearable.'

'I love it.'

'Don't you need to get into the water and cool down every once in a while?' She rubs her hair with a towel and droplets of water spray all over me. I don't say anything this time.

'Nope. I love being boiling.'

'You're weird.'

'You knew that when you married me.'

'Again, fair point.'

I sit up and pick up the suncream. 'Will you rub some of this into my back?'

She grabs it and moves round behind me. I squint out across the beach and sigh happily. Until our honeymoon last year, I hadn't been on holiday for years. In fact, I wasn't even sure I could remember coming away for a proper holiday before, not even as a young child. The odd long weekend in Devon, perhaps, and a chilly week in a caravan before Mum left, but since, nothing. We'd spent a blissful time in Portugal, sunning ourselves, and relaxing for two whole weeks, and I'd finally realised what all the fuss was about. My shoulders had unhunched, my face had un-creased, and I felt like a new man.

Until I got back to the hospital, of course.

But it meant that, when Sam had suggested another holiday for our first anniversary, I'd jumped at the chance. In the end, I hadn't been able to make it that week thanks to work rotas, but here we finally were, a month later, and I was determined not to do a single thing for the whole week.

'There you go, all done, you over-roasted piece of meat.'

'Thanks, love.' I lift my head and she kisses my nose. I shiver. I'm so relieved the attraction is still so strong. I always worried that, after we got married, things would change. But so far, so good.

I stand. 'I might go for a stroll along the beach. Coming?'

'No, it's too hot. I'm going to stay here and read my book.' She plonks an enormous hat on and lies back.

'Fine, I'll go on my own then.' I slip my flip-flops on and head off across the scorching-hot sand.

I head down to the water's edge where the sand is firmer, and feel the cool of the water on my toes. I stroll along, dodging children playing ball, splashing in the shallows, running away from the waves. They seem so happy and, not for the first time, I wonder whether Sam's going to bring up the subject of children again.

The first time had been a few months after the wedding. Well, we'd talked about it before, but only in oblique, vague 'one day' terms. This was the first time Sam had really set her stall out about what she wanted.

'I want at least two children, you know,' she'd said as we were lying in bed one morning, drinking coffee. I'd almost spat my mouthful out, and by the time I'd recovered, Sam was staring at me as if I had two heads.

'Well, that went well,' she said drily.

'Sorry. You just took me by surprise,' I said. 'I mean, it did kind of just come out of nowhere.'

'I guess so. But I've been thinking about it for ages. Haven't you?'

I felt trapped. If I said yes, I'd have been lying just to placate her, and could have got myself tangled up in making promises I wasn't sure I wanted to keep. But if I said no, I'd sound hard and uncaring and – well, like the arse I was, when it came to these things.

The truth was, having children filled me with horror. Not because I didn't like them – although some were a bit of a challenge – but because I was terrified of being like either of my parents – one who abandoned her son, the other who neglected him. I could hear Lynne telling me I wasn't my father or my mother, but it didn't matter. The fear was there, and it was holding me back from opening up to the idea.

'I have thought about it,' I'd said, carefully. 'Just not in much detail.'

Sam hadn't answered for a while, and I'd worried I'd said something wrong. But then she'd said, 'Well, maybe you can think about it a bit now. With me. You know, actually talk about something for a change, tell me how you really feel rather than bottling it all up and locking me out the way you always do.'

'Okay.' I knew I sounded unenthusiastic. I was. But she was right, too – I had to tell her the truth.

So we had talked about it that day. In fact, it was the first time I'd truly admitted to Sam how terrified I was of being a bad dad, of ruining someone else the way my parents had ruined me.

'But you're not ruined, Ted,' she'd said. 'I wouldn't love you if you were.'

At that moment, I'd come closer than I ever had before to telling her about that night on the bridge. About how close I'd come to ending it all. But something in me still held back, terrified she'd look at me differently, that she might even stop loving me as deeply as she did. So I'd agreed to think about it. Properly.

And I have been. It's just that Sam hasn't talked about it again, which is why I'm so certain she's planning to bring it up while we're away and I haven't decided what I want to say yet.

Walking along, watching these kids playing right now, I can imagine it, I really can. Lovely holidays as a family, Christmases, birthdays, fun days together. But it's the other bits I struggle to imagine. The worry, the bad days when things go wrong, and they hurt themselves, or someone hurts them, or they need me for something and I let them down.

I watch my toes splashing through the waves and take a deep breath. I have to be prepared. I owe it to Sam.

I look up and see a group of people gathering on the shore a little way ahead. The crowd is growing, and I wonder briefly what's going on. Has someone hurt themselves? Then I hear a cry go out.

'Is anyone here a doctor?'

Adrenaline surging, I break into a jog and head towards the group, ready to help out. But by the time I'm halfway there, someone else has stepped forward, and the crowd opens up to allow her through, then closes in around her again. I stop and watch for a moment, wondering whether I should still offer to help or whether I'd just be crowding if I went up too. In the end I approach, and tap the woman who'd been shouting on the shoulder. She turns with a jump.

'Do you still need a doctor?'

'Oh no, thank you. I think we're okay now, we've got a couple of people helping out.'

'Okay, if you're sure. Do you know what happened?'

'She fell waterskiing, I think,' she says. 'Injured her leg.'

'Ouch.'

'Thank you, though,' she says as I turn to walk away.

The adrenaline is seeping away now, and I turn and trudge slowly back down the beach. It's my job to help people, and I do it well every day. But the fear that I'll let them down is still there every single time I have a new patient, and it can be exhausting. This holiday has been so relaxing, and now that feeling of worry, of letting someone down, has flooded my system again and I need a few minutes to decompress, to let it seep away.

As I stroll back through the shallows and back towards Sam, I glance behind me every now and again to make sure it's all still under control. By the time I arrive back at my sunbed, the crowd has dispersed, and the patient has been taken away on a stretcher, the drama over.

'You were gone for ages,' Sam says as I arrive back. 'Did you get lost?'

'No, there was something going on over there – someone hurt themselves.'

'Oh no, really?' Sam's nursing training kicks in too, and she squints across the beach.

'It's all over now. They've gone, didn't need me in the end.'

'Oh, right.' She glances over again before settling back down. 'Do you know what happened?'

'A waterskiing injury, apparently.'

'Oh, I saw someone fall off a while back, I didn't realise they'd hurt themselves.'

'It sounds like they're in good hands anyway.'

'Well, good.' She sits up. 'I'm boiling now. Fancy going back to our room for a bit of—' She gives a comedy wink.

'A bit of air conditioning?'

'Well, that too. But I'm feeling a bit horny. Shall we?'

'You don't need to ask twice.' I stand and hold my hand out, and the drama and all thoughts of children leave my mind.

24

JULY 2001

Marianne

I stretch out on the sunbed and sigh.

'This is the life, eh?' I say, pulling my enormous sunhat down over my face and squinting at Lance who's reading on the next sunbed. She looks over.

'It really is.'

I sit up and grab the suncream. My pale skin is terrible in the sun, which is why at home I stay out of it as much as I can. But there's not much escaping it here, even if I do huddle under the parasol as much as possible. The sun is hot and white and all-encompassing. And I love it.

I've never been abroad. Ridiculous at my age, I know, but Mum and Dad could never afford foreign holidays, and since I left school, I've never really been able to either. But when Lance suggested a girls' holiday, just the two of us, I said yes immediately.

'I don't want to go to one of those awful places you see on telly where everyone is pissed and running around with their boobs hanging out, though,' I warned.

Lance had laughed. 'We're thirty, Annie, not eighteen, I'm not sure we'd even be allowed to land in one of those places.'

'Well, good.'

We'd spent hours poring over travel brochures, but when we saw this place, near Alicante, it looked perfect. A busy beach during the day, and loads of restaurants and bars in the evening. And so far, the first three days have been everything I'd hoped for. I can feel the tension leaving my body as I lie here.

'Do you fancy doing something today?' Lance says, breaking into my thoughts. I glance over at her.

'Like what?'

She shrugs. 'I dunno. Hire one of those boats? Paragliding?'

I look at her as if she's gone insane. 'Go up in one of those things, are you mad?'

She squints up at the sky where right now someone is being pulled across the azure sky by a boat. 'Yeah, why not?'

'There's no way you're getting me up there,' I say.

'It looks fun!'

'It's a bloody death trap.'

'What could possibly go wrong?'

I sit up and count on my fingers. 'You could fall from the sky for a start. Or, worse, the whole thing could fall from the sky into the water and smother you so you drown under the weight of the fabric. Or, or – I don't know. Just no.'

'Spoilsport.'

'You go. I'll stay here and watch.'

She shakes her head. 'No, I want to find something we can do together.' She scans the horizon as if looking for inspiration, and suddenly clicks her fingers. 'Got it! Let's go waterskiing!'

'You're kidding, right?'

She shakes head. 'No, I'm serious.' This time it's her turn to count on her fingers. 'One, you're already in the water so you can't fall. Two, there's no fabric to drown underneath. And three, I've done it before and it's great fun.'

I stare at her for a moment, defeated. 'Okay. But if I fall off and die, I'm blaming you.'

'I'll take that,' she says, leaping up.

'Er, where are you going?'

'Waterskiing.'

'Now?'

'Why not?'

I scrabble around for an excuse. I'd always thought of myself as brave, but clearly I'm not. In the end I can't think of a reason not to, so I haul myself off the sunbed and wrap myself in a towel.

'All right, I'll do it. As long as you try lobster for lunch later.'

'Ugh, really?'

'Really.'

She hesitates for a moment, then gives a nod. 'You're on.'

We tuck our belongings away under our sunbeds and head towards the shore where the different concessions are lined up, vying for business. The beach is busy, and we weave round clusters of sunbeds until we reach the waterskiing stand. As Lance speaks to the man in charge, I'm still secretly hoping they'll be busy today and tell us to come back another time. But to my dismay, Lance turns with a grin on her face and says, 'We can go now!'

Swallowing my fear, I plaster a smile on my face and spend the next few minutes listening to the enthusiastic young man explaining how we should hold our bodies, how to stay upright, and all the safety regulations that are obviously important but that his strong accent is making difficult to understand. I nod in all the right places, and then I'm being strapped into my waterskis.

'I'm not sure about this, Lance.'

She shakes her head. 'You can't back out now.'

'But – what if I fall off and get chopped in half by the speed-boat?' My legs are weak beneath me with nerves now and I take a deep breath to steady myself.

'Stop being dramatic. These guys know what they're doing, you'll be fine.' She must see the fear in my face because she adds, 'Honestly, it's easy.'

'Okay,' I say, defeated.

We've decided I'm going first so I don't chicken out, and I watch as the guy climbs into the boat and starts up the engine. It throbs and roars and my heart hammers in time. Oh God, I really don't think I can do this, I want to stop... and then the boat's moving forward and I'm being pulled behind it and I'm on the water and I'm being dragged along and we're getting faster and faster and faster – and I'm doing it! I'm actually waterskiing! It's exhilarating, and as I get used to the sensation of keeping my balance and holding my legs strong at the same time, I actually start to enjoy the feeling of flying across the water. I'm staring at my feet, but slowly, I lift my gaze and take in the shoreline. The beach looks so far away, the sunbathers nothing more than tiny dots in the distance, and if I didn't know better, I'd think they didn't exist. I gasp as I hit a bump in the water, and we're going deeper, further away from the shore, and the water feels choppier here, my skis skimming the surface like bumps in the road, and I can feel my legs starting to tire. And then, all of a sudden, there's a loud bang, and I'm in the air, and then my body smacks down and all the air leaves it with the impact, and I'm being dragged along, desperately trying to catch my breath as the water hits my face over and over and over. Oh, God, I'm going to die. Then my ski catches something and my leg twists and there's a searing pain in my knee and why aren't we stopping and...

* * *

I open my eyes and the sky sways above me like a baby's mobile, a bright, searing blue smudged with pale, wispy clouds. A face hovers in my peripheral vision, and I feel as though I might vomit. I try to sit up, but a warm hand presses my shoulder and I sink back down.

'Are you okay?' The voice is deep and I don't recognise it, but nod anyway.

'We're going to move you now, so take a deep breath.' I do as I'm told and then gasp as hands lift me and the pain in my knee intensifies. Then I'm being lowered down onto the warm sand and I can hear Lance's voice in my ear. I turn my head to see her face, creased with distress, getting closer.

'Oh, Annie, I'm so sorry, this is all my fault, I should never have made you do this.' She crouches down next to me and grips my hand gently. Her skin feels hot against my sea-cooled skin.

'Don't worry. It was just an accident.'

'But it would never have happened if I hadn't bullied you into this.' She rolls her eyes. 'We should have just stayed on the beach sunbathing.'

I can feel bodies round me and a low murmur of voices, and above that someone shouts, 'Is anyone here a doctor?'

'What have I done?' I indicate my knee.

'I'm not sure. I think you fell off the skis and twisted it, but I don't know how serious it is.'

I nod and close my eyes. I'm still feeling really sick, whether from the pain or the motion of the boat I'm not sure. But I'm glad when a woman arrives and crouches down beside me and announces she's a doctor.

'They're sending an ambulance, but can I have a look at your knee while we're waiting,' she says, her accent thick but her words clear. Relieved to be in safe hands at last, I nod. Her hands on my leg are gentle but the pain is intense, and I hold my breath.

I listen to the voices around me. The crowd that must have gathered after I was brought back to shore is beginning to disperse, and I'm relieved. It's embarrassing enough being in my bikini without everyone staring at me.

'Is she going to be okay?' Lance asks.

'She'll be fine. They'll probably just put this in a splint for her.'

'Oh, God, that'll be fun on the beach,' Lance groans. 'Sorry, Annie.'

'Please stop saying sorry.'

'But—'

'Really, it's not your fault.'

Before she can reply again, another woman arrives, this time holding a medical bag and looking more official. 'The paramedics are here, I'll let them take over now,' the doctor says.

'Thank you,' I whisper.

* * *

I've only been in hospital a few times in my life, and that's been to visit someone else. Despite the unfamiliarity, being here reminds me of the last time I was in hospital with my dad after his heart attack. My own heart clenches at the thought of my parents at home, oblivious to what's going on, and I hope they don't panic when the phone rings.

'Have you rung Mum and Dad?' I ask Lance, who's sitting on a plastic chair beside my bed.

'Yes. I told them it was all my fault.'

I roll my eyes. 'Honestly, Lance, are you going to spend the rest of the holiday saying that?'

'Probably.'

'Okay, I have an idea. You can make it up to me by eating that lobster tonight. And then you have to never apologise again.'

'Tonight? You might still be in here.'

'Tomorrow, then. But anyway, I won't still be here. They're going to put me in a splint and then I can go.' I giggle. 'Anyway, at least I won't need to drink because I'm off my face on all these painkillers.'

She grins. 'All right, you're on.'

Worn out from all the drama of the day, I close my eyes and drift off, happy to let the medical staff get me ready to go home. I had a lucky escape.

25

13 DECEMBER 2002

Ted

The window of the bus is so fogged up it's hard to see outside. I wipe a small circle clear with my sleeve and peer out. It's so late now there are very few people around, just the odd shopper in the late-night newsagent, a group of hooded teens passing round a cigarette by the railway bridge, a woman walking her dog, head down. A drizzle hangs in the air and it's so cold I wouldn't be surprised if it snows soon.

It's eleven years today since that night on the bridge and, although the feelings I had back then are long buried, locked away where I'll (hopefully) never find them again, it still feels important to acknowledge it, to mark it and remember how far I've come, as I have done every year since. Back then, I had nothing; no family, no one to love; I was sleeping on a friend's sofa, I had no job and no prospects. There really hadn't seemed like any other way out.

Then Fairy Girl had changed all that. She'd changed the course of my life and given me a second chance. And now here I am, eleven years later, a successful doctor in a busy hospital, a lovely wife, and lots of good friends. I have a good life, and I have a bright future, and I want to make sure I never forget that it's thanks to the girl in the fairy wings.

The bus shudders to a halt and I realise it's my stop. I grab my rucksack and stride to the front of the bus and jump down onto the pavement. I'm the only one getting off here and the street is eerily quiet as I walk towards our flat, the echo of my footsteps ringing off the houses. I hate being home this late, but there was an emergency tonight, a woman in labour who was haemorrhaging, and I couldn't leave until I knew she was safe.

I reach our flat and am surprised to see a low glow through the glass above the door. Sam must have left a light on for me when she went to bed. But when I step inside, I can hear the murmur of the TV, and I find Sam curled up on the sofa, her dressing gown wrapped tightly around her. She stirs when I walk in, and sits up, her eyes heavy with sleep.

'Hey, what are you still doing up?' I whisper, sitting next to her on the sofa.

'Sorry, I was trying to stay awake.' She rubs her eyes and yawns.

'You don't have to wait up for me.'

She looks at me, quizzically. 'What time is it?'

'About 2 a.m.'

'Oh. You're really late.' Sam knows the score, she knows what it's like when an urgent case comes in, and she never gives me a hard time about it, or asks me what happened. But tonight, I feel I owe her some sort of explanation.

'Yeah, sorry. A woman giving birth.'

She winces, and nods. Her face is pale in the dim lamplight, her dark hair scraped back off her face. She's still so beautiful and my heart lurches with love for her. But she looks troubled.

'What's happened?' I say, moving closer to her.

She looks down at her toes, then twists round and picks something off the side table and hands it to me. I hold out my hand, confused, and she places the piece of hard plastic in my palm and wraps my fingers round it. I uncurl them, but it takes me a few seconds to register what I'm looking at. When I do, my stomach flips over and I'm flooded with conflicting emotions. I look up at her, and she's watching me in anticipation, her eyes huge.

'Well?' she whispers.

'Wow.' I don't know what to say. I look back down at the innocuous piece of plastic in my hand – a perfectly ordinary-looking thing that's going to change my life forever – and I smile.

'Are you pleased?' Her voice is uncertain, and I feel guilty for making her feel so unsure of herself.

'Of course I'm pleased.' Tears fill my eyes and I reach out and wrap my arms round her. I feel her body relax against mine.

We sit like that for a moment before Sam pulls away and searches out my eyes in the semi-darkness. 'We're having a baby, Ted.' Her eyes shine with happiness.

'We are.' I hold her hands and I can feel her shaking.

'I wanted to tell you tonight. It felt too important to wait until tomorrow.'

'I'm glad you did.'

She nods.

'Shall we have a drink?'

'Aren't you exhausted?'

She shakes her head. 'Not any more. I'm too excited. I want to talk about it, talk about our baby.'

I stifle a yawn. I'm completely wiped out after a long shift, and all I really want to do is crawl into bed and go to sleep. But that feels mean, given the news Sam's just told me. After making it clear how uncertain I was about even having a baby, I owe her at least this small gesture, this small show of solidarity.

'Okay, you sit here. I'll get them. What do you want?'

'Well, wine, really, but I can't now.' She smiles and places her hand against her flat belly. 'Tea?'

I nod and head to the kitchen. As the kettle boils, I stare out of the window into the blackness of the garden beyond, and try to take in the news. Half an hour before, I'd been sitting on the bus, a husband, thinking about a day eleven years before when I thought I'd reached the end. And now here I am, a father-to-be, a whole new future ahead of me, ahead of us, and I'm not sure how to process it.

The click of the kettle pulls me from my thoughts and I fill the mugs and take a deep breath. I can do this. I can be the parent mine never were. I can give my child a good, happy life.

I'm going to be the best father I can be, whatever it takes.

26

13 DECEMBER 2002

Marianne

I've never pictured myself being a mum. I mean, I know when you're young it's not exactly the dream to have a baby, but most women seem to reach that point as they enter their twenties and beyond. But even as I've got older, and friends my age are starting to settle down, get married and pop out sprogs, I've never even once had an urge to do the same. Luckily for me, neither has Lance, otherwise I really would feel like a thirty-one-year-old freak of nature.

Which is why, right at this very moment in time, I think I might be having a panic attack. Because my period is late. Very late.

'It could be anything,' Lance soothes, trying to make me feel better. She fills my wine glass almost to the top and I down it in one. See, terrible mum. I can't even stop drinking now I think I might be pregnant.

'Like what?' I say, my words already beginning to slur.

'I dunno. Change of diet. Weight loss. Stress. There are loads of things that make periods late.'

'Has yours ever been late?'

She looks sheepish. 'Well, once. And that was only after a week-long sick bug. But that's not the point. My point is it doesn't necessarily mean you're pregnant.' She stops suddenly, almost slams her wine glass on the table.

'Wait, who do you think the father is?'

'I thought you said you didn't think I was pregnant?'

'I don't,' she says, wafting her hand around dismissively. 'But *you* think you are, therefore you must know who the father is – sorry, would be. You know, if you were. It's not *Nick*, is it?'

I feel my face getting hot. Since I promised Lance I wouldn't waste any more time on Nick almost two years ago, I've stuck to my word. Well, at least I did until a few weeks ago when I bumped into him in the supermarket round the corner and we ended up back at my flat in bed together. I hadn't dared tell her about it, but now it looks as though I've got no choice but to admit it.

'Maybe. Well, yes. If I were pregnant, it could only be him.'

'Oh, for goodness' sake, Marianne, what were you thinking?'

I shrug. 'I didn't plan it. And it was only once.'

She shakes her head. 'Oh, God, do you realise that if you are pregnant – even though you're almost definitely not – then you'll be tied to that loser for the rest of your life?'

'I know,' I say, balefully.

'How did it happen?'

'Do you really need me to explain the birds and the bees to you?'

'Ha bloody ha,' she says, topping my wine glass up again almost to the brim. 'You and Nick. How, what, when and, most importantly, why?'

'I bumped into him, we got chatting and – well, I was lonely. He was there. And that was it.'

Lance shakes her head and sips her wine. 'I can't believe you didn't tell me.'

'Can you blame me? Look how you're reacting now.'

'Fair enough. But still. You promised you wouldn't go near him again. You deserve to find someone you love and who loves you back.' Her voice has softened and I know she's forgiven me really.

'I know. Oh, God, what if I *am* pregnant?' I put my head in my hands. 'I'll never escape Nick ever again. Unless...'

'Unless what?' Lance looks suspicious.

'Unless I don't tell him.'

'You can't do that!'

'Why not? It's not as though I want anything from him. I can totally do this on my own.'

'No.' Lance is emphatic. 'You can't do that to someone. It's wrong.' She looks at me. 'Anyway, you're not pregnant.'

'I bloody hope not, or the baby already has a taste for cheap Sauvignon Blanc.' I grin and take another sip. I know I shouldn't, but if I am about to spend nine months growing another human being, then this will be the last night I can get drunk in a long time, so until I know for sure, I'm going to make the most of it.

* * *

Lance picks up on the second ring.

'I got my period.'

'Thank fuck for that.'

'Hey, I thought you said last night you couldn't wait to be Aunty Alison?'

'Fuck that, I was pissed, it would be a nightmare. I'm not ready for that sort of responsibility.'

I laugh. I know Lance would like kids one day and doesn't really mean it, but I love her for trying to cheer me up. 'So, what now? Are you going to stick to your promise never to see Nick again this time?'

'Definitely. God, can you imagine having him as my baby's father?'

'Nightmare.' I hear her suck a cigarette and the craving for one hits me hard. We wind up the conversation, and when I hang up, I go immediately in search of my purse. Even though I quit more than eighteen months ago, I'm desperate for a smoke now. Maybe it's just as well I'm not pregnant if I can't even stick to that.

But as I make my way to the newsagent to buy fags, my head pounding, my mouth hangover-dry, I can't ignore the ache in my belly that tells me that, actually, I'm a bit disappointed. Because although in an ideal world I didn't want Nick to be the father of my baby – in an ideal world, I'd have found the man of my dreams and be having a beautiful baby with him – this isn't an ideal world, and sometimes you have to take what you're given.

I've realised, for the first time ever, maybe it wouldn't have been such a disaster if I had been pregnant after all. In fact, maybe it would actually have been quite nice.

Perhaps, I realise, as I pay for my fags and slouch my way back to my flat to nurse my hangover, I am ready for something more at last.

27

NOVEMBER 2003

Ted

Churches make me uncomfortable, always have. The buildings themselves I love – cool, calm, peaceful places where I often used to go and sit for hours back in the days when I had nowhere else to go. It's the people and the culture that is contained within the churches that gets me twitching and squirming. Perhaps because it reminds me of Sundays as a child when I was forced to sit through a service every single week, come rain or shine. The tired, droning voice of the vicar, buzzing through the air like a drunken bumblebee, while I felt myself nodding off, my eyes heavy.

These days, I just feel guilty near churches. I don't believe in God and haven't for a long time. After all, my mother did, and it didn't exactly make her a great person.

The trouble is, I seem to have somehow agreed to having our son christened, despite my doubts, and today is the day it's happening.

'Are you ready?' Sam says, fussing around me like a stressed-out butterfly, flapping from one thing to another while baby Jacob sleeps on, oblivious, in his cot.

'Almost.' I slip my cufflinks on and study my reflection. My hair is shorter than I've had it for years, almost shaved to the scalp, and I know Sam isn't a fan. 'You look like a prisoner,' she complained when I came home from the barber. But I like it. There are flecks of grey in it now, and my stubble mirrors that, but my face is still relatively unlined. There is no ignoring the dark circles under my eyes, though, the identity stamp of all doctors working in hospitals these days. Sleep is not something I get in abundance, especially since Jacob arrived on the scene.

He's four and a half months old today, and he's the love of my life. That's not to say there aren't times when I just wish I could have a night away from him, get some sleep, have some time to myself. But from the moment he was born a month early, he's captured my heart entirely. And, best of all, I'm finally starting to believe that I'm never going to be like my parents. Just the thought of abandoning him, the way my mother abandoned me, makes me feel as though my heart has been ripped out of my chest. And I could never treat someone I love this much the way my father treated me either.

Speaking of my father, I finally told him about Jacob. I thought it was only fair to let him know he was going to be a grandfather. I don't know why I bothered, in all honesty. All he said was, 'Oh, your kid will be the same age as my new one when it's born.' That's how I found out he was going to be a father again at the grand old age of fifty-nine. I can't think about my half-brother, Caleb, too much, or it brings me out in a panic. I can only hope my father's softened enough to give the poor kid a better childhood than I had.

'Taxi's here!' I bundle Jacob up, his blanket wrapped round him tightly, and place him gently in his car seat. He stirs, his pink lips parting as though about to object to being disturbed and I hold my breath, ready for the onslaught. But then he thinks better of it, turns his head to the side, and falls back to sleep. I study him for a moment, my gaze following the gentle curve of his head, the widow's peak of his dark hair – darker even than Sam's, whose hair needs a little extra help to stay that shade these days – and the soft pink of his round cheeks, and I know with absolute certainty that I could never love anyone more.

'Quick, he's waiting.' Sam's hovering impatiently at the door, so I scoop the car seat up and strap Jacob into the taxi while Sam locks up, and then we're off, speeding towards the church. I feel my body tense the closer we get. Am I a hypocrite, letting my son be christened? Even Sam doesn't really believe, but she just wanted to do 'the right thing' as she called it. But it doesn't really matter now, because we're on our way, and all our guests will be waiting to wet the baby's head.

The ceremony washes over me, the words about blessing and being welcomed by God meaningless to me. I stand stiffly next to Sam, who's cradling our son in her arms.

It's not until we leave the church and head to a nearby hotel for a few drinks that I finally feel myself start to relax.

'Here, take Jacob for me a minute, will you?' Sam says, slipping our sleeping son into my arms the minute we arrive. I enjoy the feeling of his tiny body against my chest, amazed and impressed that he's managed to sleep through most of the day so far, oblivious to the fact that everyone is here for him. I spot Danny and Danni across the other side of the room, and am about to head over when there's a voice at my shoulder.

'Ted?'

I turn and find Sam's red-headed friend – Alison? – in front of me.

'Oh, hi. Sam's just popped to get a drink, I think, she won't be long.'

'Oh, that's all right, it's this little man I've really come to see.' She smiles and leans in to study Jacob's sleeping face. 'Oh, I so wanted a cuddle but I can't disturb him when he's so peaceful.'

'He's been asleep for ages, I don't think it'll be long before he's making himself known. You're welcome to hold him then.' I shift slightly, my arm starting to ache beneath his weight, even though he's still so tiny.

Alison stands there for a minute, neither of us sure what to say next. Suddenly she seems to remember her manners.

'Oh, sorry, this is my friend Annie – Marianne,' she says, tugging the sleeve of the woman next to her. And when the woman turns round, my heart almost stops.

It can't be.

Can it?

It's Fairy Girl.

I can see from the look on her face that I'm right, that she's recognised me too, and I can feel my heart thumping in my chest, throbbing in my temples. My arms feel weak and my legs like dry, brittle matchsticks beneath me, barely able to hold my weight.

'Oh!' Fairy Girl – *Marianne* – lets out an involuntary exclamation and Alison's brow creases in confusion.

'Do you—' She looks from me to Marianne and back again – 'do you two *know* each other?'

'No.' I say it quickly and Marianne shakes her head at the same time. But her flushed face must surely give her away. I'm trembling, and in my arms, Jacob starts to stir.

'I think I just have one of those faces,' I say, my voice wobbling. 'Here, Jacob's awake, did you want that cuddle now?'

Alison looks at her friend and back at me again, a frown creasing her forehead, then steps forward, arms extended ready to take my son, and for the next few minutes, all attention is focused on him. I take a moment to breathe deeply and calm down and refuse to look at Marianne. She's clearly doing the same, and is busy cooing over Jacob. I feel dizzy.

'Oh, he's awake.' Sam appears at my side and touches my elbow lightly. 'Fobbed him off, I see.'

'Oh, sorry Sam, I was desperate for a cuddle,' Alison says. 'Do you want him back?'

'No, he seems perfectly happy,' she says. 'Knock yourself out.' She turns to me.

'Everything okay? You look like you're about to throw up.'

'Do I?'

She nods, places her hand on my cheek. 'You've gone really white. Maybe you should sit down.'

I pull a chair towards me and sit, grateful for Sam's nursing training kicking in. 'I'm all right, just a bit hot, I think.' I put my elbows on my thighs and hang my head down. Sam sits beside me and rubs my back gently.

'Must be all the excitement,' she says. The pressure of her hand through my shirt feels comforting and I slowly start to feel calmer. I still don't dare to look up, though, acutely aware of Marianne standing so close to me.

Apart from the shock of seeing her again after all this time, there's something else there, a deeper hidden worry, that she might reveal how we know each other. Despite having been with Sam for seven years, I still haven't told her about that night. She knows I was suffering from depression when I came back from Kuwait, and that I underwent months of counselling. But I didn't tell her about my suicide attempt straight away, and the more time passed, the harder it became. Until I just didn't.

'You're trembling, Ted, are you sure you're all right?'

I turn to look at Sam; her face has a few more lines on it now, and months of being a new mum have given her a more drawn look. But she's still beautiful. So why, as she frowns at me with concern, am I trying not to think about another woman?

'Yeah, I'll be fine. Maybe I should have something to eat?'

'Wait here.' Sam stands and I hear her speak to Alison, ask if she can leave Jacob with her for a moment, and then she's gone. Slowly, I lift my head to see whether Marianne is still there.

And there she is.

She's watching me, and as I catch her eye, she smiles. I flash a quick smile back and shake my head quickly. I need to speak to her, but not here, not in front of everyone. I need to work something out, some way of getting away for a few minutes.

Sam comes back with a glass of Coke.

'Full fat, thought the sugar might help,' she says, and I take the cold glass and gulp it down gratefully.

'Thanks for looking after him,' she says, gently prising Jacob from Alison's arms.

'Ah, it's fine, it was lovely to hold him. He's such a cutie.'

'He really is.'

'I can't believe how much he looks like Ted.'

Sam and Alison are quickly caught up in conversation and before I notice what's happening, Marianne is walking past me. I look up and she flicks her eyes to the right. Is she asking me to follow her? Unsure, I watch her cross the room and when she gets a few feet away, she turns and gestures again. I glance at Sam, who is still deep in conversation with Alison and isn't looking at me, then I stand and follow Marianne across the room. My heart hammers as I follow her out through the main door and down the front steps, but when I get to the street, I stop. She's nowhere to be seen. Have I misunderstood completely? I look around for a moment, up and down the street, but then I hear a hissed whisper from beneath my feet.

I peer down and she's there, under the front steps. I descend and, seconds later, I'm face to face with the woman who has haunted me for the last twelve years of my life.

'It's you.' Her gaze is steady and I can't look away.

'It is.'

'Wow.'

We stand for a moment, frozen. I know I need to say something soon.

'What are you doing here?'

'I've come with Lance.'

'Lance?'

'Alison. She's my best friend.'

'Oh, right.' All this time and Sam's friend Alison has known Fairy Girl – and yet we've never met. I don't know what to say.

'So Sam's your wife?'

I nod.

Her face changes as she realises something. 'Oh, so you're the mysterious boyfriend who didn't turn up at the reunion that time?'

I scrabble around for a memory of that night. Of course, the night when Sam had met Alison again for the first time in years.

'You were there?'

She shrugs. 'I was. I left early because I threw up.'

'Oh.'

'I don't really know what to say. I didn't think you'd recognise me.'

'I didn't think you'd recognise me either.'

'I thought about you a lot after that night, you know.' She fiddles with a blonde curl, and I can barely tear my eyes away.

'Did you?' I clear my throat. 'I thought about you too.'

'You did?'

I nod. How can I explain the obsession which overcame me, the way this woman pervaded my every thought for so many years after just one meeting? 'I tried to find you, you know,' I say instead.

'Find me?'

'I put an advert in the *Standard*. You know, the "I Saw You" section, people looking for someone they've spotted on the Tube, that sort of thing. I thought you might see it.' I shrug. 'And apart from walking up and down the bridge hoping I might bump into you again, I didn't know what else to do. I didn't know anything about you. Not even your name.'

She studies me, and for a minute I think she's not going to reply. Then she says, 'I called you Bridge Man, you know.'

Bridge Man.

'I've called you Fairy Girl.'

She nods. 'Well. Now here we are.'

I switch my weight from one foot to the other and back again. 'I need—' I point upstairs. 'I can't really stay long. It's my son's christening.'

'Of course. Sorry. You go.' She fumbles in her bag and pulls out a packet of cigarettes. 'Sorry, bad habit. I'll just have this and be in.'

I hesitate for a moment. Over the years, there have been so many things I've wanted to say to this woman, but right now, none of them will come to me. It seems like a miracle that she's standing here, flesh and blood in front of me. But everything I'd thought I might say has left my mind, leaving it utterly blank.

Then something occurs to me.

'Please don't tell Sam how we met. She doesn't know.'

'About the bridge, you mean?'

I nod. 'I never told her how bad things were. It was before we met and it just – it didn't seem relevant.'

She nods, blows smoke into the air and I watch it curl up to pavement level and snake away. 'I won't say a thing.'

'Thank you.' I hover, torn between needing to get back to my wife and child, and wanting to stay with this woman who's eluded me for so many years. How can I just walk away now? What if I never see her again? I walk up a couple of steps, then Marianne says, 'Wait.'

I turn. She's rummaging in her bag again and this time she pulls out a tiny pink shell phone.

'Can I give you my number?'

I hesitate for just a second. Part of me, the pre-fatherhood Ted, wants to take her number more than anything else in the world. The other part of me knows I shouldn't. Knows it would be best to just walk away now and never see her again.

Before I can make the decision, she hands me a scrap of paper with her number on it. 'Just in case.'

In case of what I don't ask, and instead almost run up the stairs and back into the hall. My eyes search out Sam and I scurry over to where she's still talking to Alison, almost as though no time has passed at all. Jacob is in his car seat by her feet, kicking his legs happily.

'Hey.' I place my hand on her waist and kiss her cheek and she turns to greet me.

'Where did you get to?'

'Sorry, I just popped out for some fresh air. I felt a bit faint.'

She studies me. 'You've got a bit of colour back in your cheeks now.' She turns back to her friend. 'I was just telling Alison about your counselling sessions. She says her friend Marianne is a counsellor.'

'Oh...' I don't know what to say. Alison is studying me knowingly, and I'm fairly sure she knows something is going on. 'Yes, it was years ago. All fine now.'

'It was after the war, was it?' Alison says.

'Um. Yes. Something like that.'

Sam shakes her head. 'He never talks about it, do you, Ted?'

'Well, no, it's not really something I want to remember.' My voice is sharper than I intend, and Sam looks hurt. But before I can apologise, she bends down to pick up Jacob.

'Now I need to go and change this little man. Will you get me another glass of wine?'

'Sure.'

I head to the bar, relieved to have something to do and to have a moment to myself. So what if I'm scanning the room for Marianne?

* * *

It's not until many hours later when we're back at home, Jacob is tucked up in bed and Sam is dozing on the sofa next to me that I finally get a chance to properly process what happened today.

I met her.

After all these years and all the wondering, she's been there all along, just out of sight. I can hardly believe it.

And I'm racked with guilt.

How can I keep something like this from Sam? Before, it felt okay that Sam knew nothing about how bad things had become for me before we met. It was in the past, almost forgotten, so I could justify it. I had a new life now, one worth living, one that made me happy. But now it feels as though everything is bubbling to the surface again, and all the things I've tried to forget are threatening to spill over and spoil everything.

And I can't stop thinking about Marianne.

She still looks exactly the same. Before, if you'd have asked me to describe her, I'd have struggled, the details of her face long faded from my mind's eye. The picture I drew of her from memory, that had hung on my wall for so many years, has been buried at the back of the cupboard under the stairs since we moved in, dusty, forgotten.

The slip of paper she gave me containing her mobile phone number is still in my jacket pocket and it feels as though it's burning a hole in the fabric. What would happen if I picked up the phone and called her, right now? What would I say? What would I be asking for?

What about Sam?

I glance down at her beside me, curled into an S-shape at the other end of the sofa, her eyes closed, and I'm filled with another rush of guilt. How can I even be thinking about someone else when the woman I love, the mother of my child, is right here?

And yet Marianne keeps appearing, uninvited. The image of her blowing smoke from the corner of her mouth. The smile she gave me, the look as I walked away. It all keeps crowding my head until I can't think straight.

God, I need a drink.

I think about leaving the flat and walking along to the late-night off-licence a few streets away and buying myself a bottle of whisky, drinking the lot. How would it make me feel as the amber liquid slipped down my throat, into my blood stream? Happy? Angry?

Numb?

I hesitate for a few more minutes, caught between wanting to go and wanting to stay and do the right thing.

I stand and go and look for my phone. I've had my mobile a few months and it's still new to me. It's charging in the kitchen and I pick it up, and take Marianne's number from my pocket. I lay it on the counter next to my phone and stare at it for a moment. Eleven digits, which, if I use, could potentially destroy the life I've built, the life I have here.

And yet still I'm considering it.

Why? What is it about this woman that's so utterly compelling? What would I want from her? Answers? For what? Do I want to know if she thought about me as much as I thought about her? If I occupied her mind the same way she did for so many months, years? Why? To satisfy my ego? Or for something else, something I can't even quite explain?

I take a deep breath, and let it slowly out.

I can't do it.

I pick up the piece of paper and take it over to the gas hob, then before I can change my mind, I light the front ring and hold the paper over it, watching as it catches and then, in seconds, is gone, burnt to tiny black pieces of dust.

28

NOVEMBER 2003

Marianne

'Please come with me, I can't face it on my own.'

Lance's voice is pleading with me down the phone and I roll my eyes. She knows I always give in.

'Why isn't Jake going?'

She lets out a sound, half-gasp, half-tut. 'He's got to work, he says. I reckon he just can't be arsed.'

'Can't you go on your own?'

'Oh, but christenings are boring enough without standing on my own like a sad sack. But I promised I'd go.'

I sigh. 'Okay. I'll come. But I'm only coming to the reception or whatever it's called, and you're buying the drinks.'

'Deal.'

As I hang up, I shake my head. Why do I always agree to do these things with Lance? Look what happened last time she made me come to something with her friend Sam – I spent the whole night throwing up and had to take the next day off work to recover.

But still, the following day, I find myself slipping on one of my favourite sixties-style dresses, clipping my hair into a chignon, and heading into town to meet Lance. She's waiting outside when I arrive, in a body-con dress which looks amazing on her, her red curls tumbling down her back.

'Check you out,' I say, kissing her in greeting.

'Not too shabby yourself,' she replies, linking her arm through mine.

'So, how was the ceremony?'

'Pious, as you'd expect,' she grins, dragging me up the steps of the hotel. 'You didn't miss much. But thanks for coming now. I could do with a drink after all that.'

Inside it's busy, and I follow Lance to the bar where she orders a bottle of Chardonnay.

'Oh, there's Ted, do you mind if I go and say hello? I know I like to pretend to be a hard-faced cow, but I do still really want a cuddle with the little one.'

'Go on, I'll be there in a sec. I'm just popping to the loo.'

Minutes later, I'm scanning the room looking for Lance. She's easy to spot with her masses of red curls, and I head over. She's facing me, and the man she's talking to – presumably Ted, the baby's father – has his back to me.

As I approach, she grabs my sleeve and pulls me towards her.

'Oh, sorry, this is my friend Annie – Marianne,' she says. I turn round and in that moment all the breath leaves my body.

It's him.

But it can't be.

Can it?

'Oh!' I say, and Alison looks at me in confusion.

'Do you—' She looks from Ted to me and back again – 'do you two *know* each other?'

'No.' Ted says it quickly and I shake my head, not daring to speak, but I can feel my face flushing.

'I think I just have one of those faces,' Ted says, and I can hear a tremble in his voice. 'Here, Jacob's awake, did you want that cuddle now?'

Alison looks at me and back at Ted again. She looks suspicious and I think she's going to say something else, but then she steps forward, arms extended to reach for Jacob. Thankfully, all attention is focused on the baby for the next few minutes, and I breathe a silent sigh of relief, leaning in to join in. Anything to avoid looking at Bridge Man.

'Oh, he's awake.' Sam appears suddenly and my stomach flips over. Will she be able to tell something's going on? But she's smiling happily as she says, 'Fobbed him off, I see.'

'Oh, sorry Sam, I was desperate for a cuddle,' Alison says. 'Do you want him back?'

'No, he seems perfectly happy. Knock yourself out.' She turns to her husband.

'Everything okay? You look like you're about to throw up.' She's right, he does. He looks grey.

'Do I?'

She nods, places her hand on his cheek. 'You've gone really white. Maybe you should sit down.'

As he pulls a chair towards him and sits, I turn back to Lance to find her watching me intently.

'What's going on?' she hisses.

'What do you mean?'

'You know.' She tilts her head towards where Ted and Sam are sitting, but before I have the chance to say anything else, Amy joins us, and I'm saved. For now, at least. I know full well Lance is going to give me the third degree later. But I need time to process what's just happened.

Just as I suspected when I saw the wedding photo, Sam's husband Ted *is* Bridge Man.

The man I spent years thinking about. The man who, I can admit now, is almost certainly responsible for me not meeting anyone else since because nobody seems to measure up to my memory of him. Now here he is, in front of me. And I can barely speak.

While Lance is distracted, I turn to watch him. He's on his own now, and he looks up at me. I smile. He gives a tiny smile back and shakes his head. Then Sam is back and handing him a glass of Coke before walking towards us.

'Thanks for looking after him,' she says, gently prising Jacob from Alison's arms.

'Ah, it's fine, it was lovely to hold him. He's such a cutie.'

'He really is.'

'I can't believe how much he looks like Ted.'

Sam and Alison are quickly caught up in conversation, so I take my chance. I walk past Ted and gesture for him to follow me. I hope he knows what I'm saying, but when I turn round a few steps further on he's watching me, a puzzled look on his face. My heart hammers in my throat and I gesture again, then turn and walk out of the door. I have no idea whether he's going to follow me or whether I'm making a huge mistake, but I don't dare look behind to check in case I see Lance watching me. I walk out of the building, down the front steps and then notice the steps continue down beneath ground level to a basement level, which is well hidden. I go down and, to my relief, a few seconds later, Ted's standing on the steps above me, looking around.

'Down here,' I hiss, and he peers over the railing and sees me.

Seconds later, there he is. Standing in front of me.

'It's you.' He watches me steadily.

'It is.'

'Wow.'

We stand there for a moment, frozen. I know I need to say something soon, but I can't think what.

'What are you doing here?' he asks.

'I've come with Lance.'

'Lance?'

'Alison. She's my best friend.'

'Oh, right.'

'So Sam's your wife?' I say. It seems the most unlikely thing in the world that he's been married to Alison's friend all this time and yet we've never met. But he nods. Then something dawns on me. 'Oh, so you're the mysterious boyfriend who didn't turn up at the reunion that time?'

'You were there?'

'I was. I left early because I threw up.'

'Oh.'

'I don't really know what to say. I didn't think you'd recognise me.' I don't tell him I spent too much time praying he would.

'I didn't think you'd recognise me either.'

'I thought about you a lot after that night, you know.' My hands are shaking as I make the admission, and I clench my fingers tightly.

'Did you? I thought about you.'

'You did?'

He nods. 'I tried to find you, you know,' he says.

He did!

'Find me?'

'I put an advert in the *Standard*. You know, the "I Saw You" section, people looking for someone they've spotted on the Tube, that sort of thing. I thought you might see it.' He shrugs. 'And apart from walking up and down the bridge hoping I might bump into you again, I didn't know what else to do. I didn't know anything about you. Not even your name.'

He tried to find me. I can't stop and think now about the implications of that; of what might have happened, how different my life might have been if he'd have succeeded.

'I called you Bridge Man, you know.'

'I've called you Fairy Girl.'

Fairy Girl.

'Well. Now here we are.'

He nods.

'I need—' He points upstairs. 'I can't really stay long. It's my son's christening.'

Stupid me, of course he can't stand here and talk to me all day. Of course he needs to go. 'Of course. Sorry. You go.' I need something to do with my hands, so I fumble in my bag and pull out a packet of cigarettes. 'Sorry, bad habit. I'll just have this and be in.'

He hesitates a moment. There are so many things I want to say to this man I've spent endless hours dreaming about. But I don't know where to start.

And then he speaks.

'Please don't tell Sam how we met. She doesn't know.'

'About the bridge, you mean?'

He nods. 'I never told her how bad things were. It was before we met and it just – it didn't seem relevant.' I think back to that night, how resigned he was to his fate, and wonder at the strength of his and Sam's relationship if she doesn't even know about that.

I blow smoke into the air and watch it curl up to pavement level and snake away. 'I won't say a thing.'

'Thank you.' He hovers as though he wants to say something else, and I wonder if he's as flustered about this moment as I am. It seems preposterous, standing here now, that we can't snatch this opportunity to see each other again, that we just have to walk away. What if I never see him again?

Then he does walk away.

'Wait.' The word's out of my mouth before I can think about it, and I rummage in my bag for my new mobile phone. It's pink and shiny and I feel momentarily embarrassed about the girliness of it.

'Can I give you my number?'

He hesitates for just a second, and part of me hopes more than anything else in the world that he says yes. The other part of me knows it would be better if he didn't; if we both just walked away from this one moment and never saw each other again. I scribble my number on a piece of paper and hold it out to him hopefully, watching it flap in a breeze. 'Just in case.'

He takes it, then turns and almost runs up the stairs and away from me.

And I know I'll probably never hear from him again.

* * *

I can't just leave, so I wait a few minutes to let my heart rate return to normal, then hurry back inside to find Lance. A quick scan of the room reveals no sign of Ted, so I stride over to Lance. She's talking to a couple, and as I grab her elbow she spins round, her eyes wide.

'Where have you been?'

'For a fag.' I glance around. 'Can we go?'

'In a minute.' She turns back to the couple she'd been chatting to. 'These are Ted's friends, Danny and Danni. This is my best friend, Marianne.'

'All right?' Danny – the man – shakes my hand firmly and gives me a warm smile, then the other Danni does the same. 'And don't worry, everyone laughs at our names,' she says.

I like them both instantly. Which is why I'm mortified I'm about to be rude to them. 'I'm so sorry, it's lovely to meet you, but I'm afraid I have to dash off now.'

'No worries. Maybe we'll see you another time,' Danny says easily.

'That would be lovely.'

I scoop up my coat and grab Lance's arm and practically pull her out of the venue, through the door, down the steps and along the street.

'What the hell was all that about?' she says, wrenching her arm away and stopping.

I hurry on, leaving her no choice but to follow me. I spot the orange light of a black cab and flag it down. We both climb in the back, and I give my address.

As we pull out, I turn to her. Her face is fuming.

'That was Bridge Man.'

'Who was?'

'Ted.'

She stares at me for a moment as the words sink in, then her jaw drops open. 'Ted? Sam's Ted?'

I nod mutely.

'Fuck.' She rubs her face. 'I remember now – when I showed you those photos from the wedding, you said you thought you recognised him. But I never thought—' She stops. 'Shit, Marianne, you must have had a heart attack.'

'I did.'

She turns her whole body round to face me. 'Did he recognise you?'

'Yup.'

'And?'

'I gave him my number.'

'You did *what*?'

'I know, I know. I shouldn't have. But I was... I don't know. It's so long since I thought about him, but the minute I saw his face, I knew it was him and I knew I couldn't just let him disappear again.' I don't know where to look, so I stare through the glass partition at the back of the cabbie's head.

'But he's married to Sam. They've just had a baby. This was his baby's *christening*.' Her voice is getting louder and louder.

'I know, all right, I know that. I didn't – I haven't got any plans to seduce him. I was just shocked to see him again and he recognised me and he seemed pretty pleased to see me too.' I look at her again. 'I don't think he'll ring me, though.'

'I bloody hope he doesn't. For your sake as much as for his and Sam's.'

'What do you mean?'

'Don't you remember how you were back then? You were obsessed with him, with finding him. You had some weird idea that you needed to see him again. And look at you now. Still trying to find the perfect man but you push everyone away because nobody ever matches up to the images you have in your head of bloody Bridge Man.'

'I don't do that.'

'You do, Marianne. Whether you think you do or not, there's always something not quite right with every poor sod you meet. It's so obvious that it's because you've put Ted on a pedestal, and one that no one else has got a hope in hell of reaching.'

I stay silent for a moment, thinking about her words. I know I ought to be cross, but I also know, if I'm completely honest with myself, that she's right. I just didn't realise she'd noticed.

'Well, it's fine, anyway. He won't ring me.'

She grabs my hand. 'But what if he does, Marianne? What are you going to do then?'

I shrug. 'Nothing. It's fine. He's married. I was just surprised to see him, that's all.'

I can see her studying me for a minute as if she's trying to work out whether I'm telling the truth, then she drops my hand and turns back to face the front.

'So what did he say to you?'

'Not much. Just that he'd tried to find me.'

'Did he?'

'Yeah. He said he put an advert in the paper. The thing is, I always used to check those, I loved them. I can't believe I didn't spot it.'

'Maybe that should tell you something.'

I shrug noncommittally, not willing to admit anything.

'And did you tell him you looked for him too?'

'Yeah. Not for how long, though.'

'Well, good.'

We sit for the rest of the journey in silence. I feel unsettled, a weight sitting heavy in the pit of my belly. Despite what I've told Lance, I do hope Ted rings me. I don't think he will – he has Sam and the baby, why on earth would he? – but the nagging sense that somehow, what happened that night all those years ago has bound us together, has been reignited once more.

And this time I'm not sure how I'm going to extinguish it.

29

Ted

I turn over in the bed and, just for a second, I forget that it's empty, and I reach my arm out to rest it on Sam's waist. But instead, my wrist hits the cold sheet, and I wake up to see nothing but an empty space, and my heart clenches.

It's been three months since she left, taking my boy with her, and I still haven't got used to them not being around. I still listen out for the gentle whistling sound Sam makes in her sleep, the snuffles that come from Jacob's room, the happy sound of my boy giggling in the morning when I go in to give him a kiss. I miss them with every fibre of my being.

Well, it's Jacob I miss the most. The truth is, things with Sam hadn't been great for a while, and now she's gone, life is easier. And while I take some of the blame for what happened between us, it wasn't all down to me, whatever Sam believes.

It had all started going wrong after Jacob's christening. It wasn't obvious at first. The cracks that started to appear were barely even cracks at all, just tiny fissures, hardly perceptible to the naked eye.

I'd burned Marianne's number, but I still regretted it from the moment the paper went up in flames. And it didn't mean that I stopped thinking about her. In fact, despite all the years that had passed, and all the things that had changed in my life, I shocked even myself with how she infiltrated my thoughts again, after just one meeting.

'You're acting weird,' Sam had said a few days later.

'I'm just tired,' I said. 'Work's tough.'

But work was always tough, and after a few more weeks, the excuse didn't wash any more. Then one day I got in from work late – as usual. I'd taken to hanging around later even if I'd finished just so I didn't have to go back and face the increasingly awful atmosphere between us. But this particular night, Sam had waited up. Jacob was settled in his room, and she was at the dining table when I got in, an almost-empty glass of red wine next to her, the bottle half-drunk. Her eyes were bleary, and she had her arms folded across her chest.

'What's going on?' I said, searching frantically for some indication of what I might have done, what she might have found. That's how guilty I felt – even though there wasn't anything to find. She stared at me for a few beats, and then indicated the thing I hadn't noticed before, propped up on the worktop. The drawing of Fairy Girl. Marianne. My heart stopped.

'What's that doing there?' I blustered.

'That's what I'd like to know.' Sam picked up her glass and took a swig, then slammed it back down on the table.

I pulled out a chair and sat down opposite her and reached for her hands. She snatched them away.

'Sam, what's this all about? You've seen this picture before.'

'Yup. I didn't know you'd kept it.'

'It's been in the back of the cupboard since we moved. Why's it here now?'

She sighed. 'I was having a clear-out. The understairs cupboard was getting on my nerves so I pulled everything out to see what I could get rid of. I found this.'

'Right.'

'So why did you keep it?'

I shrugged. 'I don't know. I like it. I always said I was bringing it with me. I forgot it was there.' This last bit is a lie. 'Why are you so cross about this?'

She was silent for a moment, and I tried to read her expression. The hurt in her eyes when she looked at me shocked me.

'It's her, isn't it? Alison's friend Marianne, who came to Jacob's christening.'

My heart thumped. I hadn't expected her to recognise her from the drawing, which wasn't very good. But I couldn't really deny it.

'Yes.'

'I thought so.'

'I—' I stopped. 'I still don't understand why you're so upset.'

'Really?'

'Really.'

She leaned forward, elbows on the table, and rested her chin on her cupped hands. 'Ever since that day, since *your son's* christening —' She made sure to put plenty of emphasis on that last word – 'you've been acting weird. Distracted. I couldn't work it out. And then when I found this, something clicked. I suddenly remembered the strange way you'd behaved after you'd seen her that day—' She held her hand up at my objection. 'I know you thought I hadn't noticed but you went pure white, Ted. And then you kept glancing over at her, and she kept glancing at you. I knew something was going on, but not what. Then I found this.' She held her hands out, palms up. 'And now I'm asking you. How do you know her, and why have you drawn her picture?'

The room seemed to hold its breath for a moment, everything held in suspension. This was the moment when my life could go one of two ways. Just like that night on the bridge; I could jump, and lose everything, or I could stay, and battle.

I rubbed my face with my hand. I felt about a million years old. I stared at the tabletop while I spoke.

'She saved my life.'

Sam didn't reply, just waited for me to explain. She deserved that, at least. And so I told her. I told her all about that night, about how I'd planned on ending it all. About how Marianne had saved me, right at the last minute. And then I told her how I'd tried to find Marianne, how I'd always wanted to thank her for saving me. For giving me a second chance.

Sam's face, as I spoke, had given nothing away. When I finished, she finally spoke. 'I see. And you didn't think to tell me about all of this before?'

I shrugged. 'It never seemed like the right time.'

'The right time? We've been married for four years, Ted. Together for more than eight. You've had plenty of opportunities to tell me something like this.'

I nodded. I had no excuse.

'Are you having an affair with her?'

'What?'

'You heard. Have you been having an affair with this woman, since you found each other at your son's christening?' These last few words dripped with disdain.

'No! Of course not. Why would you ask me that?'

'Oh, I don't know, Ted. Perhaps because you've been acting strangely, spending longer at the hospital than usual because you're trying to avoid me.' She'd looked at me. 'Yes, I've noticed.' She'd sighed then. 'Ted, you're clearly infatuated with this woman and always have been. How am I meant to compete with that?'

'There is no competition,' I'd said. 'I barely know Marianne. You're my *wife*.'

The argument had gone on for a long time, and while I managed to convince Sam that I wasn't having an affair with Marianne, something shifted that night. Something between us – the trust that had always naturally been there, that we'd never had to question – disappeared, and in its place was an uneasy truce. I couldn't blame Sam, either. After all, I'd kept the fact that I'd tried to kill myself from her, which merely confirmed that she'd been right all along. I *did* hold things back from her, and I *wasn't* telling her everything. After all, it wasn't a small secret.

Not only that, but she knew about Marianne now, too. She knew, without me saying anything, that I'd been hung up on Marianne for years, and she suspected that meeting her again, even after all this time, had reignited that.

The worst part was, I couldn't deny it.

Marianne was in my thoughts every day, and I couldn't seem to shake her off.

As the weeks and months had passed, Sam and I drifted further and further apart. Until finally, one day, three months ago, she'd announced she was leaving.

'You can't. What about Jacob?'

'I'm taking him, but you'll see him all the time. I wouldn't do that to you, Ted. Or to him.'

'But why can't you stay? We can make this work.' I knew I sounded desperate, but I was. Marianne might be an infatuation, but that's all she was. I had no intention of ever seeing her again. But for Sam, that wasn't enough. She knew the feelings were there.

'It's over, Ted. I don't want it to be, but I can't do this any more. I can't play second fiddle to someone who only really exists in your memory.'

I begged her to stay, told her she was wrong, that she was the only woman I cared about.

But it was all too late.

Then Jacob and Sam were gone, to a flat half a mile away, while I've been left here, alone in the place we'd bought together, which had held all our hopes and dreams for the future. It feels like an empty shell without them here.

I feel like an empty shell.

I push myself up to sitting, and rub my eyes. The room looks different without Sam's stuff in it – her make-up and pots of creams cluttering up the chest of drawers, her bras hanging off the back of the chair in the corner which used to annoy the hell out of me on a daily basis. Now it looks empty and unloved, and I'd do anything to have the clutter back.

I get up and head to the shower, trying to ignore the silence of the empty flat. I have to hurry, or I'll be late for work, and it's all that's keeping me sane at the moment.

* * *

I'm almost at the hospital when my pager bleeps. I pull it from my pocket and start running. There's been some sort of incident, and they're expecting A&E to fill up in the next half hour. I'm out of breath as I race through the doors, my lungs burning, and head to change into my scrubs. While I'm getting dressed, the TV above my head flashes images of what's happened this morning and I watch it, open-mouthed.

People are filing out of King's Cross station, covered in dust and soot, blood on their hands, their faces, their clothes. The tickertape along the bottom of the screen screams news about a bomb. I stand staring as it flicks to another image, this time of a red double-decker bus, the top half blown to smithereens, leaving its twisted metal innards exposed to the summer sky. It looks like a horror movie.

'Terrorists again,' a colleague says beside me.

'Looks like it.' The words force themselves out through my blocked throat as my thoughts turn to Sam and Jacob. They were unlikely to be on that Tube or that bus at this time of the morning. More than likely, they were still tucked up safely at home, oblivious to the atrocity unfurling just a few miles away. But I don't know Sam's movements these days, and have no right to ask, so I can't be absolutely certain. I pull my mobile out of my locker and ring Sam's number, trying to stop my hands from shaking. It won't connect, the network busy with other desperate relatives attempting to reach their loved ones. I try again and again, and in the end have to settle for sending a text message, tapping out the letters I know I won't see a reply to for several hours.

I shove everything back into my locker and head down to A&E. By the time I arrive, it's already busy, ambulances screeching to a halt outside in quick succession, people scurrying, stretchers being wheeled to operating theatres. For the next eight hours, I hardly stop for breath. I treat burns, and shock and head injuries, a woman struggling to breathe, her lungs filled with smoke, a man who will almost certainly lose his sight, his eye shattered by fragments of debris from an explosion.

It's not until later that I find out more details about the utter devastation of that day; of the fifty-two people who died, and of the four bombs that had gone off all across the capital. Of the terrible, terrible things that had happened on this day that had started out just like any other.

When I finally get back to my flat and switch my mobile back on, I'm numb, and the relief I feel when I see the text from Sam letting me know she and Jacob are fine is diluted by the shock of the horrific things I've seen and dealt with that day.

I've never wanted a drink more and this time, I know I'm going to give in. After everything that's happened, I'm not strong enough to resist.

I grab my keys and head to the shop a few streets away and buy a bottle of Jack Daniel's, then scurry home, furtive, my mind already regretting my decision, while simultaneously knowing I'm going to do this anyway.

I pour the whisky into a tumbler with a shaking hand and tip it down my throat in one go. Then I repeat the action, and again. Finally, I can feel my limbs begin to relax, and the tension starts to ebb away as the alcohol enters my bloodstream. I sit at the kitchen table, the scene of that showdown with Sam all those months ago, and stare into the bottle. Images from today flicker through my mind, one after the other, and I shake them away. I haven't got the energy for this right now.

I pour another glass and sip it slowly this time, savouring the taste, the burn on my tongue and in the back of my throat. It's been months since I last had a drink, and right now I can't remember why I ever stopped. The warmth fills my body and for a while I feel as though I don't have a care in the world.

So what if I've lost everything because of a woman I barely know?

It doesn't matter.

I wonder where Marianne is, what she's up to. I down another glass and think back to the moment when she handed me her number. I had my chance then, and I didn't take it. Now here I am, single and alone and drinking whisky by myself and I have no way of finding her. What a fool.

Then it occurs to me.

She's Alison's friend. That's why she was at Jacob's christening with her. All this time, I've been so afraid to even think about her that I hadn't twigged. My chance has been sitting there all along, right under my nose. I stand and the alcohol rushes to my head and makes me sway, unsteady on my feet. All I have to do is find Alison's number, and ring her and ask her for Marianne's number. It's easy.

But of course I could never do any of these things.

I don't have Alison's number, for a start, and Sam's hardly likely to hand it over. And Alison is Sam's friend and is hardly likely to willingly give me Marianne's number either. What on earth is wrong with me?

I head into my bedroom, my feet stumbling beneath me, getting tangled up with each other, and I grab the framed picture I drew of Marianne from the back of the wardrobe and throw it onto the bed. My fingers fumble to undo the clips on the back, but finally I get it open and lift the glass out and peel the picture off it. I stare at it for a moment, and remember all the times I'd studied this face over the years. But it's wrong. It's all wrong. No longer a symbol of hope, a reminder of my second chance, now it's nothing more than a reminder of everything I've screwed up in my life.

I rip it in half, right down the middle, and then again and again until the pieces float like snowflakes around the room and settle on the bed and the floor.

Then I lie back and let the tears come. I sob for everyone who's lost a loved one on this terrible day, and I sob for what I've lost: Sam and Jacob. Marianne.

I've lost everything.

And I don't know how to come back from this.

30

JULY 2005

Marianne

The air is so thick it's like breathing in cotton wool. I take a sip from my water bottle and glance at the clock. One minute until the next train. Why don't they have air conditioning in these stations? It's unbearable.

As I wait for the next train to arrive, I let my mind wander back to this morning, and the body curled up next to me when I woke up; the still-unfamiliar lines of his torso, dark stubble creeping across his cheek; the scent of wood and lime infiltrating my bedroom so it didn't smell like my own any more. It had only been two weeks since I'd met Andy, but he was already staying over several times a week, a routine established quickly since we'd met at a comedy night at the local pub.

He'd been out with some friends, I'd been out with Lance and Jake, and she'd spotted him watching me from across the other side of the smoky room. It had been Lance who'd encouraged me to speak to him, and I'm glad now that she did.

'You need to stop thinking about bloody Ted once and for all,' she'd said for the hundredth time, exasperated. I'd been unable to stop thinking about him after meeting him at his son's christening eighteen months ago. Lance had tried to tell me he wouldn't ring me – after all, he wasn't only married but he'd just had a baby, for goodness' sake – but I was convinced he would. For weeks, I waited for a text to arrive or for my phone to ring.

But of course Lance was right, and that call never came. I told myself he'd lost my number, that he meant to call. I even wondered whether he'd try to find me, now that he knew there was an actual connection between us in the form of Lance and Sam. But of course he could never do that.

'It's ruining your life,' Lance said, several times. 'You need to find yourself someone else, move on.'

I did try. Dates that went nowhere, drunken snogs in pubs. I was beginning to think this was just the way my life was going to be. Then I met Andy, and for the first time ever, here was someone I actually wanted to talk to, wanted to spend time with.

My thoughts are interrupted by the tell-tale breeze from an approaching Tube train, the warm recycled air gathering speed as it races through the tunnel, whipping up crisp packets and discarded train tickets as it goes. The front of the train noses into the station, still travelling alarmingly fast, and I watch its approach as the brakes screech and the wheels finally come to a halt on the tracks. My heart sinks. The front carriage is packed, and a man with a rucksack is blocking my entry. I elbow my way through the crowds to the next carriage down, then stand and wait while passengers funnel off. I squeeze myself in through the door and lean against the glass partition between me and the seat beside me. It feels cool through my shirt, and I enjoy the sensation for a moment.

There's the usual beeping sound, then the doors slide shut, people pulling bags out of the way and settling back into position. I grip the pole as the train pulls away from the station, and then we're plunged into blackness, hurtling towards the next station. I close my eyes, and take deep breaths, grateful I don't suffer from claustrophobia.

BANG!

An explosion. Metalwork shaking, shards flying in all directions. A screech of brakes, a sudden stop. I slam into the woman next to me. We almost fall but then she manages to pull me up to standing. 'You're okay, you're okay,' she says. Her face is covered in tiny cuts, and I wonder whether mine is too. I look round, bewildered, and see the same expression mirrored back at me on the faces of my fellow passengers: shock, horror, confusion. For a few seconds, there's a deathly silence, then a scream rips through the air. It's coming from the carriage in front.

'Oh, God, what's happening?' someone beside me sobs.

'Help me!' a voice screams a little further away.

I'm covered in a thin layer of sweat and my hands are shaking. There's a sharp pain in my left shoulder but I don't dare look at it.

'Was it a bomb?' someone says, and my stomach flips over. The mention of a bomb has altered the atmosphere, tipped it from calm confusion to a thick, tense panic, and people are looking around now, wondering how they're going to escape.

'Should we smash the windows open?' a deep voice asks.

'Let's just wait for help,' someone else replies.

'How the fuck are we going to get out of here?'

Panic rises. Nobody knows what to do for the best. On the row of seats, people hold hands with strangers. Beside me, the woman I banged into looks at me pleadingly. 'We're going to be all right, aren't we?'

'We'll be fine. Help will come.'

I wish I believed the words I'm saying.

For a while, I can hear reassuring words passed between people, platitudes, prayers. There are whimpers and sobs, of pain, fear and confusion. But as time ticks on, the whimpers begin to fade, conversations peter out, and an eerie quiet descends over the carriage. I take deep breaths and try to block out the panic, think about Mum and Dad, Lance, and even Andy, wondering what they're doing, whether they're worrying about me, or if they're oblivious to the horror going on deep below the surface of the city.

I'm not sure how much time passes but, finally, voices cut through the silence, and there's a sudden surge of action inside the cramped carriage as help arrives. I've never been so pleased to see anyone as I am to see the paramedics when they loom into my vision. I start to shake with shock as they call out instructions. We're told to climb out of the window, and so, one by one, people start to leave, safe hands reaching up to lift them down onto the track. Finally, it's my turn, and as I exit the carriage, I take one last glance back at the enclosed space where I've just spent a terrifying slice of my life. The woman from before watches me, her eyes round, a dribble of blood sliding down her cheek from a deep cut on her forehead. I reach for her hand, and she touches mine briefly.

'Good luck.'

And then I'm gone, standing alone in the darkness. Someone is holding my arm, a bright light shining onto the tracks in front of me.

'Please make your way carefully along the tracks towards the station,' a calm voice says.

'What's happened? Is it a bomb?' I'm not sure that it will really do me any good to know even if it were, but there's an innate need in me to understand what I'm dealing with here.

'We don't know, madam. If you could walk towards the station, please, but be careful as the tracks are still live.'

In the stifling darkness, I reach out and touch the damp brick-work to my right. All I need to do is follow this, keep contact with it, and nothing can go wrong. Step by slow, painful step, I pick my way along the track. The air is getting hotter, and it's so still it feels as though I'm in some kind of vacuum. I breathe in slowly, out slowly.

In the darkness I can hear footsteps in front of me, and together, without saying a word, me and my companion continue on our seemingly never-ending journey along the pitch-black tunnel, my hand never losing contact with the curve of the wall. Eventually, ahead, there's a glimmer of light.

'We're nearly there,' the voice in front of me whispers, and relief surges through me, giving me the strength to keep going, to get out of this hellish place.

I blink as I emerge from the tunnel into the station, the lights bright here. Hands reach down and grab me, lifting me from the tracks and hauling me up to the platform. I'm grateful, I don't have the strength to climb up myself. All around me people are covered in soot and dirt; there's blood everywhere, people crying, scream-ing, doubled over. It's like a scene from hell, the acoustics of the tiled walls making the sounds of panic echo forever.

Without stopping to find out what's happened, I hurry towards the exit and clamber up the now still escalators, sucking in air like it's in short supply. My lungs burn with the effort, but I feel an urgent need to get as far away from here as quickly as possible.

I'm aware as I head towards the exit of a pain in my shoulder, but I don't stop to look. I'm only focusing on the exit sign, bright green and incongruously ordinary in the distance. Then, finally, thankfully, I stumble out of the train station and into the relatively fresh air of London. It's eerily quiet out here, and I realise the road has been closed off, the blue lights of police cars and ambulances bouncing off the surrounding buildings.

Around me, my fellow passengers disperse, pull phones from

bags and pockets and tap away desperately, trying to let loved ones know they're all right. They may not even know what happened, but it's clear to everyone that something has, that there's a threat; that we've had a lucky escape. It occurs to me I should let Mum and Dad know I'm okay, and then my heart flips over. Lance. Would she have been on the train in front, or the one in front of that? My hands shake as I look for my phone, find her number and wait for it to ring. But there's no connection, the network clogged up by the desperation of thousands of husbands, wives, parents, siblings, friends.

I put my phone back in my bag and look around now, taking in my surroundings. People are milling around, looking dazed, some like the walking dead. Then I look down at myself and realise I must look the same. My clothes are covered in a layer of black and there's blood on my skirt. Mine? I don't know.

'Excuse me, madam, would you come with me, please?' I turn to find a paramedic taking my elbow and leading me towards a nearby ambulance. I wonder how bad I look.

My shoulder feels like shards of glass are stabbing through the skin, into bone. I can feel it throbbing beneath my blouse and I know I should go and get it checked out. But more than anything else, I just want to go home. I don't want to spend hours in A&E surrounded by people worse off than me, traumatised casualties covered in blood. I just want to go home, wash it all off and forget about it. So I shake my arm free and turn away and walk briskly towards the road. Everywhere is closed – the road, the stations – and people walk, zombie-style, shirts ripped, sooty faces, glazed expressions. I join them, moving along the pavement, numb, heading north, towards home. It's a five-mile walk but I don't remember any of it. I know I must speak to my Mum, and Lance, but the details of the conversations aren't clear. And then finally I'm home, in my flat, in a hot bath. My shoulder still hurts but further inspection has revealed it's just a deep cut, nothing more, and I enjoy the sting of the warm water as it laps around it, soothing. I relax for a few minutes, trying to ease out some of the tension from my limbs but then I urgently need to wash the trauma of the day away. I scrub my skin until it's red, then step out and watch the filthy liquid drain away, taking away the horror of the day as it goes.

It's not until later that night as I lie in bed alone, eyes wide open, refusing to go to sleep in the sodium glow of my bedroom, that I truly think about what happened today. I hadn't been able to tear my eyes away from the news throughout the evening, watching the hundreds of people pouring from train stations, just like me. I saw the tangled metal of the bus on Tavistock Square, twisted limbs of black and red reaching up into the heavens, bodies scattered across the ground. I wept. I wept myself dry, until I felt there was nothing left at all.

I'd been saved, but many hadn't. Things could have been so different.

As I lie in bed in the dark, I realise that I need to stop looking back and wondering *what if*, and wondering when my life is going to start, and get on with living the life I have.

31

JUNE 2007

Ted

As I climb the familiar steps, it feels like only yesterday that I was last here. The building looks the same, I feel the same as I did that very first time. It's only once I've pushed open the office door to find a young man sitting behind the reception desk, all neat preppy hair, round glasses and white teeth, that it strikes me how much time has moved on.

'Hi, I'm Cameron, how can I help you?' he says, dazzling me with his smile as I approach.

'I'm here to see Lynne.' I place my hands on the counter to stop them shaking. Cameron peers at his computer screen, then nods. 'Ted Green?'

'That's me.'

'Please take a seat and Lynne will be with you shortly.'

I sit in the newly decorated reception area. The cream sofa has been swapped for a navy corduroy one, and I sink into the deep cushions. It's been almost fourteen years since I last came to see Lynne, and being here now feels like an admission of failure, that I couldn't do it without her. But I also knew I had no choice. I'd hit rock bottom once before, and I could feel it inching closer with each day, each week that passed. I had to get help before I got there.

'Ted!' Lynne is suddenly in front of me, and she claps her hands and ushers me into her consultation room. Her previously dark hair has flecks of grey now, and it's longer, swept back from her face and curled round her ears. But other than that, she still looks the same, and I feel comforted by the familiarity.

We sit, and Lynne leans forward, hands clasped in front of her. 'So, Ted. It's good to see you. What brings you here again?'

I don't know where to start. What does bring me here? The fact that I'm divorced, and living in a miserable flat by myself, without my son? The fact that I only get to see Jacob for a few days at a time thanks to my erratic shifts and I feel like he's drifting further away from me all the time? Or the fact that I've been drinking more and more to numb the pain and the loneliness that threatens to over-whelm me every single day?

'I'm drinking again,' I say.

Lynne nods, and waits.

I rub my nose, clear my throat. 'The last couple of years have been terrible.' I train my eyes on the corner of the carpet where it's starting to fray and continue. 'I'm divorced. I don't see my son enough. It just—' My voices hitches. 'It feels as though everything's going down the toilet and there's nothing I can do to stop it.'

There's a pause and I glance up at Lynne. She's studying me, the grooves in her forehead much deeper now than they used to be, the signs of the last fifteen years. 'And this is why you're drinking?' she asks.

'Yes. It's what I always do, as you know. It stops me thinking too much. Except that then it doesn't even do that any longer and I have to drink even more to get the same effect.' I take a deep breath. 'It's affecting my job now, and my health. Every morning, I wake up and I feel sick, my head hurts, my liver hurts. Then I have to go to work and look after sick people and I'm scared. I'm scared I'm going to make a terrible mistake and it will cost someone else their life.' I look down at my knees, the denim of my jeans pulled tight against them. 'It doesn't matter about me, really. But I can't put other people at risk.'

Lynne shuffles in her seat. 'It's interesting you say it doesn't matter about you.'

'Is it?'

She nods, but says nothing more. I close my eyes, screw them tight against her scrutiny, then open them again and expel a breath of air. 'It's true, though. I don't—' I pause. 'I don't think I'm quite ready to throw myself off a bridge yet but – well, I'm not far off.' I feel the brick of tension that's been sitting in the pit of my stomach for so long shift as I finally say the words out loud.

Lynne nods again. 'And that's why you're here.' It's a statement, not a question, but I nod anyway.

'I see.' She flexes her fingers in front of her and I wait for her to speak. Finally, she does. 'And you want me to tell you not to do it?'

I look up, surprised at her words. 'I – I don't know. I guess so.'

'Good. That means you've already done some of the work yourself.'

'What do you mean?'

She leans back and crosses her legs. 'Last time you came to see me, you came reluctantly. You didn't think this was going to work, but over time, it did.' She pauses, eyeing me up and down. 'You're one of my biggest success stories, Ted.'

'Am I?'

She nods and pushes a stray strand of hair back from her face. 'Most definitely. You came here all those years ago, desperate and disbelieving, and now look at you. A doctor. A *father*. You might have truly believed you had nothing to live for last time and that no one would miss you if you weren't here, but you can't possibly believe that now. If anything, you have too *much* to lose.' She gestures at me. 'And I think you know that, which is why you're here. To find your way back.'

I sit for a moment, letting her words settle. She's right. I do have too much to lose. My mind flits to an image of Jacob two nights ago, wanting to hug me, and me only giving him half of my attention, too distracted by my own thoughts, by the hangover that seemed to lurk at all hours of the day, and my heart lurches. *This* is why I'm here. He is why I'm here. It's all for him.

'I want to get better for Jacob.' I clear my throat, afraid my voice will break. 'He's my world.'

'Well, then, that's what we'll do. Together.'

I allow myself a small smile then. I can do this.

* * *

Over the next hour, I tell Lynne everything. I admit how my need to find Fairy Girl got out of control. I tell her how Sam was heart-broken to find out I'd hidden such a big secret from her for all those years, and then I tell her about meeting Marianne and the infatuation being rekindled.

'And you believe she's the reason your marriage ended?' Lynne asks.

'Yes. I told you last time that she was my reason for keeping going, for trying to make something of my life, as a way of thanking her. But it got out of hand. I thought about her all the time, she became like a symbol of my new life. I tried to put her behind me, to forget about her. But then bam! She turned up at my son's christening and everything unravelled.'

'And how did you feel, when you saw her again?'

I pause before answering. How *did* I feel? Excited? Ashamed?

'Guilty,' I say.

'Because of Sam?'

'Yes. And Jacob.'

'So what did you do?'

I tell her about our meeting, about Marianne giving me her phone number and how I had to burn it to stop myself ringing her. 'It was the only way I knew to resist the temptation. To burn all evidence.'

'And how did you feel?'

'I regretted it the second I did it, but I also knew it had been the right thing to do.'

'Because you knew you'd ring her otherwise?'

I nod. 'I still sometimes think of her as Fairy Girl, but that day was the first time I heard her name. Marianne.'

To my surprise, Lynne flinches, as though the name means something to her.

'Marianne?' she asks.

'Yes.'

'I see.'

I wait, wondering whether she'll say any more. But after a few seconds, she gives a small nod and carries on. 'Did it make a difference, do you think, knowing her name after all these years?'

'I think so. It made the betrayal feel more real.'

'But you didn't actually betray Sam.'

'I did. I spent the five years we were married thinking about someone else. I loved Sam. I still do. But I kept Marianne hidden from her. I don't think I could ever forgive me for that, either.'

* * *

After my session with Lynne, I feel wiped out, as though my soul has been drained from me. I stroll along in the warmth of the June sunshine and think about what Lynne suggested. She thought I needed to take some time off work, a couple of weeks, a month, to give myself a bit of space. While the thought of some proper time away from the hospital sounded like heaven, I explained there was no way I could, that I'm the most senior person there, that they can't do without me. I knew really that the only reason I didn't want to take any time off was because I didn't want time to think. My job keeps me so busy and makes me so exhausted I don't have time for delving into my thoughts. Lynne saw right through me, of course, and so I promised her I'd consider it.

But I also can't get the image of the face she pulled when I said Marianne's name. The flinch, and the look that flitted across her features, so quickly it was barely there. But I saw it, and I wonder what it means. Does she know Marianne? What would be the chances? But then again, what would be the chances of me ever bumping into her again in a city of more than eight million people?

Even if she does know her, why does it matter? It's not as though I can ask her for Marianne's phone number.

I reach the Tube station and head down into the stuffy air. Ever since the London bombings and all the horrors I saw that day, I've felt more nervous going into the Underground than I ever have before. Having lived in London my whole life, it's always just been a means of getting around, nothing to think twice about. But now, as I descend to the platform, I imagine being trapped here, not knowing whether the person next to you wanted to kill you, not knowing whether you're ever going to get out of there, and I feel my stomach knot and my shoulders tense. I wonder whether I'll ever relax again.

As I stand on the train, gripping the yellow pole, I study my fellow passengers. I look at them all differently these days. No longer just people on their way somewhere, like me, but potentially dangerous enemies. How do you recognise someone who wants to kill you? Is it the look in their eyes, the way they stand?

The man beside stands up and I recoil, my breath coming faster now, ragged, and I feel as though I might collapse. I can't seem to get any air, and the arched walls of the train are closing in around me. The train's slowing and I need to get off, but it's not stopping, it won't stop, and then a face looms in front of me, too close, hot breath on my cheek, and I think I'm going to die...

* * *

When I come round, I can see concerned faces peering at me, and the dirty grey of the Tube station ceiling beyond that. My head is propped on something soft, and there's a blanket or a coat under my back. I try to sit up, but everything is still hazy, so I sink back down again.

'How do you feel?' a voice says near my ear, and I mumble, 'I'm okay.'

A few minutes pass, and the faces dwindle, until there's just a uniformed London Underground worker, a young woman and a middle-aged man with me. The man hands me a fresh bottle of water. 'Here, take a sip of this.'

I sit up and swallow a few mouthfuls gratefully.

'What happened?'

'You collapsed just as the train pulled into the station,' he says. 'Me and this young lady stayed with you.'

'Thank you.' I rub my eyes. 'I've never passed out before. I don't know what happened.'

'Maybe it was the heat,' the woman says, and I nod. But I know, really, it was more than that. I can remember my heart racing, and the blood rushing to my head and the feeling of terror as I lurched towards the train doors, and I close my eyes and tamp the memories away.

'Well, thank you,' I say now, pushing myself up to standing. The walls sway slightly but I'm steady.

'Are you sure you're going to be okay? Do you want me to take you to hospital, it's not far?' the young woman says.

'It's fine, thank you. I'm actually a doctor, so I can take myself.'

'Oh, okay. If you're sure.' I nod again and she leaves, walking swiftly towards the exit.

'Let me walk with you,' the London Transport woman says, holding out her elbow for me. So, together, we walk out from the oppressive heat of the Tube station, up the escalators, and into the warmth of a London summer's day.

* * *

It's not until later that evening that I let myself think about what happened today. I've never had a panic attack before, not even in the Gulf, or when I thought about my father. Then, I just drank myself into oblivion and tried to block it out. Maybe Lynne is right, after all. Maybe I do need to take some time off work.

I started working at the hospital, training, fifteen years ago, and apart from the odd holiday, I've never taken a proper break. It's a tough job by any standards, and add to that what I am starting to suspect is some PTSD, my history with Fairy Girl, the breakdown of my marriage and the panic about not seeing my son, it's hardly a surprise that I'm struggling now.

I need to be kind to myself.

And I need to fight for my son.

* * *

Sam looks furious when she sees it's me standing on the doorstep – more likely thanks to the way I'd just hammered on the door like a maniac than the fact it's me, but I can't be sure.

'What are you doing here?'

'I've come to see Jacob.'

'But it's not your day.'

'I know. But I just need to see him. Just five minutes?'

She glances behind her then steps out and pulls the door almost shut. 'You can't just turn up like this, it's not fair.'

'On who? Jacob, or you?' I know I'm being snarky, but I don't really care. The need to see my son, to hold him, is overwhelming. I need to let him know, somehow, that I'm never going to leave him, that I'll do everything in my power to sort myself out. But I don't say any of this to Sam. She's not mine to confide in any more.

'Are you pissed, Ted?'

'No!' I sound offended but we both know Sam's got every right to ask given that I so often am.

'What's wrong with you, then?'

I shake my head. 'I don't know.' I stop, suddenly aware of how inappropriate it is for me to have turned up like this out of the blue. 'I'm sorry. I just needed to see him.'

Her face softens and she folds her arms in front of her and leans on the doorjamb. 'What's brought all this on, Ted?'

'I just—' I stop, shift my weight to the other foot. 'I'm struggling, Sam.'

'Oh, Ted.' She peers at me more closely. 'Are you sure you're not drunk?'

'No, really, I'm not. I had a tough day, that's all.' I don't want to tell her about passing out in case she thinks I'm not capable of looking after Jacob. 'I just wanted to spend some time with my boy.'

'You can tomorrow.' She sighs. 'I'm not being cruel, Ted. Jacob likes his routine, it's good for him to know where he's going to be and when. I don't want you to think you can just turn up whenever you feel like it and throw his routine out.'

'It's only once.'

'I know. But I'm saying no. He's having his tea and then he's going up for a bath. You can see him tomorrow as planned, okay?'

'Okay.' I know when there's no point in arguing any more and I take a step away from the doorstep.

'But promise me one thing?'

'What?'

'Tell him his daddy loves him, okay?'

She gives me a quizzical look as though she's trying to read my thoughts, then nods. 'I will, Ted. Goodnight.' Then she steps back inside and closes the doors, leaving me no option but to walk away.

* * *

Later that night, when most of the city is sleeping, I'm still wide awake, thinking about everything that's happened today. My conversation with Lynne, about taking some time off work, my panic attack, about Sam and Jacob and everything else. My mind is so busy I know there's no chance I'll get to sleep so I don't even bother getting into bed but instead sit at the kitchen table with a pen and pad of paper. It's been a while since I made a list of pros and cons, but it used to be how I made all my decisions. It seems like a good time to start again.

I draw a line down the middle of the top sheet and on the left write 'pros of taking time off' and on the right, 'cons of taking time off'. The first lines are easy, and I write quickly. When I stop, my list looks like this:

Pros	Cons
Time with Jacob	Too much time to think
Time to Rest and relax	
Time to look after myself	
Concentrate on quitting drinking	
Time to visit friends	

That's it. That's the only downside I can come up with. I don't think it will ruin my career – it's not as though I'm still climbing the ladder, and they've offered me a sabbatical before – and I've got enough money saved not to have to worry about that for a few months. Which means the only thing stopping me is fear of myself.

If I want any chance of getting my life back on track, there's only one choice. I'll ask for some time off first thing tomorrow.

32

JUNE 2007

Marianne

'I can't do this!' I scream, my whole body racked with pain.

Beside me, Andy squeezes my hand. 'You're doing brilliantly,' he says, and I want to thump him. It's all right for him, he's not the one lying on this bloody hospital bed forcing a human being out of his private parts.

'Raaaarrrgghh!' The sound is feral, like a wild animal, but I can't care. 'Just get this fucking baby out of me!'

This is the worst pain of my entire life. I don't know what's wrong with people, how do they do this over and over again? I need it to end, I'm going to die, I know I am. It feels as though I'm being ripped in half, as though I'm burning from the inside out.

'Baby's coming,' the midwife says, somewhere down near my nether regions. 'Just one more push and the head will be out.'

One more push? Is she fucking kidding me? I couldn't give one more push if you paid me a billion pounds. I'm done here. I'm done.

And then a pain worse than anything else in the world rips through my abdomen and I can't help it, I push, and I scream and then it's over. The pain has eased, and there's a beat of silence in the room, and then the air is pierced with a loud cry. My baby!

It takes all the strength I have left to lift my head from the pillow, and I see the midwife at the end of the bed, wiping my baby down and wrapping it in a towel.

'It's a girl,' Andy whispers beside me and I jump. I'd forgotten he was there. He leans forward and kisses me on the forehead. 'You're amazing.' There are tears in his eyes and I feel a flash of anger. What's he got to cry about?

My baby is handed to me, laid across my chest and my heart surges with love. It's like drowning, like sinking to the bottom of the ocean, the water folding over my head, and knowing I'll never come back up again, and not caring. This tiny person right here, right now, is all that matters.

'Congratulations, you have a beautiful baby girl,' the midwife says, smiling.

I'm crying now, the tears blurring my vision, and I brush them away with the hand that's not holding my daughter. She hardly has any hair, but what she does have is wispy and blonde. Her nose is a tiny stub, and her eyelashes fan out across her soft cheeks. She's utterly perfect. I tear my eyes away from her for a second to glance up at Andy.

'She looks just like you,' I say.

'Poor girl.' He grins.

I look back at her, trying to work out what name will suit her. How on earth can we possibly sum her up in one word?

'I like Charlotte,' Andy says.

I study her. I'm not sure. Is she a Charlotte? Will it suit her? I feel overwhelmed by the responsibility of choosing the name she'll have to carry for the rest of her life, and before I know it, I'm sobbing so hard Andy has to lean over and take our daughter from me before she slips from my chest. As I watch him standing there, staring down at his little girl with such pure love in his eyes, I know we've done the right thing, despite all the doubts I'd had while I was pregnant. Andy is a good man.

* * *

I open my eyes. It's bright in here, the warm sunshine pouring through the hospital blinds and painting stripes on the blue blanket. I turn my head and there she is. My baby.

We're alone now, just me and her, the curtains pulled round us, safe against the world. I push myself up to sitting, wincing at the pain. Slowly I lean over and push my hands beneath her, one at her head and one under her bottom, and I lift her. She's so light, it's impossible to believe she's real. I scoop her up and pull her to my chest, cradling her gently against me. She's warm, and she stirs briefly, then settles again, her lips pressing against each other contentedly. I press my own lips against her forehead and blink back the tears. What is wrong with me, why can't I stop crying?

I settle my head back against the pillow and keep my eyes trained on my daughter. I don't know where Andy is, but right now, I don't care.

I still feel surprised to find myself in the position I'm currently in. A new mum. A wife. It's all happened so fast, sometimes I forget it's happened at all. All those years I spent alone, dreaming about someone I couldn't have, and now here I am.

I never expected Andy to be The One. But after that terrible day in London when I was caught up in the bombings, I began to realise how lucky I was. In the aftermath, I discovered that the bomber on my train had been in the carriage in front, the one I almost got on. I've picked over the details of that day so many times since, turning them over and over in my mind, until I'm no longer certain what actually happened to me and what I subsequently saw on the news footage I seemed incapable of turning off.

'You don't need to keep watching that,' Mum said when she found me glued to the TV the following evening. 'It won't do you any good.'

'I do,' I'd said. I'd gone to Mum and Dad's house the day after. I'd just needed company, not to be alone with my thoughts, and yet I couldn't seem to tear myself away from the horrific images that scrolled across the screen over and over again.

That day changed me. I knew I was lucky to be alive, to be hardly injured apart from a deep gash on my shoulder, a few small cuts on my face and slight damage to the hearing in my left ear. People on my carriage and the one in front had lost limbs, had died.

Life, I realised, was too short to waste.

So I'd thrown myself into my fledgling relationship with Andy. It quickly became an intense love affair, fuelled by my need to make the most of the second chance I'd been given. Was this how Ted had felt after I'd stopped him jumping that night? I wished I could ask him, but that ship had well and truly sailed.

When Andy had asked me to marry him just six months after we first got together, I said yes. I was thirty-four years old, and Andy made me happy. He was funny and good looking and kind to me. There was no doubt in my mind that I was doing the right thing.

We got married three months later at Haringey registry office, followed by a reception at the pub round the corner. Although Mum was shocked at how fast it was all happening, I could see the pride – and relief – in her face that her only daughter wasn't going to be a spinster forever.

And then, just three months later, I'd found out I was pregnant.

'Fuck, Annie, when you decide to do something, you don't piss about, do you?' Lance had said when I'd told her. I'd burst out laughing.

'I love you and your honest responses,' I said, as she hugged me.

She'd pulled away, her face serious. 'Promise me something, though,' she'd said.

'What?'

'You won't become boring and stop coming out with me?'

'Never.'

'Well then, congratulations, my darling,' she'd said, hugging me again.

It had been harder than I'd expected, keeping my promise. The morning sickness was so bad some days I felt as though I might be better off dead. But after four months, I started feeling gradually more human with every day that passed.

'Knock, knock.' A voice makes me jump, and I open my eyes to find Mum poking her head through the gap in the curtains.

'Hello, Mum,' I say sleepily.

'Hello, love,' she says, slipping into my cubicle and bending down to kiss my forehead.

'No Dad?'

'He's just gone to get a paper,' she says. 'You know what he's like.'

I smile. More likely he wanted to give me and Mum a moment first, bless him.

'Is Andy not here either?'

'No, I'm not sure where he went. Maybe he's left us.' A look of horror flits across Mum's face. 'I'm only kidding,' I add, to appease her.

'Well, don't even joke,' she says, pressing her hand to her chest, as if to still her heart. Then she leans over the crib beside my bed and her face melts. 'Oh, my,' she says, and reaches out her finger to stroke the side of her granddaughter's face. 'She's perfect.'

I've never seen Mum's face so soft, and I can't help but wonder whether this is how she looked when she saw me for the first time. Somehow, I just can't picture it. 'Have you decided on a name yet?'

I'm about to say no, but then blurt out 'Charlotte'. It's the name Andy loves, and I realise in that instant I want to make him happy. It seems to have done the same for Mum too, who claps her hands together in glee. 'Oh, little Charlotte, that's gorgeous,' she says, her eyes filling with tears.

'You're awake,' a voice says from the doorway, and I turn to find Andy juggling plastic-wrapped sandwiches and a cardboard tray of coffees. 'I brought lunch.'

'Hello, Andy,' Mum says, taking the sandwiches from him and placing them on the small bedside table. 'Congratulations, Charlotte is gorgeous.'

Over Mum's shoulder, Andy raises his eyebrows at me and mouths, 'Charlotte?'

I nod and smile, then watch as realisation dawns on his face.

'Thank you,' he says, his face lighting up. 'Now, who's hungry?' As he pulls out a chair for Mum, hands me a sandwich, and generally fusses around, I watch him. I'm lucky to have him, I know. He's funny and kind, he loves me, and Mum and Dad love him. I love him too, of course. And yet I can't seem to entirely extinguish the tiny flame of doubt that still flickers deep in my belly; the part of me that worries that maybe, in the end, Andy isn't enough for me. But how can he not be?

'Wasn't it, Marianne?'

'What?' I look up, confused, to find Andy and Mum looking at me, waiting for an answer.

'Andy was just saying the birth was pretty straightforward.'

'For him, maybe,' I snap, and I know I'm being unkind, but part of me wants to make Andy suffer. He reaches his hand out and strokes my hair and I pull away.

'Sorry,' he says, his face crestfallen, and I relent, unsure why I feel the need to punish him.

'No, I'm sorry. I'm just exhausted.' I turn my attention back to Mum. 'Yes, it was pretty straightforward. Bloody agony, though, I don't know how people do it more than once.'

'Yes, well, you know I didn't so I can't say I disagree with you there.' Mum looks down at her hands and back up again. 'You know, I did regret it, though.'

'Regret what?'

'Not having a brother or sister for you.'

'I was all right.'

Mum shakes her head. 'No, I know. But – well, your dad and I, we just – we didn't find it very easy when you were born and, well, I suppose we just left it too late. And then you were a teenager and there was no way we were going back there again.' She stops. 'I just wish you could have had someone else to play with. You know, some company.'

'Oh.' I'm surprised. I'd never known Mum and Dad had wanted another child, and I can't help thinking how different my childhood might have been if I'd have had a sibling. But now isn't the time to pry.

'Anyway, just promise me you won't rule out having another one completely,' Mum adds.

'Er...' I shoot a look at Andy, who steps forward and places his hand on Mum's shoulder.

'Would you like to hold her? Charlotte?'

'Ooh, yes please! But – oh, she's still asleep. Maybe we shouldn't wake her.'

'It's fine, Mum. She needs a cuddle with her grandma.'

'And her grandad too,' a voice says, and I smile as Dad comes into the cubicle, a couple of newspapers tucked under his arm. He looks frail, his face drawn.

'Hey, Dad.'

'Hello, love. Hello, Andy.' He looks round. 'Blimey, it's like Piccadilly Circus at rush hour in here.' He shuffles round awkwardly.

'Just come and sit here,' I say, patting the edge of my bed.

'Are you sure, love? I don't want to hurt you.'

'It's fine, Dad. When Mum's had her cuddle, you can have yours too. Charlotte will love her grandad.'

'Charlotte? Oh, that's lovely.' Dad's face lights up.

'Andy chose it,' I say. 'But I think it suits her, don't you?'

'I really do, yes.'

I sit back and watch as Dad pretends not to read his paper, Mum coos over Charlotte, and Andy fusses around, topping up my water glass and smoothing the sheets in Charlotte's crib. This, right here with my family, is where I'm meant to be.

So why do I feel so uneasy?

* * *

Later, there's a rustling at the curtain and a face pops through the gap.

'Can I come in?'

'Lance!' I cry in a stage whisper. 'What are you doing here, it's not visiting time?'

'I snuck in like a ninja.' She kisses me on the cheek. 'Sorry I didn't make it before, work was mad.'

'Don't be silly, it's fine.'

She leans over the crib beside me and peers into my daughter's face. 'Oh, Annie, she looks just like you.'

'Do you think? I think she's the spitting image of Andy.'

She smiles. 'Well, maybe. Babies all look quite similar, really, don't they?' She perches on the edge of my bed instead of the chair, and lets her feet dangle off the side. 'So, was it horrendous?'

'Bloody awful. The worst pain I've ever felt in my life.'

'Tell me more. How long did it last? Was Andy there? Did he see *everything*?'

'I don't really remember the details, just the pain. And then Charlotte, of course.'

'Charlotte.' She turns the name over in her mouth. 'Yes, I approve. I didn't know it was on your list, though.'

'It wasn't, it was on Andy's. But I realised I didn't really mind, and I thought it might make him happy.'

'Are you worried he's not, then?'

I sigh heavily. 'I don't know, Lance. I don't know whether it's just my hormones, but I look at him at the moment, and I feel nothing.'

'What do you mean, nothing?'

'Just that. I see him there, fussing with Charlotte, and I wish he'd just stop and leave us alone to be together. It's like he's just a man, passing by, rather than my husband.' I look at her. 'What's wrong with me?'

'Oh, Annie, I'm sure this is completely normal. Your body's just spent nine months growing a new human being, and another few hours pushing her out into the world. Of course all you want to do is be with her. Anyone else must feel as though they're just a distraction.'

'I'm sure you're right.'

She takes hold of my chin and tugs it until I'm looking her directly in the eye.

'I'm always right. This will pass, okay?'

'Okay.'

'And if it doesn't, dump him and come and stay with me.' She grins and I slap her arm away. 'Where is Andy, anyway?'

'He went home to get some sleep.'

'Hang on, aren't you the one who needs sleep?'

'He was awake all night too. He looked terrible. I told him to go, he didn't want to. Of course.' The truth was I'd wanted to get rid of him for a few hours, and although I'd assured Lance I knew it was hormones making me feel that way, I was still scared there was more to it than that.

'Where's Jake?' I say, before Lance can ask any more questions about Andy.

'At home. I told him I needed to come and see you on my own. I think he was more than happy with that.'

'Everything all right with you two?' Lance and Jake had been together for four years, and although he'd made it clear he wanted to get married and have children, Lance was still resisting it all. It had been causing a bit of tension between them for the last few months.

She looks at me now. 'Yeah, it's all fine. He still keeps telling me he wants to marry me, but I just don't want to. I'm not there yet. I don't know that I ever will be. You know what I'm like. I just don't see the point.'

'I know. I thought Jake was all right with that, though?'

'He says he is, but you know.' She shrugs, traces her fingers along a line of pattern on the blanket. She looks shifty.

'Is there something else you're not telling me?' I say, and the moment she looks back at me, I know I'm right.

'I wasn't going to tell you now. I don't want to spoil your moment.'

'Come on, out with it.'

She swallows. 'I'm pregnant.'

'What? Lance, that's brilliant! Isn't it?' The look on her face tells me otherwise.

'I don't know, Annie. I mean – me, with a baby? I just – it's not what I'd imagined.'

'Well, no, me neither. But we're thirty-six now, it's not the most unusual thing to ever happen.'

'I know. And that's what worries me. Everyone else thinks it's brilliant, that I must be thrilled. But I'm not, and I'm worried there's something wrong with me.'

I place my hand on her arm. 'There's nothing wrong with you, my darling. You're just scared, that's all. Same as I was. But look, it's worth it in the end.' I glance over to where Charlotte is stirring in her crib, and Lance follows my gaze.

'You're right, I'm being ridiculous.' She stops. 'Can I hold her?'

'Of course you can. She's just waking up, why don't you pick her up?'

As I watch my best friend cradle my tiny baby girl in her arms, my heart floods with love. I might have my doubts about Andy – about whether we rushed into getting married, having a baby – but without all that, I wouldn't have Charlotte, and now that she's here, I know she's my reason for living. She's my everything. It's time I stopped feeling sorry for myself.

33

SEPTEMBER 2009

Ted

I might not have seen my father for more than twenty years, but it doesn't mean his voice has diminished in my head. In fact, I swear that as I get older, it only gets louder, more critical. Today the self-flagellation is stronger than ever.

The reason is standing right in front of me. A beautiful, intelligent woman, who I know is far too good for me and yet she doesn't seem to have noticed, is asking me to move in with her. And I'm hesitating.

You're not good enough for her, the voice says.

Why would someone like that want you?

Stop being such a loser, Ted.

Stop it! I shake my head to get rid of the thoughts, and force a smile. A small crease folds across her face, getting deeper the longer I take to answer.

'Yes, okay,' I say. *Okay?* Is that the best I can come up with?

Sophia's disappointment is clear on her face and guilt swamps me. *Why can't I just be normal?*

I clear my throat, try again. 'That would be great,' I say, stepping towards her. I feel her relax in my arms as I hold her, and tell myself I've done the right thing.

I don't know what's holding me back. Sophia and I have been dating for more than eight months, ever since Danni introduced us.

'It's not going to end up the same as it did with Sam,' she reassured me. 'Sophia is totally different to Sam.'

It turned out she was right. Sophia worked as an HR consultant in an accountancy firm in Harlow, she was divorced as well, and had a son, Archie, who was the same age as my Jacob.

'Okay,' I'd reluctantly agreed.

I was glad I had, in the end. Danni had been right, Sophia and I did get on. We did have more in common than I'd expected, and I enjoyed her company. Were there sparks? Not really, not for either of us. Did I fall head over heels in love? No. But after the last few years, I knew none of that mattered. What mattered was that Sophia was lovely, we cared about each other, and our children got on well. Whatever was holding me back was pushed to the back of my mind, and shut away forever. On paper, we were perfect.

Now here she is, asking me to move in with her – which, in all honesty, would be amazing as her house is a lovely little three-bed in Essex and I'm still in my cramped flat. I spend most of my time there anyway. But something about not having my own space, somewhere to escape to when I feel as though things are getting too intense, terrifies me.

But I agree anyway. I'm sure I'm doing the right thing.

* * *

Every time I pick Jacob up for our time together, I feel nervous about seeing Sam. Maybe it's the way she's cool and pleasant with me, as though I'm a delivery person or a neighbour, someone she only knows in passing and is just being polite to, rather than the woman who shared my bed, my life, for seven years, the mother of my son. Or maybe it's the more obvious reason, that I feel guilty about the way I treated her. She didn't deserve it, and I'll never forgive myself for making her feel second best.

'Come in,' she says as she opens the door, and I follow her into the flat. There's something different about the place today, and at first, I can't put my finger on what.

'Daddy!' Jacob says, windmilling towards me and launching himself at my stomach.

'Hello, gorgeous boy,' I say, scooping him up and covering his face with kisses, even though he's six now and insists he's far too old for that sort of thing. He pulls his face away and hides it in my shirt until I finally stop. 'How are you, my little man?'

'Good.' He wriggles until I relent and put him gently back down on the floor. Every time I see him, I feel amazed. When I'm not with him and picture him in my mind, he's still a tiny toddler, following me round like a shadow, asking me endless questions. But he's growing so fast now, almost up to my chest, that I feel a jolt of shock every time I see him, and remember how big he is already.

'Mummy's friend stayed last night.'

'Oh?' I raise my eyebrows at Sam and she flushes.

'Yeah, I—' She wipes her hands on a tea-towel and looks at Jacob. 'I've met someone.'

It's completely unjustified after everything I did, and especially now I'm with Sophia, but my heart twists with pain at the thought of her with someone else. Or rather, at the thought of another man spending more time with my little boy than I do.

'Jacob, why don't you go and get your stuff ready, and we'll get going,' I say, ushering him out of the room. When I'm sure he's out of earshot, I turn back to Sam.

'Who's this?' I say.

To her credit, Sam looks awkward. But then she lifts her head, chin up. 'Just a friend.'

'Male, I presume?'

'Yes, not that it's anything to do with you.'

'It is when he's in the same house as my son.'

'For God's sake, Ted, who do you think I am? I'm not just going to let anyone stay here. And anyway, Jacob's spent time with your new fancy woman.'

She's right, and I have no right whatsoever to say anything about how Sam chooses to live her life or with whom. And yet I can't help myself. I don't like it.

'Well, just make sure you know what you're doing, and that he's nice to Jacob.'

She doesn't even answer, just rolls her eyes and turns away, making it clear the conversation is over. Jacob returns with his backpack, and I turn my attention to him.

'Ready to go then, buddy?'

'Yep.'

'Got your special socks?'

He lifts his trouser leg and proudly shows me his trampolining socks with the rubber bobbles on. 'Check.' He grins.

'Right then, let's go. Say bye to Mummy.'

'Bye, Mummy,' he says, hugging her briefly, then he follows me to the car and climbs into his seat in the back.

As I pull off into the traffic, I watch him in the rear-view mirror and my heart swells with love. It's almost impossible to believe he's mine sometimes, and even more impossible to imagine that I ever dared contemplate leaving him behind, even for a moment.

'Are we going with Sophia and Archie?' he pipes up from the back.

'Yes, is that okay?'

'Yes, Daddy, I like them.'

I've been worried about telling him I've agreed to move in with them, but now seems like as good a time as any.

'That's good. Daddy's going to be living with them soon.'

I see him frown in the mirror. 'With who?'

'With Sophia and Archie.'

'And me?'

'Well, no. But you can come and stay, just like you do now.'

'Will I have my own bedroom?'

'No, you'll probably have to share with Archie. But that will be fun, won't it?'

I watch him thinking for a moment. He has his own bedroom when he comes to stay with me at the moment, and I'm worried it could be a deal-breaker. Finally, he says, 'Yes, we can have sleepovers.'

I should feel relieved, but in fact I'm torn. I had enough doubts of my own about this move. If Jacob had opposed it, for whatever reason, I would have backed out immediately. It would have been like my get-out clause. But now there's no get-out clause.

* * *

What I haven't told Jacob is that we're also meeting Danny and Danni at the trampoline park, and as we pull up outside and he spots their kids Chelsea and Bo in the car park, he almost falls out of the car in his excitement. They're a few years older than Jacob and he worships them.

'Jacob, careful!' I yell as he launches himself at Chelsea and nearly knocks her over.

'All right, small fry?' Danny says, ruffling Jacob's hair as I approach. 'All right, Ted?'

'Yeah, great, you?'

'Yeah, perfect, aren't we Dan?' He pulls her close and plants a smacker on her lips.

'Oi, get off,' she says, but it's clear she doesn't mean a word.

'All right, you two love birds. I can't believe you're not sick of each other after all these years.'

'Nah, he's not too bad, our Dan,' Danni says, patting his bottom as we walk into the trampoline park. As the doors slide open there's a wall of sound, a soup of yells and screams and machinery.

'Sophia not coming?'

'Yeah, she's meeting us here,' I say as we reach the desk to pay.

'And things all right with her, are they?'

'Not bad. She's asked me to move in with her.'

'What?' Danny's stopped what he's doing and is looking right at me. 'And are you?'

'I said yes.'

'You don't look very happy about it.'

I sigh. 'I don't know, Dan. I just – I don't know if it's what I want, but I don't know why.'

'She's a lovely girl, Sophia.'

'Exactly. I know she is. And I really care about her.'

'That sounds like something you say about your nan.'

'I know. I think that's the problem. I just don't know if I feel strongly enough about her.'

'So why are you doing it?'

'Why not? What else am I going to do? Stay on my own in that flat, waiting for the weekends when I'm allowed to see my son, working all week and never moving on?' I pull my shoes off and the orange trampoline socks on. 'I just feel like, if I do this, I'll learn to be happy.'

Danny's standing stock still, his socks still in his hand.

'Ted, are you sure about this? I mean, it doesn't sound like the best plan you've ever had. And don't you think Sophia deserves better?'

'I've thought about nothing else since she asked me. I said yes because I didn't know what else to say, and she looked so sad when I didn't answer straight away. But I reckon this will be a good thing, in the end. Plus it's a nice house, and it will give Jacob someone to play with when he's there.'

'Sounds like you've made up your mind, then.'

'I suppose so.'

'Just don't hurt her, Ted. Don't ruin this because of a girl you never had, like you did with Sam. Sophia's too nice to be treated like that.'

'I know. I won't.'

'What are you two gossiping about over here?' Danni appears at my side and leans her elbow on my shoulder.

'Sophia's asked Ted to move in with her and he's said yes.'

'What? That's brilliant!' Danni claps her hands and throws her arms around me. 'Oh, we can do all sorts of things together, it'll be amazing.'

'Thanks, Danni,' I say, untangling her arms from my neck.

'Where is she, anyway?' she says, looking round. As if on cue, Sophia and Archie fall through the door, looking flustered. They rush over to me, Sophia almost dragging her son behind her.

'So sorry we're late, the traffic was awful,' she says, rising up on her toes to give me a kiss.

But before I can respond, Danni has grabbed her arm. 'Ted told me the news!' she says excitedly. Sophia gives a small shake of her head and indicates Archie. She clearly hasn't told him yet, and I wonder how he'll take the news. As we file into a small side room for the safety briefing, I try not to meet Danny's eye, afraid of the disapproval I'll see there. I know he thinks I'm doing the wrong thing – and the problem is, I'm worried he's right.

34

SEPTEMBER 2009

Marianne

I sit on the toilet lid, my face in my hands, not daring to look. It's like a game of roulette – one line I go, two lines I stay.

I breathe in deeply, in and out, in and out, and try to stop my head from spinning. I can hear Andy playing a game with Charlotte in the living room; her shrieks of delight when she's winning, her whines when she's not. I check my phone again. Two minutes. One more minute to go. I keep breathing steadily, and let my mind wander. I think about the last couple of years since Charlotte was born. Life has changed beyond recognition, revolving entirely around this new person. I'd never imagined myself being a mother before, but the moment it happened, it felt as though it was always meant to be. Not that it's been easy – God, no. The sleepless nights, the constant demands, none of it has been a walk in the park. But if I ever wonder why I did it, I just look at my daughter, and I don't need to question anything. Mum has been amazing too. She might not always have been an affectionate mother to me – at least, not the way I remember it – but she can't get enough of her granddaughter. Her and Dad look after Charlotte twice a week and I swear I've never seen either of them as animated about anything.

The only thing that hasn't changed is the way I feel about Andy. He's a lovely man, and he's good with Charlotte. He's kind and trustworthy, and I know he'll never let me down. But I'm not in love with him. He doesn't make me feel alive.

In fact, so much so that, just a week ago, I was on the verge of leaving him. He hadn't done anything wrong. He rarely does. But I just suddenly felt overwhelmed by it all. By the pretence of playing happy families, of pretending to be love's young dream. Because while I have no doubt that he loves me, I know for a fact I don't feel the same way. I wish I did. More than anything. But I don't, and I didn't think I could do it any more. He deserved better, if nothing else.

The only thing that stopped me telling him it was all over there and then was Charlotte. The thought of having to leave her with him every few days, to only spend half of my time with her, instead of all of it. My heart couldn't contemplate it. And so I stayed.

Then this happened. My period didn't arrive. And I knew.

I open my eyes and let them drift over to the piece of plastic balancing on the edge of the bath. I keep my vision blurred at first, not daring to look properly. Then slowly, I let the focus return.

Even from this distance there's no doubt. There are two lines. Two clear, definite lines.

I'm pregnant.

My stomach lurches with fear and excitement simultaneously. Two lines I stay. Fate has decided.

'You don't believe in fate,' Lance says, later, on the phone when Andy's taken Charlotte to the park.

'Not usually. But fate or not, my decision's made. I'm not going anywhere.'

'I don't think this should be the deciding factor.'

'Of course it should! I can't leave Andy now. It's fine. I'll be fine.'

I hear the suck of breath and I know Lance is smoking. She hadn't smoked for years, then, after the birth of Milo last year, she took it up again and is now more addicted than ever. 'I hope you're leaning out of the window with that cancer stick,' I say.

'So far out I'm practically flying,' she replies, her voice raspy.

'Well, good. At least you're only killing yourself.'

'Yeah, I know.' She sucks deeply again. 'I'm going to quit.'

'Again?'

'I know, I know. But I do mean it. I can't go round stinking of fags all day when I'm looking after Milo.'

'It's not the best look.'

'It's not.' She's quiet for a moment and I know she's thinking. 'So there's no doubt then?'

'That I'm pregnant?'

'That you're keeping it.'

'Lance!'

'I know but hear me out. You've got Charlotte. You've got Andy, but you don't want him. This baby – this tiny little embryo that you've never even met – is going to tie you to him for years. It doesn't matter what you say, you won't be able to leave him if it means not seeing your children. I've seen you with Charlotte.'

I want to argue with her, tell her she's wrong. But the truth is, she's got a point. As usual. Although the thought of another baby to love as much as I love Charlotte is exciting on the one hand, on the other, the idea of being trapped for even longer terrifies me.

'I can't do that,' I say, my voice quiet.

'I know. I just needed to put it out there. I won't mention it again.'

'Thank you.' I sniff. 'So, how's Milo?'

'Milo's great. Jake's a pain in the arse, though.'

'Oh no, why?'

'You know, the usual. He's decided now he's going to ask work to go part time so he can be at home more with Milo, because he doesn't want him spending more time with the childminder than he does with his parents.' I can almost hear the quotation marks she's drawing in the air.

'What's wrong with that?'

'Oh, nothing, really. It just makes me feel guilty that I'm not doing that too. But I don't want to, dammit, I worked too hard for this job.'

'Nobody's saying you have to, Lance. Not even Jake, by the sounds of it.'

She sighs. 'I know. I'm being a twat. I just – I do feel guilty about not being with him more. You know, being one of those mummies who's always at the park with their kids, who takes them to singing classes and on playdates and to the zoo rather than just dumping them in a nursery all day. It makes me feel like I'm a terrible mum.'

'Oh, Lance, you're not a terrible mum. You're amazing, and you're teaching Milo a brilliant lesson, showing him that people have to work hard to make a good life. Anyway, you're there the rest of the time. He adores you.'

'I know. I don't know what's wrong with me. I just – I hate the thought that he's going to grow up and remember bloody Gloria more than he remembers me.'

'Who's Gloria?'

'The childminder.'

'He won't. You know that. My mum and dad always worked and I'm all right.'

She snorted.

'What? I am!'

'You are. But you used to moan that your mum and dad were often too busy to spend time with you. And I – I don't want that.'

'Yeah, you're right. But now I do remember the times we spent together, and I know they love me. And Milo knows that you love him.'

We finish the conversation, both trying to console each other, and hang up. As we do, I hear the key in the lock and my heart sinks. I'm going to have to tell Andy about the baby – and as soon as I do, that will be that. The next fifteen, twenty years of my life will be decided. I take a deep breath and walk into the hall to meet them.

35

DECEMBER 2011

Ted

When you've done this job for as many years as I have – as a junior
doctor, a consultant, and now a surgeon – you become pretty
immune to most things. You have to, or it would drive you mad.
Harden to it, or crumble. But it doesn't stop my heart clattering like
a jack hammer every time the phone rings an emergency in. When
that bell chimes out, the tension in A&E racks up a notch, and
there's an air of uneasy anticipation as everyone awaits the new
arrival. Until they get here, we have no way of assessing how bad it
is, or whether we can save them. All we can do is prepare for every
eventuality.

So when the phone goes tonight, I have my usual reaction. A
woman, early forties, has been hit by a car while crossing the road.
She has a suspected broken pelvis, a broken left arm but, most
worryingly of all, she hit her head and is unresponsive. The ambulance carrying her is due in two minutes' time, and the wait feels

like forever.

Then, instantly, the tension is shattered as the back doors swing open and the stretcher is wheeled in, a woman strapped tightly to it. Her head is bandaged round the top, and her eyes are closed. An oxygen mask covers her mouth and nose, which looks as though it's badly bruised.

We race along to the operating room where I plan to assess her. Beside me, the paramedic who attended the scene of the accident is reeling off the details of what he found, and I slot each piece of information into place in my mind, ready to call on later. My heart's still hammering, but I know once I get down to work, once I start to figure out how serious the injuries are, I'll forget my fear and adrenaline will take over. It always does.

We crash through the doors and come to a stop in Majors, then I start my examination. Visual at first, to see if there's anything obvious just from looking. Then I begin the physical examination, checking the areas of injury the paramedic has already told me about, then assessing the rest of her body for anything less obvious. My team wait for my decision, but I won't rush. This bit needs to be done properly and thoroughly. There's no room for mistakes.

Despite the bruising and the broken bones, it's soon clear that the head injury is the biggest worry, as I'd feared. After checking her over, I send her for a scan, and moments later, she's wheeled off with a nurse and an anaesthetist for an MRI, giving me time to check the notes. I pick them up to see whether we know who this woman is, and what else they've been able to ascertain about her. I scan quickly over her name and age, then flick down to the list of suspected injuries. It all pretty much tallies with what I've found but I check the details over one last time, and that's when I notice it.

Her name.

Marianne Cooper.

Marianne. My hand that grips the paper is sweaty, and my heart lurches. I glance up, but there's no one around. I stare back at my patient's name and age. Marianne. Age forty-one.

I shake the thought from my head. Marianne's not a common name, but there will still be hundreds of them in a huge city like London. I'm mad if I think that this is my Marianne. I roll my eyes. *My* Marianne. What am I thinking? Even if it is her, she couldn't be further from being mine.

I roll my shoulders and click my neck to relieve the tension. This is ridiculous. Even if it is her – which it won't be – what difference will it make? I've only met the woman twice, and the last time was eight years ago, for a few minutes. What am I expecting to happen – that I'll save her life, she'll fall madly in love with me, and we'll live happily ever after? Get a grip, Ted, this isn't a Hollywood movie.

I leave the paperwork on the side and make my way to where Marianne is having her MRI. 'Anything?' I say as I enter.

'There's severe bleeding on the brain.' The radiographer indicates the area of Marianne's brain that's shaded dark. It means blood has collected and is getting worse.

'Subdural hematoma?'

He nods. 'I'd say so.'

There's no time to lose. A subdural hematoma means the pressure on the brain is enormous. Time is of the essence if I want to try to save her life before the pressure causes too much damage.

I try not to think about who this woman is. All that matters is that we get her to surgery and drain the blood and try to stem the bleeding.

The next four hours are a blur as tubes are fed into her skull, and me and my team do what we do best. The world shrinks away and all that's left is me, the medical team and this woman on the bed.

* * *

I slump into the hard plastic chair, exhausted, and put my head in my hands. They smell of cleaning products and bleach, and my pulse is pounding.

But I'm relieved too. The operation was a success. At least in terms of what we needed to do immediately. What happens next – whether she comes out of her coma or not, whether she's suffered any long-term damage to her brain – still remains to be seen. But, for now, my work here is done.

It's hours past my clocking-off time and I should be pulling on my civilian clothes and heading home to eat some dinner and pass out in front of the TV. But something is keeping me here.

Although it didn't matter who this woman was while the operation was happening, now I need to go and see her and confirm what I already know. I stand and my legs feel wobbly beneath me, like I've just run a marathon. I guess I have, in a way. Leaving the cafeteria, which smells like burned coffee and greasy chips, I head back to Intensive Care. Before I worked in a hospital, I never really gave the places much thought, but if anyone had mentioned Intensive Care, I would have pictured a hushed atmosphere, people creeping round so as not to disturb patients. But the reality is very different – visitors come and go, nurses race around, people chat and laugh and machines beep and whir and hum. It's noisy and lively and busy and it feels wrong that it's a ward full of very sick people.

I nod at the nurses as I pass and head straight for Marianne's bed in the corner. She's lying flat, only her head propped up slightly by a pillow, and the wires and tubes needed to keep her stable – to keep her alive, right now – snake all around her body, linked up to heart monitors and saline drips and breathing apparatus. I can see why relatives find this so distressing, but all I can see is hope – hope that these machines will do their job and keep this woman alive.

She doesn't have any visitors at the moment, and I'm glad. I approach her bed and stand over her, watching her chest rise and fall, rise and fall. She looks peaceful now, so different to when she came in a few hours before. Her head is wrapped in bandages, but some blonde curls slip out of the bottom, and I lean over and study her face. Despite the bruising and the swelling, I know it's her. It's Marianne. The woman who saved me all those years ago, who gave me a second chance to do this job, to try to save other people, is lying in a coma on this hospital bed. Her life is, quite literally, in my hands. The responsibility is overwhelming, but more than that. It seems fitting, somehow, that it's me that has to save her. I vow I'll do everything in my power to do so.

Marianne

It's a cold night, and the air feels crisp as I step out of the house. I'm leaving Charlotte and Ava with Andy tonight, and am off for a night out with Lance, just the two of us. Since I had Ava and Lance had Milo, we've barely seen each other, and I can't wait to go out drinking, just like the old days. Except this time we'll both be mothers, and I'll be divorced – so not quite the same.

I pull my coat tighter round me and pick up my pace. I'm slightly late – as always – and I know how much Lance hates my consistent tardiness. The wind is bitter and seeks out gaps in my clothes so that it feels like needles prickling my skin. I put my head down and hurry towards the bus stop. The Tube would be quicker, but ever since that day of the bombings, I can't go near it. Just the thought of it makes me feel dizzy and my legs weak. I've spoken to Lynne about it, but we've both agreed avoidance may be the best thing for now, rather than trying to push the issue.

The bus windows are steamed up with breath and bodies and I'm overheating in my coat as I wend my way towards the back where I spot a spare seat. I sit, puffs of air flumping out of the seat fabric, and breathe a sigh of relief. As long as the traffic isn't too bad – never guaranteed in north London – then I should be there on time and will dodge the wrath of Lance. I stare straight in front and drift off, letting my thoughts roam to pass the time. Despite the excitement of a night away, I can't help my heart aching for my girls, and I wonder how they're getting on with their dad putting them to bed. Despite our separation, Andy's a pretty hands-on dad. Sometimes, when I watch him with them, I wonder whether I made a mistake, leaving him. But then I think about the way he made me feel – or rather, didn't feel, which was more the point – and I know it was the right thing to do, however tough. What's the point of a loveless marriage these days? It's not the 1950s.

Ava had only been six months old when I realised I couldn't stay any longer. I'd tried to start a row to make it easier to tell him, but as usual, Andy refused to take the bait.

'What's the matter, Marianne?' he said as I stomped and raged around the flat.

'You!' I screamed, unnecessarily cruelly, and immediately regretted it. He was a lovely man, and didn't deserve to be treated badly. Really, I was angry at myself for not being able to love him enough, and so it had come out as anger directed at him.

I felt guilty as I saw him flinch, but he still didn't rise to it.

'Well, there's not much I can do about that then, is there?' he'd said, scooping up a crying Ava and doing a walk-jig around the living room to soothe her. I'd watched as he'd paced up and down, up and down, and slowly felt the anger subside in me.

'I'm sorry,' I'd said, crossing my legs and leaning forward with my elbows on my knees. 'I just – I can't do this any more.'

'Us, you mean?'

I nodded and even though I knew it was hurting him, he didn't stop, just carried on walking calmly.

'You don't seem very upset.'

'What did you want me to do, fall at your knees and beg you to love me?' Up, down, up, down, walk, jig, walk, jig.

'No, I—' I stopped. Had I wanted that, or something like it? Some show of affection, of passion? Who knew? But I knew I'd never get it from Andy.

'It doesn't matter. I've known this was coming for a long time.'

'You have?' I looked at him, his jaw set. He nodded.

'I thought it was coming before Ava but when you found out you were pregnant, I hoped it might mend things. But that was just a sticking plaster in the end, wasn't it? Because I'm not what you want, and I never have been.'

'Andy, that's not true,' I started, but he cut me off again.

'It's fine, Marianne. Well, not fine, but it is what it is. You married me because you thought no one better was going to come along, and because you realised life was too short after the bombings. I get it.' He shrugged. 'I'm just sad I couldn't be the man you wanted me to be.'

My heart felt as though it might rip in two. Poor, lovely, kind, sweet Andy. How did he always know he wasn't enough for me? Hadn't we been happy, once?

He stopped in front of me and handed Ava over. 'She's asleep now. I'm going out for a bit.' Then he'd calmly pulled his jacket on and walked out of our flat, and that night everything had changed. We'd agreed to split custody of the girls fifty-fifty. I didn't want him to miss out on them growing up, and I also wanted them to have their dad around. So he found a flat round the corner and we made it work. That was a year ago, and it's mostly fine. Andy's even found someone else, Sarah, a slightly younger woman who seems quite happy to spend time with someone else's children, and I'm glad he's happy at last. He deserves so much more than I could ever have given him.

Tonight is my first night out since the split, and I'm not sure how I feel about it or what to expect.

The bus is barely moving and I peer through the front windscreen. I'm meeting Lance in Soho, and we're still a good mile or so from there. At this snail's pace, it will be quicker to walk. I can see the glow of a bus stop just ahead, so I make an instant decision to get off. I stand, press the bell then make my way to the door in the middle of the bus. It inches along, frustratingly. I could get there faster on foot, and I tap my fingernails impatiently against the yellow pole. Finally, the bus comes to a stop, releasing a gust of air and jerking forward so suddenly that I almost fall into the man beside me. I smile apologetically, then wait for the doors to open. Stepping out into the cold night air feels refreshing, and I breathe it in, letting it fill my lungs. I check my watch. I'm still not late but I need to get a move on. I walk towards the back of the bus. My bag slips off my shoulder, and I feel a gentle vibration inside it, so I stick my hand in and rummage around for my phone, one eye on the road, one eye on my bag. I glance round quickly. Nothing coming. My phone has stopped ringing now and I pull it out and notice it was Andy. And at the very moment when I wonder what's happened, whether I should ring him back, I step out into the road and...

BANG.

Nothing.

37

DECEMBER 2011

Ted

Marianne has visitors now, so I've left them to it. Her mum and dad arrived earlier, her mum sobbing, her dad stoic and brave, but I could see it was breaking his heart to see Marianne the way she was.

'She will be okay, won't she, doctor?' he asked me quietly, and all I could do was reassure him that we were doing all we could. I know it's not what relatives want to hear – they want reassurance, proper reassurance, for you to say, 'Yes, they will be absolutely fine in a couple of days, you'll never know there was anything wrong.' But the trouble is, we can't know that. The truth is, after the injuries Marianne sustained, she has a fifty-fifty chance of making it, and even if she does, we won't know the extent of her injuries until later.

I try not to imagine how I'd feel if it were Jacob lying there. I wouldn't be able to do my job if I thought like that.

Instead, I'm staying around, just in case anything goes wrong.

It's not as if I've got anyone to go home to. Sophia and I had ended it a few months ago – Danny had been right all along, moving in with her had been the wrong thing to do – and I'd moved back into London and rented a flat near to the hospital. When Jacob's not with me, it's a pretty sad, soulless place to be.

Besides, I need to make sure I do everything I can here. It feels like fate, that I've been given the chance to save Marianne after everything that's happened.

Later, her friend Alison arrives, and I give her some space. I'm fairly certain she's recognised me from the couple of times we've met, but I may be wrong. I'm meant to be off duty now, but I decide to stay, and spend the day checking in on other patients in Intensive Care while Marianne's parents come and go. I can't help noticing there's no husband visiting her, and it hasn't escaped my notice that she isn't wearing a ring either. But I'm furious with myself for even thinking about these things. Marianne's condition is critical, and the next forty-eight hours will help us understand how serious her injuries are. This is no time for inappropriate thoughts.

Eventually, it's time for my shift again and I change into a fresh pair of scrubs and start my rounds. Marianne is stable, and I try to concentrate on my other patients as I make my way round the hospital. I deal with a broken ankle and a teenager who I decide needs to have their stomach pumped after someone spiked their drink, then send a woman home who came in with a sore finger that it transpires she simply burnt on the toaster. Sometimes I wonder at people's common sense. The whole time I'm with them, my mind is elsewhere, up in the ICU.

Finally, I make my way back to Intensive Care. When I get there, there's nobody by Marianne's bed and I stand for a while, deciding whether or not I should speak to her. I know there's a chance she can hear me, and there's so much I could say. But none of it feels right, so instead I just stand with her for a while, making a show of checking her over whenever a nurse comes near, and studying her notes.

I know nothing about this woman lying on the bed on front of me, and yet it feels as though I know so much. She's occupied so much of my mind for so many years that it feels impossible I don't know who she is. What's her favourite TV show, who's her celebrity crush? Does she have a hobby, a boyfriend, is she married, divorced, does she prefer cats or dogs, what's her favourite drink, or flavour of crisp, or pizza topping... I sit heavily on the plastic chair beside her and put my head in my hands. There's no way I can tell her who I am or how much I want her to wake up. I can't tell her about my feelings for her, or how much it would destroy me if the person who saved me died under my care.

So, instead, I sit by her bedside until her parents return, and Alison comes back. But when her loved ones arrive, I make myself scarce, try not to get in the way.

Two days pass this way, and I only pop home briefly for a change of clothes and to snatch a few hours' sleep. All the time, I'm wondering what's happening at the hospital, and am almost pulled back there magnetically, to Marianne's bedside in the ICU. I answer questions from her parents, and discuss solutions and possible outcomes with other members of the medical team. But all I can think about is that night on the bridge, the night when Marianne pulled me back from the brink and gave me my life back. I *have* to do the same for her. I have to.

Then, on the third day, something happens. Until now, Marianne has been stable, if unresponsive. But all of a sudden, an alarm sounds and half the nursing staff are by my side at her bed.

'What's happening? What's wrong?' her mum sobs, and a nurse leads her away to comfort her. All I can focus on is Marianne.

Her body seems to be spasming, the first sign of movement I've seen since she arrived into my care. Her legs are twitching but she's holding her arms straight out beside her, rigid. Sounds drip from her parched lips but I can't make out any words as her head shakes from side to side. I watch the monitor that's counting out the rhythm of her heart and wait to see what happens. Slowly, her heart rate climbs, and she stiffens more. I wonder what she's seeing, what going on in her mind.

'Hello?' I say, and she stops briefly, twists her head.

'Come on, Marianne,' I whisper. Behind me, I'm aware of feet shuffling and voices hissing questions, but I ignore them all and focus on trying to bring Marianne's mind back to the here and now, to bring her back from the brink.

'You need to come back to us now,' I say, louder this time, and there's a brief moment when I wonder whether she's even heard me. Then, slowly, she reaches out for my arm and grips it tightly, and her body begins to relax, the tension seeping down into the bed and away from her limbs. I feel as though everything is holding its breath; even the machines that previously hissed and puffed beside her seem to stop for a beat.

Marianne's eyes flicker open.

'She's awake!' someone cries behind me. Marianne's eyes close again, the light obviously blinding her, and then open more slowly, blinking as she focuses on the room.

'Marianne,' I say. And then she sees me.

38

DECEMBER 2011

Marianne

I can hear voices, muffled at first, the occasional one piercing through the cotton wool so that I can make out the odd clear word. But there's nothing that makes sense, that helps me to work out where I am and why. I try to open my eyes, but they seem to be stuck down. Why would they be stuck down? I try again but nothing happens, and I can feel panic rising in my chest. Perhaps I should get up. My body feels stiff, parts of it numb while other parts ache. Maybe getting out of bed would help. I lift my foot off the bed and go to sit up, but my body doesn't respond. I try again, but I seem to be pinned down.

I feel panic surging through me, turning my whole body to jelly. What's happening to me, why can't I move?

I tell myself to slow down and take some deep breaths. But even that doesn't help, as I don't seem to have control over my breathing either. I close my mind down for a moment and try to take stock.

There are only a few possibilities here. One is that I've been kidnapped and I'm tied up. But it seems unlikely. The other – what is the other? That I'm in hospital, unconscious? But why would I be? I try to think of the last memory I have. I remember saying goodbye to the girls – oh, God, the girls! – and leaving the house. Where was I going? To meet someone. Lance? That was it. I was going out to meet Lance. But after leaving the house, I have very little recollection of the night. Did I get my night out? Did something awful happen to me on the way home? Why can't I remember anything?

I force my mind back to the present, to focus on the here and now. I could hear muffled voices before, and they're still there, but they're less muffled now, as though a fog is slowly lifting. I can't tell whether they're talking to me or whether the room I'm in is just full of people. There's a constant background noise, and I focus on that instead, trying to pinpoint sounds. There's lots of beeping, like supermarket tills. Have I collapsed in a shop? But I don't think it's that. There are urgent voices, and low hums, and squeaky shoes on lino and wheels on trolleys, and then there are sudden shouts and footsteps running and a sense of panic. And then it hits me. I *am* in hospital.

But why?

'Mum!' I try to shout her name but I'm fairly certain nothing comes out. I need to find out what's happened to me. 'Lance!' I try, but still nothing.

Again, I try to still my breath but it seems as though it's beyond my control, as though, for the first time in my life, it's not me controlling my breathing but someone else, something remote.

'Marianne, can you hear me?' My body sings with joy – it's Lance! Oh, Lance, why am I here? Please tell me what's going on. I feel the touch of her hand on mine and I want to squeeze it, let her know I can hear her, that I'm here. But I'm quickly realising that's not going to happen. That whatever my mind wants to do, my body won't cooperate. Instead, I focus very hard on listening for her voice, on hearing her next words.

'I'm going to pretend you can hear me,' she says next, and I think her face must be quite near mine as her words are clear, and everything else has faded into the background. 'The girls are fine, they're with Andy. We're not letting them come and see you, we thought it was best. But when you're feeling better, they're desperate to come and have cuddles.' Her voice cracks and I wonder why. Does she think I might not ever feel better? Have doctors said that's a possibility? Surely not. I try and ignore the rising panic, and keep listening.

'Oh, Annie, I can't believe this has happened. Why didn't we meet somewhere else? Anywhere. I hope you weren't rushing so you weren't late.' She sniffs and I wonder whether she's crying or if she has a cold. 'Anyway. Enough of that. I'm meant to be cheering you up, not depressing you.' She gives a nervous giggle, and I can feel her hand rubbing my forearm over and over.

'I'm here,' I want to yell. I long to stand on my bed and shout it out across the whole of the ward, the hospital – the whole of London. I'm here and I'm fine!

'Your mum and dad have gone to get something to eat. I made them, they looked so knackered and I knew you wouldn't mind if they weren't right here when you woke up. Your mum looks dead on her feet, bless her. What else? Oh, Jake sends his love. He's told me to stay here as long as I need to and he'll look after Milo, so if it's all right with you, I'll do that. Not that you can tell me to go away anyway.' I can hear the smile in her face and can picture her lipsticked smile, her fiery red hair and her twinkling eyes, and I long to give my best friend a hug.

There's a rustling sound and some subdued voices and I can't focus on what anyone is saying for a moment. There are a few beeps and someone fiddles with something in my arm, then moves away, leaving, I assume, me and Lance alone again.

'That was just the nurse, come to check on you,' she says, pushing my hair away from my face and holding her hand to my cheek. 'She says there's no change. I think that's a good thing, right?' She sighs. 'Anyway, I've got something really amazing to tell you. You'll never guess what.' She pauses and I almost scream for her to carry on. 'The doctor who—' But then she stops short, and I hear the scrape of a plastic chair across the floor, and some unfamiliar voices hover above me, a deep one, and two others, one male, one female. It's hard to decipher the words, but after a while they seem satisfied, and everything goes quiet again. I wonder how long I'm going to have to wait for Lance to come back and finish telling me whatever it is she was excited about.

'Marianne, it's Mum.'

Oh, Mum, I'm here, I long to say, but instead I lie here, helpless.

'Love, can you hear me? The doctors say you might be able to, they said I should speak to you as if you can, but I don't half feel silly. What if you can't hear anything, what if—' She stops, a sob escaping on her next breath and I hear Dad's voice, gentle and low.

'Come on, Wendy, don't get upset. Why don't you get a cup of tea, let me stay with her?'

'I can't – I don't want to leave her. What if she wakes up and I'm not here, what will she think then?'

'She'll think you've gone to get a cup of tea,' Dad says, and after a few more minutes, I hear footsteps walking away and the creak of a chair as, presumably, Dad sits down next to me. He leans on the edge of the mattress and I feel myself tipping ever so slightly towards him, and feel his forearm rest against my shoulder. He doesn't speak, but I can hear his breathing, slightly rattly on the way out, and it strikes me how awful this must be for him and Mum. I think back to the day we rushed here with Dad all those years ago with his suspected heart attack and how frightening it was. How awful must it feel to think you might lose your own child? I long to reach out and comfort him, but all I can do is sit and listen to his breath and hope he knows I'm here with him.

I don't know how long passes or who else enters and leaves the room. I must drift in and out of consciousness – let's call it sleep, to sound less frightening – and sometimes the bedside feels full of people, while at other times it feels as though I'm entirely alone, with just the humming and whirring of the machinery for company. It might be minutes, or hours or even days that pass, but I don't think it can be too long as Lance hasn't come back and finished her story yet – or at least I haven't heard her – and I don't think she'd stay away for too long. I just wish I knew what was wrong with me. I've heard snatches of conversations between the medics, but I don't understand a lot of it, and presumably, if they think I might be able to hear, they say anything worrying out of my earshot.

There's something else, too. Something that's bothering me and if I could just put my hands on what it is, if I could grab hold of it, I'd feel better. It's a voice. One of the voices that keeps coming and going around me. It's more of a constant than the others and I can only assume it's my main doctor. Consultant, is that what they're called? Whatever. There's something about this man's voice that's triggering a memory in me, that's making me feel as though I know him. But I can't quite grasp the right memory from my mind and slot it into place.

Beep. Beep. Beep. Beep. I register the rhythmic beating of my heart as recorded by the heart monitor, and I wish someone would switch the noise off, give me some peace, just a few minutes of complete silence to reset my brain. I want to scream and shout. But I can't.

I drift off into yet another sleep. Snatches of memory float through the haze, some fleeting images, some more detailed pictures like silent movies. Me as a child going to the shop with Dad to buy his paper, him treating me to a bar of chocolate and telling me not to tell Mum... me and Lance ironing our hair for a night out and Lance leaving a chunk behind on the ironing board... sleepovers at Lance's house, scaring ourselves witless with totally unsuitable horror films... and then my stomach drops, because I'm standing on the edge of a bridge, dark water thundering below me, and just my slippery, frozen hand clinging to the barrier, tethering me to the earth. Wind whips through my hair and my clothes, and my whole body feels stiff with cold. This memory is powerful, and I can feel everything, as though it's happening to me right now, even though I know it can't be. I feel the icy metal beneath my fingers, my breath coming in gasps, and then there's a presence next to me, a hand on mine, pressing my flesh into the sharp metal below.

'Hello.' The voice sounds thin in the freezing air, and I turn my head quickly to find a man standing beside me, on the wrong side of the railings. I can't see his face, but his voice sounds familiar, just that one word. Who is he? I squint through the darkness to see. I'm still leaning over the water, and I don't seem to have the strength in my arms to pull myself upright again. They're shaking, with cold and fear. Then he speaks again.

'Come on, Marianne.' How does he know my name? Who is he? What am I going to do? I don't think I could even pull myself back if I wanted to. Goosebumps mark my skin as the wind whips round me again and I see his body shiver beside me. He's wearing fairy wings, I notice, and a memory jolts me. Fairy wings? What was that? But the memory seems beyond me, just out of reach.

'You need to come back to us now,' he says gently, coaxing, and I wonder why he cares whether I jump from this bridge or not. I glance down. It doesn't look like water below now, it looks like sheer blackness, as though if I dropped down into it, I would never come back up. Fear prickles at my neck. That's death, that way. Suddenly I know it, as certainly as I know my own name. I don't want to go that way, I want to get off this bridge and carry on living.

Suddenly my girls flash into my mind and from somewhere, somehow, I manage to find a strength I didn't know I had. I straighten my arms and try to pull my body upright, away from the raging water below. But there's not enough there. I can't do this on my own.

Then the stranger holds out his hand and it looks like a lifeline. I don't know what will happen if I let go of this railing and grab hold of his hand, but I do know for certain that it's a risk I have to take. And so, slowly, I unpeel my fingers one by one from the metal and then I take a leap of faith, and grasp for his hands, his fingers. I miss. My heart leaps into my throat, and I try to scream as my hands flail around blindly in the air. But then, suddenly, miraculously, his fingers are there, within my grasp, and the warmth of his skin is radiating through mine, and I feel myself being tugged slowly, slowly, back to standing, back into the light... back into the room.

I open my eyes and blink wildly. All I can see are lights and they're blinding, and I close my eyes against them again, red glowing through my eyelids.

'She's awake!' someone says, and I think it's Lance, and then there's shuffling around me, and another voice, the voice I was struggling to place, says, 'Marianne,' again, and suddenly I know who it is.

I open my eyes again and blink slowly until they adjust to the glare of the strip lights overhead. Everything is so bright and at first I can only make out silhouettes, blurred features where faces should be. But slowly, slowly, details start to come back into focus again. There's Mum, standing beside my bed, her hands clasped to her chin, her eyes shimmering with tears. She's smiling, and has lipstick on her teeth. Dad is behind her, with Lance, and they're both watching me, the relief clear on their faces. But it's the other man there, on the other side of my bed, who I really need to focus on, and I slide my gaze over until it's resting on the man in the white coat who's standing over my bed and holding my forearm in his hand.

'Bridge Man?' I whisper, my voice hoarse.

'Fairy Girl,' he replies.

EPILOGUE
13 DECEMBER 2012

Ted

I check my watch and huff loudly. The bus has been inching along for the last twenty minutes, barely making any progress at all. I'd get out and walk if I wasn't still miles from my destination. I'm going to be so late.

I tap my fingers against my knee as I squint out of the window. It's steamy in here, breath fogging up the glass and ice beginning to crystallise on the outside of the window so it's hard to see through it. I rub a patch clear with the sleeve of my coat and peer out through the smudge at the grey day beyond.

As the bus continues its stop-start journey, my mind wanders back to this day, twenty-one years ago. A bus journey like this one, snow threatening the December sky, a pocket full of rocks. It's almost impossible to imagine now how low I'd come that day, so low I was prepared to throw myself into the Thames. That man is far behind me now.

The bus chugs round a corner and, as if on cue, the river looms into view, a grey slab of water glimpsed between black railings. I swallow. How could I ever have thought of ending it like that?

Then I think about the conversations that got me here, to this bus, to this journey; I think about the year that's passed since Marianne came back into my life on a hospital bed, since she woke up and recognised me. The days and weeks after that as she recovered under my care, and then the agonising months when I thought I'd lost her all over again, when she backed away, terrified of what we were doing.

Then, just last week, an email had landed in my inbox, and when I'd seen the name, my heart had stopped beating for a few seconds.

Marianne Cooper.

I need to see you. Can we meet up? M x

That was it. Nothing more. It had taken me hours to reply, to decide what to say so as not to scare her away again. I'd worried that suggesting meeting here, on this day, would terrify her. I mean, it wasn't exactly something I'd ever wanted to remember either. But that was just the point. I needed to make this day and this place mean something else. I needed it to help me put it in the past once and for all. And, to my relief, she'd agreed.

We pick up speed now and the river slips away beside me, dotted with the occasional barge, the tourists staying away today, the iron sky not what they want in their holiday snaps. As we get closer, I feel my heart rate start to quicken and my hands become sticky. Will she be there?

I breathe in deeply and let the air fill my lungs, calming me down. It's fine. This will all be fine.

Finally, it's my stop and I climb down, my boot slipping on the pavement. I stand for a moment to gather my thoughts as the bus roars away, and then I glance up and see the time on the imposing clock face of Big Ben. I'm five minutes late.

I hurry along the pavement, the snow falling in fat flakes now, people scurrying with hoods pulled up tightly, the unprepared holding newspapers above their heads. I stare at the ground, watch the lines of the pavement disappear beneath my feet with every step that takes me closer, my heart thumping, my breath coming in rapid puffs. And then I'm there: the steps of Waterloo Bridge loom above me and I take them quickly, my heart pumping as I reach the top. As I catch a glimpse of the white railings that had been the only thing stopping me from falling into the depths of the water that night, I shiver involuntarily. Then, lifting my head to see along the bridge, I walk, slowly at first, then speeding up as I reach the middle of the bridge. I see her, standing with her hands in her pockets, her blonde hair whipping wildly in the wind, and in my mind's eye, I see the fairy wings, the halo bopping about in the breeze, and I shiver. She hasn't seen me yet and I take a moment to let my breath settle, steady my nerves. Then she looks up, and she smiles, and I step towards her and wrap my arms around her. And I know that I'm home.

* * *

Marianne

It had sounded macabre when he'd suggested meeting on this bridge, on this day. But now, as I wait for him in the freezing wind, I know it was the right thing to do. Despite the memories it evokes, despite everything that's happened in between, it feels fitting, some-how, to be here, on this day.

I can see him striding towards me, his long black coat flapping in the wind, flakes of snow landing on his shoulders and instantly melting into the fabric, and I can't believe what a different figure he cuts compared to all those years ago. He looks older and wiser and, most importantly, sure of his place in the world. It makes me realise how far we've both come.

He doesn't know I've seen him yet, and as he looks up, I turn away and wait for him to arrive. As the seconds tick by, my heart leaps around in my chest, and my vision tunnels, until there's no one here but me and him. Now here he is, and I turn to face him and smile, and he smiles back, and, after a second's hesitation, he steps towards me, filling my vision and wrapping his arms around me. Right here, on Waterloo Bridge where it all began, on this freezing December day, I know I'm where I belong.

I'm home.

ACKNOWLEDGMENTS

I love this bit – saying thank you to everyone who has helped me to bring this book to life. But I'm also always petrified I'm going to miss someone out, so if you helped me and you're not mentioned here, I'm VERY sorry. It's my terrible memory, not you!

Firstly, I want to thank my lovely, lovely editor Sarah, for letting me write this book in the first place. It's a story I've wanted to write for many years, and to have you believe in me and let me finally get it out there has been fantastic. Plus, your brilliant editing skills have helped make it the best it can be. Thank you also to everyone at Boldwood, especially Nia and Claire, who are simply amazing at getting books into the hands of readers.

I do like to try and make things as authentic as possible when writing a story, and this time round a couple of people very kindly helped me with the details of NHS life, including how to train to be a doctor, and how things work in A&E when there's an emergency (so it didn't just end up sounding like an episode of Casualty), and they were Liz Nash and the gorgeous Cathy Harwood. I'm certain I have used a little artistic licence in the actual telling of the story, but your help was invaluable – and any mistakes, deliberate or otherwise, about how hospitals work, are entirely down to me. I also read quite a bit about PTSD during the course of my research for this story, and hope I have done justice to the way so many former soldiers felt following combat. I'd never want to make light of something so life-changing.

I have some very lovely, supportive friends, some of whom are authors themselves and others who are just simply brilliant and unwavering in their support – I'm not going to name any of you so that you can't get upset if I miss you out, but you all know who you are! There are also some wonderful groups on Facebook, full of enthusiastic readers (my kind of people), including the Friendly Book Community, the Fiction Cafe Book Club and Chick Lit and Prosecco. Thanks for all your support ladies, and never stop reading! And thanks of course to Rachel Gilbey of Rachel's Random Resources for organising such a brilliant blog tour.

I can't leave without saying my thanks, as always, to my brilliant family. Mum and Dad, Mark, and of course, Tom and my boys, Jack and Harry, I love you very much. And thank you, Tom, for letting me pursue my dream, and for always believing in me. I'm determined to let you retire one day soon!

MORE FROM CLARE SWATMAN

We hope you enjoyed reading *The Night We First Met*. If you did, please leave a review.

If you'd like to gift a copy, this book is also available as an ebook, digital audio download and audiobook CD.

Sign up to Clare Swatman's mailing list for news, competitions and updates on future books.

https://bit.ly/ClareSwatmannews

A Love to Last a Lifetime, another book full of love, laughter and tears from Clare Swatman, is available to order.

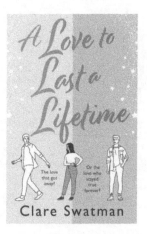

ALSO BY CLARE SWATMAN

Before We Grow Old

Dear Grace

The Mother's Secret

Before You Go

ABOUT THE AUTHOR

Clare Swatman is the author of three women's fiction novels, published by Macmillan, which have been translated into over 20 languages. She has been a journalist for over twenty years, writing for Bella and Woman & Home amongst many other magazines. She lives in Hertfordshire.

Visit Clare's website: https://clareswatmanauthor.com

Follow Clare on social media:

 facebook.com/clareswatmanauthor

 twitter.com/clareswatman

 instagram.com/clareswatmanauthor

Boldw∞d

Boldwood Books is an award-winning fiction publishing company seeking out the best stories from around the world.

Find out more at www.boldwoodbooks.com

Join our reader community for brilliant books, competitions and offers!

Follow us
@BoldwoodBooks
@BookandTonic

Sign up to our weekly deals newsletter

https://bit.ly/BoldwoodBNewsletter

Lightning Source UK Ltd.
Milton Keynes UK
UKHW040051291222
414353UK00007B/386